Breaking the Circle

Breaking the Circle

S.M. Hall

F

FRANCES LINCOLN
CHILDREN'S BOOKS

First published in Great Britain and in the USA in 2012 by
Frances Lincoln Children's Books, 4 Torriano Mews,
Torriano Avenue, London NW5 2RZ
www.franceslincoln.com

A catalogue record for this book is available from the British Library.

ISBN 978-1-84780-122-7

Set in Palatino LT

Printed and bound by CPI Group (UK) Ltd, Croydon, CR0 4YY
in December 2011

1 3 5 7 9 8 6 4 2

Thank you to Colin, for always being there – S. M. H.

Chapter One

The girl stood stone-still in the middle of the pavement. She was small and thin, dressed in black – scuffed leather jacket, tight, frayed jeans and worn boots. Her clothes were too heavy, her face too pale for such a hot late summer day. Beneath a strand of lank, gold hair, her eyes moved restlessly, scanning the people hurrying home.

As Maya drew closer, she was aware that the girl was watching her. When she was level, the girl stepped into her path.

'Got any spare change?'

Maya stopped, patted her pockets, gave an apologetic shrug and shook her head. She couldn't give money to everybody. This area was getting worse, full of crazy people living on the edge.

The girl repeated her request, her voice sharper, more insistent.

A sour smell of sweat came off her as she raised a cupped hand in front of Maya's face. Irritated, Maya reeled back, ready to walk away, but the girl whispered something – words in a foreign language, words that were strange yet also familiar. The words were no doubt curses, but they sent Maya's thoughts spinning. She looked into the girl's face; the eyes that stared back were a startling, luminous gold. Maya felt as though she'd been zapped.

Despite the heat, a shiver ran through her. She tore her eyes away from the girl and stumbled forward. As she walked away, she felt the girl's eyes burning into her skin.

A few steps ahead, Maya knew the girl was following; she could hear her leather jacket rustling, her black boots scuffing the pavement. A split-second decision – should she take the short cut? Her heartbeat quickened as she turned into the narrow alleyway – she wouldn't be bullied into going the long way round.

Keeping her steps deliberate and measured, she walked along the hard dirt path between high walls, a skinny girl at her back – a girl who looked unwashed and in need of a good meal. Maya wasn't worried, she could sort her out if she had to.

The alley was littered with broken glass, plastic bags and weeds. As Maya dodged the debris, the girl's boots scraped behind her, kicking at a bottle and sending it spinning. A thin tabby cat sprang from the shadows and clawed up the side of the wall. Moving to the edge of the path, Maya stopped and switched her heavy bag to the other shoulder, alert, listening – the girl had stopped too.

Up ahead, the sun was still shining, silhouetting blocks of tall flats against blue sky – beyond them, the park and home. With determined steps, Maya strode forward. If she hadn't stayed at school for athletics practice, she'd be home by now, finishing schoolwork, looking forward to watching *Hollyoaks*. She had no regrets about the races, though – she'd thrashed everybody. A thrill of pride ran through her as she remembered the last race; five hundred metres and she'd clocked a personal best. Soon it would be the inter-schools championship. Bring it on! She was ready.

Head down, plotting a race strategy, she forgot about the girl following. She didn't see the guy behind a screen of bushes, was totally unaware of the girl taking out a mobile and speaking into it softly, urgently. The first thing she knew was a swish of movement at her heels, a tug at her blazer, a bony hand clamping her shoulder.

'Give me the money. Give me the mobile.' The girl's eyes were like a cat's, liquid amber glowing in her face. 'You, you give me.'

'No!'

Slow to react to a sharp push, Maya was sent reeling. She hit the ground – *whack!*

Fight back, fight back!

Fingers clutched her hair, twisting and wrenching; her schoolbag was ripped from her shoulder.

Charged with anger, Maya swung into action, lashing out, lunging for her bag, grasping the strap. The girl tugged hard but Maya's training kicked in. Reeling the girl in like a fish, she held her tight, then relaxed her grip for a vital split second. Sensing victory, the girl pulled back, but at that precise moment, Maya yanked her down, put an armlock round her neck and rolled her onto her stomach.

'You can't have my bag, right?' Maya said, pushing the girl's head down.

The girl mumbled, her mouth full of dirt.

'Who are you?' Maya asked, jolting the girl's head.

'Get off. Let go!' the girl spluttered, kicking wildly.

Maya held her down. Then a man's voice shouted, 'Leave 'er!'

Hoping for help, Maya glanced over her shoulder. She gulped. A snarling dog was charging towards her, ears pricked, eyes like laser pens, its slavering jaws bared in a vicious snarl. Her eyes were riveted, muscles tensed, but she couldn't move – there was nowhere to run. The dog was so close that any moment now it would sink its teeth into her skin. At a command from the man, the dog dropped into the dirt. A low, savage growl came from its throat, clumps of froth fell from its mouth.

'What's up? Scared?'

A young guy in a black hoodie ambled towards her, his face sharp and bony, eyes half-hidden by the shadow of the hood. As he bent to clip the dog onto a silver chain, she noticed his long, thin nose; his lips turned up in a mocking smile.

A snappy response to his stupid question went through Maya's head.

Too right I'm scared. Isn't that the reason you have that rabid dog with you – to scare the guts out of people?

But she couldn't speak. The dog was hypnotising her with its mad stare, and all the time it was snarling and slavering as if contemplating its next meal. Fear sang through her bones.

They can smell you, they can smell fear.

The boy sniffed and spat as Maya slowly, very slowly, eased herself off the girl, who was still underneath her, and rolled away from the dog.

'Gimme the bag,' the boy ordered.

Maya hesitated – there was no way she was putting her arm near that crazy dog.

'Give it 'ere.'

He yanked the dog away from her as he reached out his hand. The dog pulled sideways, sending the guy slightly off-balance. Fast as lightning, Maya dipped a hand into the bag and grabbed her mobile. It was just going into her pocket when he spotted it.

'I'll 'ave that,' he said. 'Get it, Kay.'

The girl, who'd been silent and still ever since he appeared, levered herself up, limped over and went to take the mobile, but Maya clutched it to her chest.

'It's mine. You can't take it!'

The girl backed away, looking puzzled and uncertain. She tugged at the zip of her leather jacket, hunched her shoulders and stared down at the ground, biting her knuckles. The fight had gone out of her, but the boy was on a mission and he took charge.

'I can 'ave what I like, or Gunner'll 'ave you. You don't wanna mess with Gunner.'

On cue, the dog snarled. Defeated, Maya opened her hand.

'Take it, Kay,' the boy said, laughing cruelly as the girl limped over and took the mobile. 'What you done to yourself?' he snapped.

The girl, Kay, winced as she put weight on her foot. 'My ankle is hurt.'

'Serves you right. What you doin', robbin' schoolgirls?'

'It's your fault, you ask me for money.'

'So, what you messin' at 'ere? Get back to base an' earn some proper cash.'

Kay sniffed. 'No. I will not do that. I am your girl.'

He leaned forward. 'You're too particular. Think you're special?' He laughed. 'Come on, give that 'ere,' he added, indicating the mobile.

'No, it's mine, it's good. I will sell it, give you money.'

A fist slammed into the girl's arm, sending the phone flying. Maya saw her chance and didn't hesitate. She caught the mobile, veered round them and ran for her life. In a flash she saw the wall was slightly lower towards the end of the path and threw herself at it, leaping up, fingers clawing at the top of the wall as the dog came roaring towards her. Barking and yelping, it snapped at her heels. She kicked out, her foot connected, thudding into the dog's jaw, sending it reeling.

In the split second it took the dog to recover, she managed to get one elbow on top of the wall. She was just swinging her legs up out of danger when the dog leapt wildly below her, catching a piece of her skirt in its teeth. It hung suspended by the cloth, a bite away from her flesh. She had to do something or it would mangle her leg. Jerking her body sideways, she smashed a fist down on Gunner's forehead. With a strangled gasp, the dog fell.

Triumphant, she hoisted herself up on top of the wall but her mobile slipped out of her hand. There was no time to retrieve it; the dog wasn't down and out. It was yelping and snapping again.

Time to jump!

Landing amongst big tufts of spiky grass, she scrambled to her feet and lurched forwards. There was nothing to use as a weapon – no stick or anything

– but, over in the far corner, she spotted an old brick outbuilding. Racing towards it, she slipped on a sheet of glass. It shattered and a shard of glass razored her foot, but the pain only urged her onward. Behind her, she could hear the dog barking itself into a frenzy, scrabbling over the wall. In the nick of time, she threw herself against the door of the building; mercifully it gave way, catapulting her into the sanctuary of the shed. She turned and kicked the door shut as the dog's nose appeared round the edge. Then, with trembling hands, she picked up a brick from a pile near the door and hammered home a rusty bolt.

Loud commands boomed over the wall. 'Gunner. 'Ere, Gunner!'

Leaning against the door, she listened hard. On the other side, the dog was panting, hot breath seeping through gaps in the door. Would the boy come after it?

Another command. 'Gunner, 'ere! Come 'ere, you useless piece of meat.'

The panting stopped. The grass rustled, broken glass crashed; there was a loud yelp. She waited, every nerve trembling, but the boy didn't come.

Standing in the empty building, she cursed the girl who'd followed her, the scumbag in the hood, the mad dog and her own stupidity. Torn skirt, bleeding foot, scratched legs, nerves in shreds – why had she been so stubborn and taken the short cut? What an idiot! She should have trusted her instincts – she knew that girl was trouble as soon as she'd laid eyes on her.

Another shout came from a distance.

'What the. . .?' There were more words, the translation lost in the air. What felt like a lifetime passed. Several times she nearly pulled back the bolt on the door, but the thought of the boy and his killer dog lying in wait kept her inside. Pressing her ear to the wooden planks of the door, she heard the shout of children in the playground, and the distant drone of traffic. She turned her head and peered through a crack – nobody was visible, there was no sign of the dog, the guy, or the girl. Finally she screwed up her courage and ventured out, easing the door open bit by bit until she was sure there was no one waiting to ambush her.

Squinting into the evening sunlight, she scouted for an escape route. The waste ground was enclosed by high walls – the way she'd entered seemed the best way out. Carefully avoiding shards of glass and stopping to look and listen every few steps, she picked her way over to the wall. The ground was lower on this side, the wall high, but a few flying attempts to get a foothold paid off and she was able to swing her legs up and over and drop down onto the path.

A nervous glance up and down the track confirmed that there was no sign of the hooded thug or his dog. So, top priority was to search for her mobile, but she knew right away it had gone. Of course, the boy had spotted it and picked it up. He'd taken her schoolbag containing books and money, her purse containing her bank card, but most upsetting was the loss of the phone that Pam had given her just before she left. It was a secure number which Pam, her mum, might call at any moment. Now she wouldn't be able to answer. A mixture of sadness and anger welled up as she looked again in the spot where she was certain she'd dropped it. It wasn't there. She kicked at a bottle and swore loudly.

Damn him for stealing her mobile! It was complicated enough to stay in touch with her mum without added problems.

There was nothing for it but to head home. She walked warily towards the playground at the end of the path. Children were playing on swings, a couple of men were walking dogs. It was a lovely summer's evening. Gran would be waiting for her in the flat, but she couldn't even call to tell her she'd be late.

As she crossed in front of a playground on the edge of the estate, a couple of young boys ran up to her – shaved heads, cheeky grins.

'Give us fifty p!' the smallest one demanded.

'No, go away.'

'Go on, tight arse.'

'Shove off. I haven't got any money. Some thieving yob just nicked my purse.'

The boys started to laugh. 'That'd be Gerard. We just seen 'im.'

'He went that way with 'is dog. He's cool, Gerard.'

'Oh yeah. Very cool, with his mad dog and thieving girlfriend.'

'His girlfriend's over there.'

A stone whistled past Maya's ear as she walked towards the place the boys had pointed to. Skirting round some straggly bushes and two upturned shopping trolleys, she emerged into a concrete square and saw the girl, Kay, sitting on a low wall in front of a block of flats. She looked miserable, and made no effort to move as Maya walked up to her.

Chapter Two

Any traces of a tough streetwise kid had disappeared – Kay was a picture of despair. The collar of her leather jacket was turned up, framing a pale face, her skin stretched tightly over sharp cheekbones so that it looked transparent. From deep hollows, her golden eyes shone out wide and luminous, too big for her face and full of unshed tears. She looked dazed and lost, fragile as a trapped bird.

It would have been easy to feel sorry for her, but Maya reminded herself that this girl had mugged her.

'Where's my mobile?' she demanded.

Kay sniffed and said sullenly, 'Gerard, he take it. He rob me. He take everything.'

'Oh, tough luck! Poor you, but actually it was my stuff, not yours!'

Kay sniffed again, wiping the back of her hand across her face. 'You do not understand. I owe him money.'

Maya shrugged, 'Not my problem.'

A tear rolled down the girl's face. 'Gerard is angry, very angry, with me, with you.'

Maya gulped. 'Angry with me, what's he angry with me for? He's got my money, my mobile!'

'His dog cut its foot, so he is angry with you. He take him to the vet.'

'Oh dear, very inconvenient. I can see that would be my fault.' Maya took hold of Kay's arm and hauled her to her feet. 'Come on.'

Kay didn't resist, but groaned in pain. 'Where will you take me?'

'To the vet. I want my mobile back.'

Kay looked as if somebody had just told her she was standing next to an unexploded bomb; her eyes widened, her mouth gaped. 'Gerard is not a good man; when he is angry, he make the dog bite – he is very crazy.'

Yeah, Maya thought, I'll buy that – anybody who walks about with a dog like Gunner has a screw loose. 'Don't worry, I'll think of something,' she said. 'Where's he taken the dog? Which vet?'

'On the high street, next to the bank. We went there last week when the dog was sick.'

'Right, we'll have to hurry.'

Kay pulled back. 'I will not go. I cannot.'

'If you don't help me, I'm calling the cops, I'll tell them you robbed me.'

'No!' Kay looked terrified, throwing her arms over her head as if to defend herself. 'If you call the police they will arrest me.'

She was totally panicked and made to run off, but as soon as she put weight on her foot, she stopped and crumpled in pain. Leaning back, she grabbed onto the wall for support and hung there, one leg in the air.

Maya was just about to reach out and pull her along when Kay suddenly lifted her head and said with a gleam of triumph, 'How can you call the police? You have no mobile.'

Maya gave a wry smile. 'Erm. . . OK. You're right. Look, I'll help you, if you help me.'

The girl screwed up her face, eyeing Maya doubtfully. 'How can you help me?' She winced in pain as she tried again to stand on her damaged leg.

Putting out a hand to steady her, Maya said more sympathetically, 'After we get my mobile, I'll take you home.'

There was an immediate change in Kay's expression. 'Home?' she queried, eagerly. 'You will take me to your home?'

'Not my home, yours,' Maya replied.

Immediately the light in Kay's face died. 'I do not have a home.'

'You must live somewhere.'

Kay answered with a dismissive snort, then slumped down on the wall. 'Yes, I live somewhere,' she said, bitterly. 'Doorways, subway, park, a horrible apartment. Sometimes, if Gerard lets me, I stay at his place.'

'But that's horrible.'

Kay shrugged while Maya stood silently, thinking how awful it would be to be homeless. She looked down at the dark roots showing through Kay's stringy hair, noticed the multiple piercings in her ear.

'Can't you get a job, find somewhere proper to live?'

Kay shot her a challenging glare, her eyes blazing fire. 'Why, why do you think I live like this? I am illegal, I come to the UK to work, six months I work as a cleaner. I clean every day for many hours, then they tell me I do not work hard enough. I owe them money. They use me, so I run away. Now Gerard use me. I have no control – no papers for work.' Her lips pouted and trembled and she gazed off into the distance. 'Before I come here I was a good girl. Now I am a thief and a junkie.'

For a moment Maya was silent, she didn't know what to say. Then, moving closer, she placed her hand firmly under Kay's arm. 'I could try to help you.'

A face full of suspicion looked back at her. Maya saw shadows of past disappointments and betrayals. Suddenly her offer of help seemed empty and worthless, a promise she couldn't deliver on.

'Perhaps I won't be able to. I'm not sure,' she said. 'But at least let me try. My mum works for the government. She knows a lot of people.'

Kay sniffed dismissively. 'If the government know about me, they will arrest me.'

'My mum got me into this country, she adopted me. I'm legal.'

A sudden flash of hope brightened Kay's face. 'OK,' she agreed. 'You help me walk. I will show you the vet but how will you get the mobile?'

'Not me – you! You stole it, you get it back.'

'No! If Gerard finds out I help you he will beat me.'

'Important you don't get caught then. Come on.'

* * *

Along the high street, evening traffic was piling up and motorists stared curiously at the two girls stumbling along – one a tall schoolgirl with a mane of blue-black hair, hobbling slightly, her leg streaked with blood, and her companion, a thin, waif-like, blonde girl with a more pronounced limp.

As they made their way towards the vet's, Kay was whimpering in pain and Maya asked herself if she was being stupidly stubborn about retrieving her mobile. But she couldn't give up. The phone was her only direct link to her mum, top security agent, Pamela Brown. A week earlier she'd watched Pam pack a suitcase with light summer clothing, sandals and long silk scarves. She'd guessed she was heading somewhere east, but Pam was cagey about her assignment.

'The fewer details you know about my destination, the better, don't you think?' Pam had said. 'Look what trouble it got us into during the summer.'

'Oh yeah? And who would have saved you if I hadn't?' Maya shot back.

Pam had dropped the clothes she was holding, wound her arms round her daughter and hugged her tightly.

'Never think I don't value what you did,' she said, kissing the top of Maya's head. 'But I want a normal life for you – school, going out with friends, having fun, not worrying about me.'

But how could Maya not worry when Pam was far away from home, most likely in some dangerous, inhospitable place? Her work as head of a government counter terrorism unit with links to MI5 and MI6 was crucial to the country's security, her expertise always in demand. Maya hadn't heard from her in six days except for one brief call to say she'd arrived – wherever she was. Since then, Maya's mobile had been switched on day and night, because with different time zones Pam might call at any moment. Even at school, although she was breaking the rules, she carried her phone in her pocket.

* * *

The vet's surgery was fronted by darkened shop windows that gave onto the street. Maya tried to peer in but couldn't see a thing. She had more luck peeping through the notices on the clear glass door and saw a couple of people sitting with baskets at their feet, but there was no Gunner or Gerard.

'Don't let him see you,' Kay urged, standing behind Maya.

'He isn't there.'

'He must be.'

'Could be in with the vet. They wouldn't keep Gunner hanging about – not with those guinea pigs and rabbits.'

Suddenly the door opened and a huge beefy guy carrying a white rabbit came out. Maya held the door open then stepped inside.

'Can I help you?' a woman behind the reception desk asked.

'I . . . er. . .'

'Are you sure you don't need a doctor?' the woman said, eyeing Maya's bloody leg.

'Oh, no, I'm fine, I . . . er . . . sorry, I just wondered. . . I'm looking for somebody.'

'Young man and a dog with a cut paw?'

'Yes.'

'He's in surgery. It was an emergency. Could be a while yet,' the woman said pointing to a door at the back of the waiting area.

'Thank you,' Maya said, backing away.

Outside, she grabbed hold of Kay. 'Come on, we're going round the back.'

Kay protested but Maya drew her down the alleyway between the surgery and a betting shop. 'It's hot, yeah?' Maya said.

Kay gave her a puzzled look.

'So they're bound to have windows open.'

'You are crazy,' Kay whispered.

At the back of the surgery were a small car park and a brick extension. Maya put her finger to her lips and slowly and silently moved towards the biggest window, which was slightly open. Flattening herself against the wall, she edged forward and peered in.

In the middle of the room was a high metal table and on it was Gunner. There was no mistaking the dog, but the fear factor had gone – he was laid out cold. Music played in the background as a young woman, presumably the vet, sewed up his cut paw; the sheet underneath was soaked with blood.

Her hand on the window, Maya waited, then, putting her faith in a blast of louder music, she dared to lever the window open a little wider. A pair of skinny legs disappearing into black studded boots came into view to one side of the window – they had to be Gerard's – and, next to them, just under the window, was her bag.

Tilting her head, she managed to see Gerard's face.

He was gazing forwards, his attention focused on the operation. Never taking her eyes off his profile, she eased the window open a little more and slid her arm down over the sill. Groping with her fingers, she found the strap to her bag, gripped it and pulled. Suddenly Gerard shifted, he flicked back a long strand of hair and sat forward. She froze. The bag dangled in the air. At any moment she expected him to dart towards her, but then he spoke.

'Gunner will be all right, won't 'e?'

The vet, intent on her work, didn't look up as she answered. If she had, she would have seen a girl's arm hoisting a bag through an open window. The slight scuffing noise it made as Maya pulled it over the sill sent her into a mad panic and she grabbed it with both hands and dodged down beneath the window. Crouching on the gravel, she hardly dared breathe. Blood beat in her ears as she waited for a shout or a head to be thrust through the window above her. Nothing came, no sound, nobody appeared, so, cautiously, she wriggled sideways, shimmied upright and tiptoed away.

Before rounding the corner, she flung a quick glance over her shoulder. Kay hadn't moved, she was standing at the other side of the window, frozen and white as a ghost.

In the alleyway, Maya stopped for a moment to dip her hand in her bag. Fumbling between the books and loose papers, her fingers grasped a small solid block. Yes – she had her phone! Now all she had to do was leg it up the road and disappear.

The first obstacle was to get past the vet's front door. Peering cautiously round the corner, she dodged back as the door opened. A thin woman carrying a cat basket emerged. She waited, then, just as she was about to take off, Kay grasped her shoulder in a vice-like grip.

'We must go. We must go before Gerard finds out and comes after us.'

'Us? I'm going home,' Maya said.

'No, you cannot leave me. I have a bad foot.' Kay's eyes were wild with fear. 'I cannot run. Gerard, he will. . .' She stopped suddenly and her face became sulky, her voice accusing. 'You promise to help me.'

Maya sighed. 'All right, come on, I'll take you to a friend's café.'

'I cannot walk. I try but the pain is bad.'

Aware that at any moment Gerard could come rushing out of the surgery, Maya bit back her irritation, hitched her bag onto her shoulder and bent down.

'Jump up. I'll give you a piggyback.'

Kay clung on like a limpet as Maya stumbled along the high street. Victor's café was only a short distance, but to Maya it seemed further than all the races she'd run that day. Her schoolbag was heavy, Kay's bony fingers were like claws digging painfully into her shoulders and her foot was hurting. And, for all she knew, Gerard could be right behind them – it wasn't possible to turn round to check. When she finally lurched in through the open door of the café, she was filled with relief.

After depositing Kay in the nearest chair she slumped down herself.

'Oh, my God, I'm whacked. I thought any moment he'd come running out and catch up with us,' Maya said. 'That was exhausting.'

'I am not heavy,' Kay said.

'I was carrying you and my bag!'

Kay lifted her damaged leg onto a vacant chair, settled back and unzipped her leather jacket. 'Why do you care so much about your mobile?' she asked, fixing Maya with her gold stare.

The question took Maya by surprise. She bit her lip, gazing into the distance a moment before answering. 'My mum's away, I don't know where she is. She calls

me on my mobile. Without it . . . I won't know . . .
I won't know if she's safe.'

'Safe?'

'My mum's work is special. She can't always tell
me where she's going. If I don't answer my phone
then she might not have another chance to call me.
And if I don't answer she might think something's
happened to me.' Her voice went quieter until it was
barely a whisper. 'You wouldn't understand.'

Kay's amber eyes were bold and challenging. 'No.
I do not understand. I have no mother, no family.'

Maya swallowed. 'I'm sorry.'

A dark shadow fell over Kay's face and Maya
saw her withdraw into herself. Silence stretched
between them. Maya felt responsible, wishing she
hadn't mentioned her mum, but then she thought
with a twinge of irritation, shouldn't it be Kay who
was feeling bad? She'd stolen her bag and mobile and
caused that mad dog to chase her, scaring the pants off
her. She ought to keep away from guys like Gerard.

'Is Gerard your boyfriend?'

Kay sniffed. 'Sometimes.'

'Why do you owe him money?'

'He gives me stuff to deliver.'

'What sort of stuff?'

Kay slid her hand up to her hair, tugging at the thin blonde strands. She looked down, blinking. 'He is a dealer.'

'What, you mean drugs?'

'Of course.'

'You sell drugs?'

Kay shrugged. 'Mostly I just carry stuff for him. But this time he ask me to get money for him – five thousand pounds he want for this package and I lose it. I must pay him back.'

Maya's eyes opened wide. 'Five thousand pounds!' She shook her head. 'You're not going to make five thousand pounds stealing a few mobiles.'

'I know. He wants me to do something worse than steal. He says I must go with men but I say no, never.'

Maya looked at Kay with horror. What on earth was she mixed up in?

Victor, the owner of the café, came over to take their order – tea for Maya and strong black coffee for Kay. While he went to fetch their drinks, Maya was trying to imagine what Kay's life was really like.

'Earlier – you said some words in another language,' she said.

'So?' came Kay's sharp response.

26

'Where are you from?' Maya asked.

Kay's face went blank, all emotion scrubbed away from it. Then she said firmly, 'I do not talk about it. None of your business.'

'I'm sorry. I just thought, well . . . I was adopted, so. . .'

'So you were lucky.'

A sharp, stony silence divided them, while Maya struggled with questions she dared not ask.

Finally she said, 'When my mum comes back I'll talk to her, she might be able to arrange something.' Her voice tailed off – they both knew it was a slim hope. 'Have you got a mobile?'

Kay shook her head. 'Gerard take it.'

'Here, I'll give you my number.' Maya picked up her bag and searched for pen and paper. All her books were still there, purse, papers, pencil case, then her fingers clutched a soft package that wasn't familiar. She drew it out.

Kay's eyes opened wide. 'Oh, my God! Give it to me, give it to me!'

Maya handed over the package and Kay bent and examined it. Inside the polythene was a square foil packet.

'Look, see the number written on back.' She kept

staring at the parcel like she'd found treasure. 'I lose this, so why did Gerard have it and put it in the bag?' She frowned. 'Maybe he trick me. He have package all the time. He want me to think I lose it.'

Maya watched as Kay wrestled with the problem, but then her face cleared, she shrugged and looked happier.

'No. Gerard did not do that. I think he find the package. He want to tell me but you are there, then his dog was hurt – he forget.' She grinned. 'Everything is OK now.' She levered herself up. 'You have the mobile, I have the package. I will go.'

'All right. But, look, take my number.' Maya wrote down her mobile number and the house phone. 'Call me,' she said handing Kay the paper.

Kay put the paper in her pocket. Then, with boot in hand, she limped towards the door.

'You can't walk home like that,' Maya said.

'Don't worry, I will get a taxi. See you.'

As she disappeared from view, Maya stared after her. If Kay had money for a taxi, why on earth had she accepted a piggyback ride to the café? She sipped her tea gazing at the door and wondered if she'd ever see Kay again.

Chapter Three

A warm waft of spice-scented air greeted Maya as she entered the kitchen. There was some compensation when Pam was away – Maya's grandmother Helen came to stay and cooked fabulous food.

'What's on the menu tonight, Gran?' Maya asked, putting down her schoolbag.

'Chicken tagine,' Helen answered, setting a large casserole dish on the table. 'I thought you'd be here hours ago.'

'Sorry. Athletics practice, then the coach wanted to talk to me. I didn't realise how late it was.'

Helen turned, glanced quizzically at Maya, then looked more closely. 'What's happened to you?' Her eyes swept over Maya's dishevelled state. 'You've got blood on your leg and your skirt's torn. You look as if you've been in a fight.'

'I know. I'm an idiot.' Maya made a face and went over to the sink to wash her hands. 'I fell on the pavement – wasn't looking where I was going.'

Helen's sharp eyes followed Maya as she dried her hands then moved to sit down at the table.

'You're limping. Are you sure you're not hurt?'

'Scraped my foot, that's all. It's fine. I'll have a shower after I've eaten.'

'As long as you're OK. No broken bones?'

'No. It's just a scratch, a bit painful, that's all.' Maya helped herself to some rice. 'I did great tonight – shaved three seconds off my best time.'

'Well done!' Helen said. 'That's amazing. You must have a good chance of winning the inter-schools.' She spooned a heap of chicken onto Maya's plate. 'I'm glad you're home now, though. I was beginning to worry. You should have called me.'

Maya apologised. It had been a split-second decision not to tell Helen about what had really happened on the way home, but she was pleased she hadn't. It was only a few weeks since Helen had had to cope with terrorist threats made to her daughter and granddaughter and the terrifying events that had followed – Maya figured her gran deserved a break.

But though she didn't talk about being mugged or the whole episode afterwards, she couldn't stop thinking about Kay. Time and time again she saw Kay's tiny, haunted face. She listened to Helen explaining about her new yoga class and an interesting radio play, but as she tucked into Helen's delicious cooking, she couldn't forget how excited Kay had been when she thought she was going home with her.

You're crazy, she told herself, she's just a thieving, smelly street kid. Rank hair, pale face, thin as a rake – and she said she's a junkie. But, she couldn't help thinking, if Pam hadn't adopted me, I could have been Kay – homeless and desperate.

'I wonder if Mum will call tonight,' she said to Helen, as they cleared dishes from the table.

'I wish I knew where she was,' Helen said.

'Me too,' Maya answered.

Homework took up most of her time after dinner. Pam didn't call and later, when she was lying in bed, it took a long time for Maya to fall asleep.

Meeting Kay had stirred up memories. In her dreams, fragments of images fluttered around her head like circling moths – the heavy bolt on a cellar door, numbers etched on a stone wall, icy water slopping from a bucket, a covered head bobbing in prayer.

Feelings long buried took shape and tugged at her as she fell in and out of sleep – the cold clutch of hunger, the sweet melody of a song, the fearful boom of falling shells. And, most vivid of all – the sharp stab of terror when they came – ringing footsteps descending, coming closer and closer to the cellar door, men with rough hands, pushing and shouting, the dark heavy metal of guns and her father, tall as a tree, forced to the ground.

Then came the familiar sense of panic – separated from her family, she was running, searching, shouting out their names. She tossed and turned as the images flickered and faded. There were no faces, just shadows, until the shadows were consumed by flames – fierce, flaring flames lighting up the night sky. It was a recurring dream – flames silhouetting a church roof, flames licking at a locked door and inside the flames people screaming.

The dream ended as it always did with Maya shouting out in her sleep, but this time, just before she woke she saw something new – a girl, a small girl, thin with straggly blonde hair. She grabbed Maya's hands and pulled her away from the fire, muttering words in a language Maya couldn't understand. The girl's hands were hard and firm on her back, and then she was falling. The last thing she saw were the girl's eyes, lit by the fire – they gleamed with a golden light.

When she awoke, Maya's face was wet with tears, her breath hot as she sat up in bed, clasping and unclasping her hands.

Helen, who'd come running at the sound of Maya's cries, switched on the light. 'Maya! What's wrong?'

'A dream, the same one I always have. It was horrible – I was holding my mum's hand but, she let go. I couldn't find her and then people were screaming – they couldn't escape and the fire was getting bigger.'

Helen took Maya in her arms and hugged her. 'Oh, my love, you're safe now.'

Maya shuddered, burying her head for a moment in Helen's shoulder. 'I'm sorry, sorry to make so much fuss. Sorry I woke you.'

'It doesn't matter one bit. I'm glad I heard you.' She kissed the top of Maya's head. 'Do you want to talk about it?'

'No. It's gone. I'm fine now. I'll go back to sleep.'

Helen nodded and stood up. Maya lay back on her pillow and briefly closed her eyes but just as Helen was about to leave she spoke.

'I saw something new. There was a girl. She saved me – pulled me away from the fire. She was shouting. I couldn't understand her, but I think she was telling me to move, and when I didn't, she dragged me away. And I saw her face, I'm sure I did but now. . .' Maya rubbed at her eyes. 'I can't remember, I can't see her – she's gone.'

'She pushed you into the ditch?'

Deep furrows etched Maya's face. 'I think so, I was falling and then I woke up.'

Helen smiled and squeezed her hand. 'And that was where you were found – in the ditch.'

'Yep, Maya, the bog child. Pam said I was so dirty, they didn't know if I was a boy or girl.'

'Well, whoever that girl was, if she did save you from the fire, I will thank her forever.'

Maya squinted up at Helen and smiled. 'Me too,' she said, turning onto her side. 'I'm OK now, Gran. Go back to bed. Sorry, I was such a baby.'

Helen shook her head. 'Give yourself a break. You can't be superwoman all the time.'

For the rest of the night, Maya fell into a deep sleep. When she woke, her dreams were forgotten. It was Saturday and uppermost in her mind was the party her best friends Leona and Evie were giving to welcome her back to school.

A few weeks before the summer holidays began there had been threats to kidnap Maya and she'd had to quit London to hide in the countryside at Helen's cottage. What should have been a nice long relaxing holiday before GCSEs kicked in properly had turned out to be a harrowing, dangerous adventure, and she hadn't been able to return to London or see her friends until the new term began.

To make up for all the fun times she'd missed, there was to be a big party at Leona's house, so Maya's morning was spent getting ready and deciding what to wear. After several phone calls to Leona, she discarded a dress bought for her by Pam, deciding it was gorgeous but too posh, and instead she chose a red silk top and new jeans – casual with a touch of glamour was the look she was aiming for. The cut on her foot was a nuisance, but there were some new high-heeled sandals she just had to wear.

It was these sandals she was cursing as she hobbled through Parkland Estate towards Leona's house – and that blasted dog for chasing her. Holding onto a gate, she lifted her leg and was busy inspecting her foot to see if the cut had reopened when she was startled by a sudden whirring of wheels and loud shout. She reared up as a bicycle raced towards her, mounted the pavement, then wheeled away.

'Hey, watch it!' she yelled.

The cyclist pedalled off, then turned and came back. It was one of the crop-haired boys who'd asked her for money the previous day. He skidded to a halt in front of her.

'You're the girl Gerard robbed yesterday, ain't ya?'

Maya shrugged.

''E's looking for you.'

'What?'

''E reckons you took your stuff back, and took something else that belongs to 'im.'

'Rubbish! He's a liar,' Maya shot back.

The boy laughed. ''E's after you and 'e'll get you.' Then, turning the handlebars of his bike, he scooted off, shouting over his shoulder. ''Is dog'll eat your 'ead.'

'Thanks,' Maya called after him. 'Thanks for nothing.'

Suddenly the estate seemed like enemy territory. In the distance a dog barked and Maya doubly cursed her elegant sandals as she tottered and tripped towards Leona's house. If Gerard appeared with Gunner, she had no chance of running.

With relief she reached Leona's gate and closed it

firmly behind her. Music spilled out of open windows as she knocked on the door and then Leona was there, welcoming her with a friendly squeal.

'Hey, babes! Brilliant, you're early. Come on in!'

She was grinning widely as she ushered Maya through to the living room.

'Wow! I can't believe you've done all this for me!' Maya exclaimed, looking round the room festooned with balloons, streamers and 'Welcome Back' signs.

'You're my mate. It was a lousy summer without you.'

'It wasn't exactly wonderful for me,' Maya said, with a wry smile.

'I know.' Leona gave her a pat on the back, then climbed onto a chair to tie up an escaping balloon. 'It must have been horrible wondering what was happening to your mum.'

'Yeah,' Maya agreed. 'It was.'

'You were amazing,' Leona said, jumping back down from the chair.

'I didn't really stop to think. It happened so fast.' She scrunched up her face. 'What I told you is secret. Don't go spreading it around, will you?'

'No, course not, but if it was me, I'd want it all over the papers.'

'I wouldn't have minded – front page headlines, celebrity.' Raising her hands, Maya went into action hero pose and commented in exaggerated newsreader style. 'FIFTEEN YEAR OLD SCHOOLGIRL THWARTS TERRORISTS. MOTHER SNATCHED FROM THE JAWS OF HELL BY. . .' her voice softened, 'drop-dead gorgeous, super-intelligent daughter.'

'Go, girl!' Leona laughed.

Maya lowered her hands and made a disappointed face. 'Sadly not to be. Pam has to keep a low profile.' She picked up a red balloon and started to blow. 'Did I tell you she wanted me to change schools?' she continued between puffs.

Leona looked horrified. 'No! You didn't tell me that!'

'She wanted me to go to a boarding school. Said it would be easier to protect me if any trouble kicked off again.'

'Well, I'm glad you didn't.'

'Me too,' Maya said as she finished blowing up the balloon. She tied it and batted it to her friend. 'Couldn't leave my old mates, could I?'

Leona batted the balloon back. 'Nah, me and Evie couldn't survive Maths without you. Who'd do our homework? And you'd be a walking disaster without us – you'd turn into a right nerd.' She turned to look at herself in the mirror, adjusting a string of giant white beads. 'Like your top by the way, and your sandals. '

'Thanks. You look great, as always.'

Leona gathered up her hair and let it fall again. 'Up or down?'

Maya laughed. 'Definitely down, it looks sexier.'

'Thank the lord for hair extensions,' Leona said, posing.

Maya went up behind her and pulled faces in the mirror. Turning round, Leona gave her a hug.

'I'm so glad you didn't get hurt or nothing. And don't you think about going to another school – you, me and Evie, we're the Fearsome Threesome, always.'

Maya laughed. 'Fill me in on who's coming tonight.'

'All the usual suspects from school, plus Jimbo and Danny from year twelve, Petra from next door, my cousin Serena.'

'Oh right, so that's all the guys spoken for, then.'

Leona nodded. 'Yep, nothing compares to Serena. She's bringing her new boyfriend. He's cool, he's been hanging around with us all summer – you've missed loads.'

'Thanks, that makes me feel a whole lot better,' Maya said.

Leona laughed. 'Come on, let's organise some drink.'

They went into the kitchen where plates of food covered in cling film sat on the work tops. Leona opened a cupboard and took out a jug, pulled a big pack of ice from the freezer and fished two rolling pins out of a drawer.

As they banged away at the ice, Leona asked, 'So, where's your mum gone now?'

Maya whacked the cluster of cubes with a hefty blow. 'She wouldn't tell me.'

'Sometimes I wish my mum would disappear,' Leona said. 'She's always on at me.'

'Your mum's lovely.'

'Hey, did I tell you I've got a Saturday job?' Leona asked. 'I'm starting next week. It was Serena's, but she's working full time now – chucked school and she's working in Topshop.'

'Maybe I should get a job,' Maya said.

'You don't need it. You've got money.'

'I'm not rich,' Maya protested.

'No, you live on the estate like the rest of us, yeah?' Leona answered.

Maya didn't take offence. She knew Leona envied her elegant two storey apartment on its quiet leafy street, but Leona also knew there were times when Maya would have swapped with her to have a family life with a mum and dad at home and two older brothers who adored her.

'I think these are small enough now,' Maya said, inspecting the plastic bag of broken ice.

She limped over to get the jug.

'What's wrong with your leg?' Leona asked.

'Cut it, last night. I was mugged.'

'What?' Leona gasped, open-mouthed. 'Why didn't you tell me? I called you three times this morning and you never mentioned it.'

'I was going to, but I don't know, it was weird . . . strange. I met this girl and well, I got my stuff back and. . .'

There was a sudden movement behind her and Maya turned to see Leona's mum Sadie enter the kitchen.

'How's my beautiful Maya? Welcome back! We thought we'd lost you forever!' Sadie said, as she enfolded Maya in a big bear hug. 'Good to see you. Now you enjoy the party, huh? I cooked your favourite bean patties.'

Breathing in Sadie's familiar scent of lavender soap and spices, Maya put her arms round Sadie's ample middle and hugged her back. 'Thanks Sadie!'

Kissing Maya's forehead, Sadie broke away and gestured to the food and drink. 'Don't you be too busy dancin' and canoodlin' that you forget to eat. And watch if anybody's smugglin' in alcohol. Don't want nobody passing out on my bathroom floor.' She rearranged a couple of cupcakes, then span round towards the door, skirt swaying, long scarf floating behind her. 'Any problems, I'm four doors away. You have a good time, now.'

'We will,' Maya and Leona answered.

They heard voices in the hallway. 'Some guests have arrived,' Sadie shouted, on her way out.

'Go on. Tell me,' Leona said. 'Quick before everybody comes in. What happened?'

Maya poured some ice into the jug. 'It's a long story. I'll tell you later.'

* * *

Some of the first guests to make an appearance were Evie and her friend Zac.

'I told you I'd bring him,' Evie said, ushering Zac

in and smiling smugly as if she'd turned up with precious treasure.

Zac gave a general, 'Hi,' to everybody then stepped towards Maya and held out a long thin arm to solemnly shake her hand. 'Hi! I'm Zac,' he said, smiling broadly.

Mm! That smile could melt chocolate, Maya thought.

And she liked him instantly – perfect teeth, smooth, nutty skin and eyes that sparkled with a hint of mischief. She wasn't sure about the wild Afro hair and the attempt at a goatee, but he was certainly better than average.

'Maya, right?' he asked, holding onto her hand. 'Evie tells me you run.'

Maya smiled. 'Not all the time. Sometimes I stand still.'

Zac threw his head back, light glinting on his cheekbones and laughed. 'Not a great openin' line.'

'It's OK. Evie's always teasing me about running, and how much I miss out on by not going shopping instead.'

'Dead right,' Evie said. 'You can get all the exercise you want walking up and down Oxford Street.'

'Oh yeah, lifting all those carrier bags,' Maya said,

seizing Evie's arm. 'Feel these muscles.'

'Maya!' Evie shrieked.

'You *are* friends?' Zac asked, in mock seriousness.

'Been together since junior school,' Evie said, thumping Maya's arm. 'She's a bit of a freak, but can be a good laugh, if you get her in the right mood.'

With a pat on first Maya's then Zac's shoulders, Evie moved away. 'I'll find Leona. Leave you two nerds to get to know each other.'

They watched Evie sashay into the kitchen, where a growing number of people were chatting loudly.

'Evie talks about you a lot,' Zac said. 'She admires you.'

'Really?'

'Yeah, says you're focused. Know what you want.'

Maya raised her eyebrows. 'Maybe. Well, yeah, I suppose I do.'

'And what would that be?'

'To pass my exams, go to uni, work for the government – like my mum.'

'Top security agent.'

'Somebody's been talking.'

'Only a little bit. Just enough to get me interested.'

'Well, I hope I live up to expectations.'

Zac smiled. 'More than.'

They laughed, their eyes meeting.

I like him, Maya thought. He's not afraid to say what he thinks.

A lot of boys she knew were so guarded, so worried about saying the wrong thing, or then there was the opposite type, who thought everything they said was world news. But Zac seemed easy with himself, and had a sense of humour, was good-looking – and that smile was dynamite. She also liked the fact that he was taller than she was.

They moved into a corner and sat down, Zac stretching out his long legs in front of him. Conversation flowed easily and they found they had lots in common – they liked the same music, sports, food and TV programmes, and could have carried on talking non-stop if Leona hadn't reappeared and dragged them up to dance.

'I've got a bad foot, remember?' Maya moaned, but really she was pleased to dance with Zac. And he turned out to be an all right dancer – not one of those guys who hardly moved and just sort of twitched when they were supposed to be dancing, or one of those stupid macho types who thought dancing was just another way to show off. He moved naturally, elegantly.

When a song with a slower beat started to play, Zac moved forward and put his arms round her and she was only too pleased to rest her head on his shoulder. For a moment she closed her eyes. The rhythm was slow and sensuous and for the first time in ages she felt relaxed. The feeling didn't last long. A hand touched her arm, she opened her eyes and over Zac's shoulder saw Leona leading her cousin Serena into the room.

Whenever Serena walked into a room it was an event. She was stunningly beautiful and everything about her was perfect – her hair, her clothes, the way she walked. Maya had seen her only a few times over the past couple of years and had to admit she'd grown even more gorgeous.

She was so busy admiring Serena, looking at her cool hairstyle and make-up, that it took a moment to see she was holding somebody's hand. When her eyes flicked away from Serena's shimmering dress to the slim, dark-haired guy by her side, she gasped. His face was tilted away from her, a strand of long, black, silky hair hung over one eye, giving him a shadowy look – just as the hood had done last night. She only had a moment to recover before Serena introduced him. 'This is Gerard.'

Maya tensed as Gerard glanced at her. She saw his eyes narrow, a flicker of recognition, and then he smiled. 'So, this is where all the good-lookin' girls have been hidin',' he said.

'Smooth talker, ain't he?' Serena said, gripping his arm.

'Yeah, real smooth,' Maya answered, the words sliding slowly out of her mouth, her tongue curling upwards as she stared him fully in the face.

The Gerard that looked back at her was transformed. This guy who was Serena's boyfriend smiled in a friendly, open manner. His brown eyes fringed with dark lashes gleamed with good humour. Instead of the dark hoodie, he was wearing a white sports shirt, his black hair carefully combed so that it curled over the back of the collar, just one silky strand framing his finely-sculpted cheekbones. Maya remembered his skin as sallow, but in the soft light of the living room, it took on a bronze sheen. The whole image added up to a cool, stylish guy, with an air of ease and confidence – someone you'd definitely want to be seen with.

'So, do you . . . er . . . wanna dance?' Gerard asked, nodding towards Maya. And, before she could collect her thoughts, he had hold of her arm.

'Hey, are you leavin' me?' Serena protested.

Gerard turned and laughed. 'You told me, "Don't be shy – make friends."' He twirled Maya round. 'So I'm makin' friends.'

'Yeah, you just watch yourself!' Serena retorted.

He gave Maya no chance to escape, pulling her away from the others and locking his arms round her back. 'Say anythin' and you're dead,' he whispered.

'Like to bet?' Maya snapped. 'The last person who tried it ended up splattered.'

'Think you're so smart? I know who you are, Serena told me – Mummy's some kind of cop, a government agent or some such crap, but she's not 'ere now, is she?'

'You want to be careful. You're lucky I haven't shopped you. Have you told the beautiful Serena you nick bags for a living?'

Gerard glanced over his shoulder and saw the others had retreated into the kitchen. Quick as a flash, his fingers snaked round Maya's neck, digging painfully into a nerve, making her feel dizzy. 'You've got somethin' of mine,' he snarled.

'I don't know what you mean,' Maya said weakly.

He grasped a handful of her hair, covertly twisting the strands and pulling her close. 'You think I'm stupid. Kay told me you stole your bag back. That package was in it for safe keepin'. Thought you'd come into a fortune, did you, or, were you gonna dob me in to Mummy?'

'I haven't got. . .'

'Don't bullshit me. Bring it tomorrow to the ice rink – two o' clock. If you're not there, I'll come lookin' for you – me and Gunner.' He screwed her hair tighter. 'Don't think you can get away with it, I got eyes everywhere, my mates keepin' an eye out for me. Every time you walk down the street you are watched. Next time you won't escape.'

He jabbed his fingers hard into her neck before suddenly letting go and walking out of the room. Left reeling, Maya stumbled backwards and sank down onto a sofa. Gently massaging her neck she heard Serena laughing in the kitchen.

'Maya too fast for you, darlin'? Come and chill with me and Leona, we're more relaxed, ain't we, girl?'

When Leona giggled in reply, Maya felt betrayed. And Kay! She'd dumped her in it by telling Gerard that Maya had the drugs.

Her neck hurt. She wriggled her shoulders and attempted to make circles with her head but it was too painful. Gerard must have had training – he knew how to use minimum force for maximum effect.

More people were arriving, talking and shouting, and she drew into a corner of the sofa where she could sit unnoticed. Part of her was angry she hadn't hit back at Gerard or publicly denounced him, but she knew why she hadn't – as much as she was accepted by Leona, Evie and the other kids on the estate, ultimately she wasn't one of them. She was different, an outsider. And Serena was top of the heap, as far as the girls were concerned. What Serena wore was cool, what Serena said was listened to, her boyfriends admired – she had respect.

'You OK?' Zac bent down in front of her.

'Yeah.'

'Do you wanna dance?'

'Not really.'

He held out his hand. 'Come on through to the kitchen, then,' he said, pulling her up. 'Let's get a drink.'

The kitchen was packed. Leona and Serena were sipping some lethal-looking cocktails.

'Have some,' Serena said, 'it's wicked.' She was giggling as she poured more from the jug into the stemmed glass Leona was holding.

'I'm not good with alcohol,' Maya said.

'Chill, girl! There's only a bit of vodka in it. The rest is juice, but don't tell no one.' Smiling, Serena pulled a glass from the worktop, filled it and handed it to Maya. 'Nice to see you. You look cool. I like that top. I can tell Gerard's well impressed.' She turned and looked over her shoulder. 'Hey, baby!'

Gerard had appeared in the doorway. He came over and draped an arm around her.

'How long have you two known each other?' Maya asked.

'Seven weeks, five days,' Serena answered, with a smile. She looked up at Gerard, nuzzled into his neck and whispered something to him.

He kissed her hair and said softly, 'Yeah, babe. Course I did.' His fingers stroked her cheek. 'Wouldn't let you down, would I? Bring your friends outside.'

Maya watched as Serena whispered something to Leona and Evie, then they all went out of the back door.

'What do you think's going on?' she asked Zac.

Zac shrugged. 'Some kind of surprise, maybe.'

Maya looked doubtful. 'Don't think so. I'm going to see what's happening.'

Putting down her glass, she motioned to Zac to follow her and they hid behind the half-open door, peering through the crack. Her friends were gathered round Gerard, standing with their heads bent, eyes focused on something he was holding. Then Leona leaned back slightly and turned to look at the house. In the split second before she dodged back, Maya saw Gerard drop something into Evie's hand.

Maya didn't hesitate. 'Hey, what's happening?' she asked, charging out into the yard.

Her friends looked guilty. Leona shrank back, shuffling her feet.

'Oh, er . . . nothing. Gerard's just . . . telling us . . . stuff.'

'Stuff,' Gerard echoed, with a wide grin.

'Sure,' Maya nodded, tugging at Leona's arm.

'What?' Leona asked.

'I want to tell you something.'

'So, tell me.'

'Bit of a disaster in the kitchen. Help me sort it.'

She dragged Leona inside, past Zac's startled eyes and into a corner. 'Don't trust him,' she said urgently.

'Who, Gerard?'

'Yeah. He's vile. Yesterday, when I was coming home from school, he was the one, the thieving moron who nicked my schoolbag – took everything, mobile, money.'

'No way,' Leona exclaimed. 'Gerard's not like that!'

Maya shot her an impatient glance. 'Listen! I took a short cut down the alley to the estate and he was waiting – Gerard. He had a vicious dog and he threatened me – if I didn't give him my mobile and schoolbag he'd set his dog on me.'

Leona looked stunned. 'No way, not Gerard. He wouldn't want your stuff. He's always got money and he's generous with it. Must have been somebody else. Did you get a good look at him?'

'Yes, I did and I'm sure it was him. Does he have a dog?'

'Well, yeah, he does but. . .'

'That's him then,' Maya said. 'You should warn Serena.'

'She's crazy about him, reckons he's the one.'

Maya raised her eyebrows. 'I kind of got that by the way she was draped all over him.'

'What's got into you?' Leona asked, picking up on Maya's stinging tone. 'You never used to be so suspicious.'

'Suspicious! The guy robbed me! And he's a dealer. Have you looked at Serena's eyes lately, her pupils are like marbles.'

Leona pursed her lips and looked away. 'She's excited is all, got a new man, yeah?' She made a pleading face. 'Give Gerard a chance, he's cool and he's a laugh.'

Maya bit her lip, thinking of things she'd like to say, but before any words were spoken, Leona broke contact, turning away and shouting over to Zac, 'Hey, Zac, give this girl a drink.'

'What's goin' on?' Zac asked, as Leona slipped back outside.

Maya shook her head. 'I'm not sure, but I don't trust that Gerard guy.'

She slid behind the door again, watching the girls clustering round him. Serena had both her arms clasped round his shoulders and Leona was laughing hard at something he'd said. She leaned forward to catch his words.

'Seein' 'ow it's you – a tenner.' He tapped her gently on the nose. 'Now you can really party, girl.'

Chapter Four

Maya stood in the kitchen, feeling lost and helpless, as her friends came trooping back in.

'Come on, let's go and dance,' Leona shouted, making a grab for Maya's arm.

'Yeah, in a minute,' Maya said, fending her off. 'I'll just finish my drink.'

'OK, baby,' Leona giggled. She lurched forward and reached for Zac, dragging him towards the music, with Serena and Evie following. The back door slammed and, turning round, Maya saw that Gerard had come in. Moving forward, she barred his way.

'Are you selling drugs to my friends?' she asked quietly.

He rocked back on his heels and smiled smugly. 'What's that got to do with you?'

'I want you to leave them alone.'

'I don't think they want me to leave them alone. They're just learnin' 'ow to enjoy themselves.' He grinned, but when he stepped closer, his eyes were as hard as stone. 'You don't belong on this patch. Bring me my stash tomorrow – then keep away. I got somethin' goin' 'ere and you are not gonna mess it up. Understood?'

Maya glared at him. 'There are plenty of people you can sell drugs to – not my mates. I know people – cops, I could. . .'

Gerard's face sharpened, his eyes narrowed, his hand reached into his pocket. 'You don't wanna try that, girl.'

Suddenly his fist was in front of Maya's face. She reeled back when she saw a knife blade glinting.

Gerard grabbed her arm. 'Mummy can't protect you now, can she?' He dug his fingers into her flesh. 'Deliver that package to me, two o' clock tomorrow or you're dog meat.' Then, after looking over his shoulder, he leaned forward. Maya felt his hot breath on her cheek. 'You owe me. I got a big bill to pay to fix up Gunner's paw. I told Kay you was trouble.'

Maya stood her ground, trying to stop trembling

and keep her voice controlled. 'Where is Kay?' she demanded.

'She ain't comin' out tonight,' Gerard laughed, his spit landing on her cheek. 'She's got business to take care of.'

'I thought she was your girlfriend.'

He smirked. 'Kay? She's anybody's.'

'You don't care, do you? You don't care about anything or anybody,' Maya snapped.

'Smart, ain't you?' Gerard sneered. He touched the knife blade to the tip of her nose. 'Two o' clock sharp tomorrow, or I'll have to punish your friend Kay for tellin' me lies.'

Cold shivers ran over Maya's skin. As if from a great distance, she heard Leona's voice behind her.

'Oh great, you two have made friends,' she trilled, seeing their heads so close together.

Gerard's face softened. He closed his fist, slipped the flick knife quickly back into his pocket and patted Maya's shoulder. 'We was just talkin' over what 'appened last night. My mistake. Should 'ave known that girl Kay was up to no good. She's scum. We understand each other now, don't we, Maya?'

Maya just stared.

* * *

What felt like a million hours later, Maya sat with Zac in the garden. The warmth of the day had gone and she shivered. Zac took off his jacket and placed it round her shoulders.

'So, how do you feel now?' he asked her.

'Don't know. Not much different, a bit hyper, twitchy. Somebody must have spiked my drink.'

'Make sure you have plenty of water before you go to sleep or you'll have a stormin' headache tomorrow.'

'Yeah, thanks. I hate feeling like this; I like to be in control.'

'I gathered that.' Zac took her hand, gently massaging her fingers. 'How come you've stayed friends with Leona and this crowd – you're so different.'

'Am I? Sometimes I'm not sure where I belong,' Maya said, 'not sure I fit in anywhere. But at least Evie and Leona accept me for who I am. We've been best mates since junior school, ever since I punched a boy who kept throwing sand in their faces.' She laughed at the memory. 'We've always done stuff together – picnics, skating, sleepovers, netball – we were the best netball team, no other school could beat us. Actually, Evie's brilliant at sport, a good hockey player, but don't let on I told you. We've got more in common than you might think.'

Zac nodded. 'OK. I get it, but you aren't from round here, are you?'

'Close. I live the other side of the high street.'

'The posh side.'

'I suppose so,' Maya admitted.

'Other side of the tracks – different world,' Zac said. He looked suddenly thoughtful, staring out at the rose-scented garden. 'I grew up in the same street as my friends, one of them lives next door, but he don't want to know me now. He's in a gang, heavy stuff. Things change, I guess.'

He let go of Maya's hand and got to his feet. 'I have to go. My mum worries.' He squeezed her shoulder. 'Don't sit out here, OK? Go inside, drink more water.'

For a moment he stood looking down at her. She didn't want him to go. She wanted to tell him about Gerard, about how he'd threatened her if she didn't deliver the package of drugs. It was so tempting to ask him for help, but she had no right to involve him. Gerard was vicious – she'd seen the hate in his eyes – he wouldn't hesitate to knife Zac if he tried to interfere.

Zac smiled and bent close. She thought he was going to kiss her, but instead he ran his fingers lightly over her hair, his fingers brushing her cheek.

'You're cool,' he said.

She handed him his jacket. 'Good to meet you, Zac.'

'See you soon.' And he was gone.

Staring at the almost-full moon that hung above the shadowy trees and bushes, she felt worried and lonely. The night hadn't turned out at all as she'd expected and she wished she were going back to her own bedroom, snuggling down in her own bed, instead of sleeping over. The threat from Gerard was real, no doubt about that. She rubbed at her arm where his fingers had dug into her skin. Tomorrow he was expecting her to deliver the drugs and, of course, she didn't have them.

By telling Gerard that she, Maya, had the drugs, Kay had put her in danger. She didn't doubt what Gerard had told her was true – wherever she went she'd be tracked, anytime, anywhere, by Gerard or one of his gang. A sick feeling welled in her stomach as she remembered how he'd held the knife blade in front of her face. Was the best thing to tell the police, or contact Simon, her mum's deputy – ask him for help? But then, how safe would she be on the street tomorrow, and what would Gerard do to Kay? She needed time to think.

The best plan was to find Kay before two o'clock tomorrow, get the drugs and deliver them to Gerard. That way he'd be satisfied and he wouldn't beat Kay up. If she managed that then she'd have time to think – to plan how to stop Gerard selling drugs around her friends and, more than that, how to stop him dealing completely.

* * *

Waking up in the morning, Maya had a raging thirst and her head felt as if it were filled with cotton wool. Stumbling out of her sleeping bag and into the bathroom, she met Sadie coming up the stairs with bucket in hand.

'Not a pretty sight in there,' Sadie said. 'Can you wait while I clean it up?'

When Maya nodded, her head swirled. She leaned back against the cold painted wall and listened to Sadie, swishing and rattling stuff around in the bathroom, as if she were on another planet. She was desperate to pee and stood with her legs crossed until finally she heard the toilet flush and Sadie came out.

'I think somebody drank too much last night cos I know it wasn't my food; nothin' wrong with my food,' Sadie declared.

'No,' Maya mumbled, diving for the bathroom. 'Your food was great.'

Returning to the bedroom, Maya found Leona and Evie were still asleep. Leona was in her own bed with one leg flung out at the side and Evie was buried inside a sleeping bag, on top of an air mattress that seemed to have deflated in the night.

From her sports bag, Maya fished out jeans, T-shirt, cardigan and trainers, dressed, packed away the previous night's red silk top and sandals and went downstairs. Sadie was in the kitchen clearing plates and loading the dishwasher.

'Not too much mess,' she said cheerfully.

Maya looked around at the smeared dishes, the half-eaten food, the glasses toppled onto their sides and the stains all over the work surfaces and table.

'Sorry, I'd give you a hand but I have to get back to Gran – she's expecting me. Tell Leona I'll call her and thanks for the party. It was cool.'

'You're welcome, girl, you're welcome any time,' Sadie replied, holding out her arms for a hug.

'Remember, when your mum's away, my door's always open.'

Leaving behind the comfort of Sadie's kitchen, Maya felt suddenly nervous, and glanced around cautiously as she set off down the road. She was being stupid, she told herself, there was no way Gerard would be up and about at this early hour. It was nine o'clock, curtains were drawn and outside doors were firmly closed to morning sunshine. When she reached the little concrete square where she'd found Kay two nights previously it was empty, apart from piles of litter and the two rusty shopping trolleys. Nobody was around, it was too early for most of the 'Parkies', as residents of the Parkland Estate were known.

Sauntering past three boarded-up shops, she saw that the last one was open and decided to buy some gum to freshen her mouth. Inside the shop, a couple of boys were standing in front of the counter, cramming their bags with papers. She thought she recognised the back of a head and, sure enough, when the smallest boy turned round, it was the cheeky crop-haired kid – Gerard's messenger. He didn't say a word, just gave her a funny look as he passed. She followed him out of the shop and grabbed his bike.

'Oy, what you doin'?' he yelled. 'I gotta deliver me papers. I'm late already.'

'I want a word.'

'It'll cost ya.'

Maya seized his hand, pressing his little finger back. 'I don't think so. I'm specially trained, see, know all the tricks. See this place?' She touched the back of his ear. 'This is your weak spot, I press there and you're dead in three seconds.'

The boy shrank back, shuddering.

Maya leaned forward and muttered sharply in his ear, 'Tell me where Kay hangs out – the girl who was with Gerard, the one who took my stuff.'

'I dunno, I dunno.'

Her hand moved towards his ear.

'All right, all right. I'll tell you what I know, but don't tell Gerard you got it from me.'

'I won't if you tell me the truth.'

'She sometimes shacks with Gerard, in them boarded-up 'ouses, top end of the estate. Dunno which one exactly.'

'You do.'

'Can't remember, somewhere in the middle, "Beware of the dog" sign on the gate.'

'Yeah, that figures,' she said.

Moments later, Maya stood in front of a row of old brick semi-detached houses, the only ones left standing when rows of similar homes had been cleared to make space for the flats. The houses looked derelict – windows boarded-up, heaps of rubble and corrugated iron fencing strewn around in front gardens. Heavy graffiti covered the walls and on one of the houses, a letter O with a cross through it featured boldly. She moved towards this house. A gate hung so crazily on its hinges it wouldn't have stopped any dog getting out or any pedestrian getting in. But behind it, there was wire fencing and a sign attached to it shouted: *Beware of the dog!*

She waited, wondering what to do. She had to see Kay, but what if Gerard were inside? She stepped back, looking up at the windows on the upper floor; they were grimy and she couldn't make out anything or anybody inside. When a dog barked she jumped and shivered, remembering Gunner's slashing jaws. It would be sensible to turn away, but that wasn't in her nature. Footsteps sounded, a figure loomed behind the wire fence. Through the gaps she saw a pair of boots; they were red and shiny – definitely not Gerard's.

A loud grating noise sounded as the fencing was pulled aside. A girl in a pinstriped jacket and very short skirt opened the gate and closed it behind her. She didn't seem surprised to find Maya standing there.

'You want stuff?' she asked.

'Is Kay in?'

The girl's eyes swept over Maya. 'You are her friend?'

'Yes,' Maya answered. 'I'm a good friend.'

The girl eyed her suspiciously. 'You do not look like a friend.' She glanced back at the house and shrugged. 'Kay is gone, there was a big fight. Gerard is angry.'

'Do you know where I can find her?'

The girl glanced over her shoulder. 'Maybe the warehouse at the canal.'

A dog barked again, closer this time. Maya's heart pounded; that gate wouldn't withstand a Gunner attack. She felt in her pocket, pulled out a ten pound note and held it out to the girl.

'What canal, where?'

The girl grabbed the note and gave her directions. Maya sped away, aware of Gunner barking, aware of the clock ticking.

Chapter Five

Jumping down onto the towpath, Maya walked in the direction the girl had described, past carefully-tended houseboats festooned with flowering plants, grass clipped neatly at the water's edge, the backs of smart, newly-renovated flats – on to a point where the water became brackish and green. Here she stood in front of shabby warehouses built of crumbling and blackened red brick with wide doors and peeling paint. A truck stood outside one of them and there were deep tyre tracks in the mud. Signs hung above the doors – *Bullock's Body Works, East End Electricals* – and then she spotted the sign she was looking for – a simple O with a cross through it.

The wide door was solid and padlocked. A smaller, narrow door, set into the big doors, was closed. Maya knocked, stood back and waited. Nothing, no answer, no sound came from inside. She turned and looked across the water wondering what to do, then she heard a faint scraping sound behind her.

'Kay? Kay?' Maya said, moving closer.

She saw the narrow, inset door judder and open a few centimetres. When she put her hand on the door to pull it open, another grabbed hers and she was yanked inside. The door slammed shut behind her.

It was murky inside, the only glimmer of light coming from a lantern set on a work bench.

'Why are you here? What do you want?' With relief Maya recognised Kay's voice. 'Did Gerard send you?' she demanded.

'No.'

Kay stood in front of the lantern so Maya could only see her silhouette.

'Why are you hiding here?' Maya asked.

Silence stretched out into the darkness, making a wall between them. Maya heard Kay sniff, then she spoke haltingly, breathing heavily in between words, as if the explanation were costing her too much effort.

'Yesterday I see Gerard with a new girl. I say he cheat on me. He is angry. Then he start shouting, he say I steal his drugs. He say he put the packet in your bag and I help you steal the bag from vet's. He say I have the drugs.'

Maya leaned forward, peering into the dim void. 'Well you do, don't you?'

Kay didn't reply. She moved away and her face was suddenly illuminated in the glow of the lantern. Maya saw that her lip was bloody, one side of her face swollen, her right eye slightly closed.

'Did Gerard do that?' she demanded.

Kay gave a harsh, bitter laugh. She ran her fingers over her swollen face, wincing as she touched her split lip. 'He ask me where I put the drugs but I do not tell him. I say I know nothing.' She dropped her hand and gave Maya a challenging stare. 'But then he kick me so I tell him you have the drugs. Now I am free. He thinks you have the package, and I have a plan.'

'What are you doing to do?'

'I sell the drugs, keep the money, get away, escape.'

Maya's stomach tightened. 'Good idea,' she said. 'Except you've put me in a load of danger.'

Kay shrugged. 'Not my problem.'

'I could just go to the cops,' Maya said, moving closer.

Kay looked at her with hatred.

'OK, that was a stupid thing to say,' Maya admitted. 'Actually, I came here to try and help you.'

'No!' Kay shot back. 'You come because you are afraid. You come to ask me for the drugs. If you don't give the package to Gerard, he will slit your throat.'

A cold hand of panic clutched at Maya's heart. For a moment she couldn't speak.

Kay was silent too, retreating to the work bench and pulling a shoulder bag close to her. 'This is my chance,' she said, holding the bag in front of her. 'I sell the drugs and find a place to live.'

Putting the bag on her shoulder, she limped to the door, her head down, avoiding Maya's gaze. Desperately, Maya followed.

'How can you? Who're you going to sell the drugs to without Gerard finding out?'

Kay put her hand on the door and pushed it open. 'It is possible,' she said, defiantly.

'Kay, I'm sorry,' Maya said gently. 'I understand why you want to get away from Gerard but. . .'

Kay sniffed, leaned back against the door and pulled up the zip of her leather jacket. 'How do you understand my life? You are a rich girl.'

'That's not true. I'm not rich.'

Kay looked sullen and tense. Her shoulders stiffened, she folded her arms and spat words out like broken teeth. 'You know nothing. You have a good life. I come to the UK lying in the back of a truck. Five days and nights, seven people in a tiny space – we cannot see, cannot breathe – the smell of the truck nearly choke me. But I hang on because I think I will have a new life – then, I find only bad things.'

As Kay spoke, Maya thought she'd never seen anyone look so wretched – her battered face looked tortured. Reaching out a hand, she tried to touch Kay's arm, but Kay shrugged her away and started to cry.

'I am stupid. I cannot escape, I cannot even walk properly. Gerard, he will find me.' She touched her swollen lip, wiped her hand across her nose and sniffed. 'If he think I cheat him he will kill me.' Then her head dropped, she leaned back against the door and crossed her arms, hugging herself. 'I will never escape, it was a stupid dream,' she muttered.

'Don't give up,' Maya said gently. 'Trust me, I'll help you. I have a plan. Give me the drugs and I'll take them to him.'

'No!' Kay's head reared up and for a moment, Maya thought she was going to hit her.

Maya backed away. 'Please, just listen. If I take the

drugs to Gerard, he's happy. You go back to him, he's got what he wants.'

'And me?' Kay snapped. 'My life is the same.'

'Yes, but only for a few days – enough time for me to tell the cops about him. They'll trap him, lock him up and you're free. And when my mum is back, she'll help you.'

Kay looked at Maya with a pitying stare. 'You are stupid. You think Gerard work alone? Who do you think give him drugs? He is part of a big operation – many countries. You think like an idiot. If the police arrest Gerard, somebody will take his place.'

The news hit Maya like a slap in the face. She bit her lip and stared gloomily at the peeling paint on the door.

Kay carried on. 'It is dangerous to fight Gerard. This is a big business, not just drugs, many things. It is a big circle.'

How naive she'd been, Maya thought, she should have realised Gerard was just one link in a chain. What an idiot! But then there was a twinge of excitement – this was big, she was on to something. No way could she tackle a group of international criminals alone, but she could play a major role in helping track them down.

Her mind raced, trying to plot a course of action. First she'd contact Simon, her mum's deputy. He'd know the right people to set up surveillance on Gerard. Plain clothes detectives might act as customers, wait for Gerard to take delivery, note his contacts then arrest all the gang. It was important Gerard suspected nothing. Kay had to go back to him, pretend things were normal, only for a few days, just until enough evidence was gathered. More immediately, the drugs had to be delivered to him.

While Maya's brain was in fast mode, Kay had been leaning against the door, dabbing at her lip with a tissue. She looked exhausted, and, when Maya put her hand on her arm, this time she didn't move away.

'Gerard might be part of a big ring of dealers. But I can't let him turn my friends into druggies,' Maya said softly. 'I can see what he's doing, grooming them, giving them stuff so they get hooked. And I see what he's done to you.'

Kay looked at her with glistening eyes. 'Why do you care about me?'

'I don't know.' Maya smiled. 'Maybe I'm crazy, but I think it's because, well . . . because I've been lucky. If Pam hadn't rescued me and adopted me I could be in the same situation as you.'

Kay gave a dismissive sniff and started to walk away.

Maya's hopes fell. 'Please, help me!' she flung at Kay's back.

Kay's head went down. Then she wheeled round. 'Why should I help you? Why should I care if Gerard kill you?' Her eyes were wild, her face full of scorn but she didn't continue walking away – instead she stood still in silence, staring.

Maya didn't move or speak. She knew her fate hung in the balance. She watched conflicting emotions flash across Kay's face. Then Kay's shoulders drooped and she sighed.

Holding the bag out towards Maya, she said, 'All right. I will help you. I know I will never escape, anyway. It was a stupid dream. Maybe I will be sorry, but yes, you take this to Gerard. Then you help me.'

Maya took the bag and put it over her shoulder. 'I won't let you down. I promise.'

Chapter Six

It was raining lightly when Maya jumped off the
bus. A few pigeons were pecking at the pavements, a
group of girls were up ahead, giggling and dawdling
their way towards the ice rink, but apart from that,
the street was empty. She didn't see the two men in
big anoraks and beanies sheltering in the doorway of
the library until she was almost level with them, but
they'd clocked her and moved fast to block her path.
She side-stepped, they changed direction and formed
a big solid wall in front of her.

'You Maya?'

She looked down, willing herself not to make eye
contact. A hand grabbed her shoulder and another
gripped her chin forcing her head back. 'You ignorin'
us?'

Her instinct was to knock the clamping fingers away, but two of them, as big and solid as rocks? It was better to try to ride this one out. She closed her eyes, but it was difficult to stay calm with the guy's sour breath on her face, his gurgling laugh next to her ear. The other man grabbed her cardigan, ran his fingers down her arm and over her breast.

Her resolve snapped. 'Get off me!' she yelled, and grabbed the guy's wrist, trying to pull his groping fingers away. Her arm was seized and twisted up her back. Shrieking curses, she kicked out. Her foot connected with a shin. Her hair was grabbed and twisted, her head pushed down.

'Give her a smack,' one of the men said.

His mate laughed. 'She ain't worth it.'

With a strong push, she was sent reeling across the pavement. Clutching fiercely at the shoulder bag containing the drugs, she just managed to avoid falling into the gutter.

When she righted herself, her two attackers were walking away. Over his shoulder, one of them shouted, 'Gerard's expectin' ya.'

* * *

The ice rink was a place Maya usually felt at home. She'd been going there since she was a little girl; the skid of skates, the echoing voices, the cold air and faint smell of sweaty feet were so familiar to her. But today was different. Gerard's mates would have alerted him that she was on her way – somewhere in the crowd of people he was watching out for her, and in Kay's bag slung over her shoulder, she had a package worth thousands of pounds.

The clock showed two-twenty and she spotted him right away, talking with two of his gang, who stood either side of him like bodyguards. He dismissed them as Maya walked up.

'You're late. I don't like bein' kept waitin'.' Lounging back against the wall, he stuck his hands in the pockets of his leather jacket and looked at her through half closed eyelids.

'Sorry. Bus was ages in coming,' Maya said.

He made an exaggerated tutting noise. 'Too bad.' Then, moving away from the wall, he stepped towards her. 'You brought me candy, baby?'

The words span from his lips like poisoned silk, whilst his eyes bored into her, brutal, merciless. She remembered the flick knife he'd threatened her with at the party and had no doubts he would use it – not here, not now, but sometime he'd stalk her and find her alone.

Edging slightly away from him, she lifted the flap of the bag and showed him the top of the package. 'It's all here. I haven't touched it. I don't want anything to do with it.'

He moved in front of her; they were the same height and as he spoke he leaned close, his mouth almost on hers. 'So Kay wasn't foolin' me, you did take it. What were you gonna do with it? Sell it? 'And it to the cops?'

'No. I was going to throw it away, destroy it,' she said, trying to hold her voice steady. 'Drugs mess with your mind and I don't want you dealing to my friends.'

His hand shot out, gripping the strap of the bag. 'You'd be very stupid to destroy my stash.' He lifted the strap slightly off her shoulder, twisting it until it was tight. 'You see my mates on your way 'ere?'

'I saw two idiots, if that's who you mean.'

He pulled the bag from her shoulder. 'Remember, I got spies everywhere.' Keeping a grip on her wrist, he opened the flap of the bag and looked inside. Then he nodded. 'Seems to be OK, but . . .' he pointed a finger at her face, '. . .you cross me and you're dead, understand?'

Maya nodded.

'You say nothin'. No snitchin' to Serena or your mates and definitely no blabbin' to your mum or *'er* mates or . . . you're dead meat.'

Maya looked at him, keeping her eyes level. 'I won't say anything.'

'If you want to livc, you won't.'

Stepping back, she glared at him. 'I'm always true to my word. As far as I'm concerned, it's over with, finished.'

She was breathing rapidly, aware of his eyes on her back as she walked away. She hoped he couldn't see how much she was trembling.

It was a relief to see Leona and Evie, skates in hand, waving at her.

'Been on the ice yet?' Leona asked.

'No, I only just arrived.'

'Come on, then, get yourself sorted.'

It took longer than usual to undo her trainers – her fingers wouldn't cooperate, they were like frozen sausages pulling at the laces, while Gerard's threats echoed in her head. If she was sensible, she'd walk away – forget Gerard, the drugs and Kay. She was more shaken by Gerard than she liked to admit. That look of absolute menace in his eyes, the cold glint of cruel hatred – he was somebody you definitely shouldn't mess with. But she knew she'd have to deal with him sooner or later. He was selling to her friends, he was controlling Kay – he was an evil presence in her backyard.

Only when she got on the ice did she feel more like her normal self. It was a relief to glide across the surface, and when Leona and Evie skated up to her, she felt their old familiarity return as they linked arms. Practised skaters, they prescribed wide circles, keeping close to the barriers, then moving to the middle and swirling to a halt in a flurry of ice chips. They were busy laughing at some nerdy kid who'd got himself into the middle and couldn't stand up, when Maya spotted Zac.

'Back in a minute,' she told her friends and skated over to him.

'Hi, fancy seeing you here.'

'No accident. Evie called me, told me you'd be here.'

'How did she know?' she asked and then she realised – Gerard. He'd been sure she'd turn up, then.

Zac was grinning. 'Come on, I'll race you!'

They buzzed around the ice, weaving in and out of

people. Maya out-paced him and turned triumphantly to wave, but as she did so, a man crashed into her and sent her spinning to the side. Zac caught up with her as she was peeling herself off the barrier.

'You all right?'

'Yeah,' Maya answered brushing down her cardigan.

'Come on, let's go and get a drink.'

He held out his hand and they skated to the exit. Over by the window she saw Gerard talking to two little kids, and then Leona and Evie joined them. She put her hand on Zac's arm.

'What's Gerard up to now?' she muttered.

The way Gerard was holding court made her want to throw up. He was laughing and joking, all smiles and charm and it was sickening to see how her friends were taken in by him.

'How can they like him? He's scum,' she spluttered, her fingers clenched tightly round Zac's forearm.

'Do you reckon he's the one who spiked your drink?'

'Yeah, probably. I want to know what he's saying.'

She and Zac took off their skates and went over.

'Well, if it isn't Miss Maya – darin' and dangerous to know.' Gerard turned to her with a dazzling smile.

'Just doin' a little business with your friends, but sadly I gotta go, meetin' Serena.' He clapped Leona on the back and clasped her hand. 'Pay me anytime, no worries.'

Leona and Evie exchanged glances and giggled.

'He's cool, isn't he?' Evie said. 'Serena's well in.'

'Yeah,' Maya agreed, 'he's cool.' Zac shot her a questioning glance, but she continued singing Gerard's praises. 'Nice for Serena to have somebody who really appreciates her. He's cute.'

'You've changed your mind about him,' Evie laughed.

'He's not my type but all right, I agree, he's got charm.'

Now Zac looked really puzzled. 'I thought you. . .' he began to say, but Maya jumped in before he could finish.

'Let's get a drink.'

In the café area, she waited until Zac went off to the toilet before she asked her friends the question that was burning in her brain.

'What did you get from Gerard?' she said, trying to sound casual.

'Oh, just some stuff to give to Serena,' Leona said.

'But Gerard said he's going to meet her.'

'Oh, yeah, I forgot.' Leona giggled, then she leaned forward, putting her hands flat on the table. 'Look, Maya, it's not that we're taking stuff all the time – we're not stupid. It's just a bit of experimenting. How do you know if you don't try, eh? You not gonna be arsy about it, are you?'

Maya smiled. 'No, course not. Might try some myself. They say it's bad for you, but they're probably just trying to put us off.'

'Yeah, right,' Evie said. 'I felt so good last night, I was flyin'.'

Leona jumped up suddenly. 'We gotta go now.'

'Shall I come with you?' Maya asked.

'No, you stay and keep Zac company. He likes you.'

Maya watched her friends walk off arm in arm, wondering if she should follow them, wondering what they were actually up to. They'd always shared their secrets, there'd always been three of them – now, it seemed, there were only two.

'I don't know what to do,' Maya told Zac when he came back. 'If I dob them in they'll be in real trouble. If I don't tell and something happens to them, I won't forgive myself.'

'So you were puttin' it on when you said Gerard was cute?'

'Yes, of course.'

Zac nodded. 'I don't think you need worry too much. Gerard's probably sellin' them a few Es and a bit of blow. It's, like, not serious. More people get wasted by alcohol than drugs.'

'Yes, I know but it doesn't feel right. And I can't work out whether it's more about them or me. I wasn't around this summer and since I've come back everything seems to have changed. It feels different, I feel like an outsider.'

'They're just tryin' stuff – it'll pass.'

Maya sipped her drink. 'But what if it doesn't? What if they get hooked and get into hard stuff and I stood by and did nothing about it?' She made a sulky face. 'OK. I know you think I'm weird.'

Zac shook his head. 'You're not weird.'

'You don't know me,' Maya said. 'It's like I see something's wrong and I can't leave it. I always want to sort it, to make things right. I don't know if it's because of my mum's job or what happened to me when I was little, but I have this massive need to interfere. Realistically, I know I can't sort everything out, but it doesn't stop me trying.'

Leaning across the table, Zac took hold of Maya's hand. 'Because you're brave and special.'

'Not really,' Maya said.

'I think so. I heard a rumour that you nearly got yourself killed this summer savin' your mum from terrorists.'

Maya smiled. 'Yeah, but I'm still here, still crazy. Come on, let's go. I need some fresh air.'

* * *

The rain had stopped and the sun was shining. As they walked up to the park, Zac took Maya's hand and it felt good. People had come out onto the streets to enjoy what could be the last of the summer sun. A dark, dangerous place by night, the park was claimed by families and joggers in the daytime. A little kid in bright red anorak came racing past them on her tricycle, an anxious father running along after her. A couple of dogs sniffed at each other then trotted past.

By the edge of a lake, they stopped and sat down on a park bench. Above them, the leaves of a weeping willow rustled softly in the breeze, two swans glided on the water. It should have been a romantic spot, but both were occupied with their own thoughts. Relieved to have delivered the drugs and got Gerard off her back, Maya sat gazing into the distance, planning her next move.

Meanwhile, Zac was glancing sideways, admiring Maya's profile and wondering if a girl like her could possibly fancy him.

He slipped his arm around Maya and she leaned her head on his shoulder, looking down at his long, delicate fingers. She longed for him to kiss her. It would be great to have a boyfriend who'd come round to the flat on cold winter nights – they'd study together, listen to music . . . get close. But she couldn't relax and stop her mind working. Nagging worries about Kay and Leona and Evie invaded her mind. Where had they gone, what were they up to? And where had Gerard gone with his stash of drugs?

'If Gerard makes trouble, you can count on me,' Zac said, as if he were reading her thoughts.

'Thanks,' Maya replied. 'But Gerard's a real nasty piece of work. I don't want him going after you. The first time I saw him, he threatened me.'

She started telling Zac about her first meeting with Gerard and Gunner, but her story was interrupted by her mobile buzzing.

'It's Leona. I'd better see what she wants.'

When she put the phone to her ear, Leona's voice came screaming through.

'Maya! Thank God! Come quick. It's Serena. She's ODed, won't open her eyes.'

'Call an ambulance!'

'I can't. I'll be in trouble.'

'Get an ambulance! Now!' Maya ordered.

'All right I will, but please come. I'm frightened.'

'Where are you?'

'Serena's flat.'

'Is anybody else there?'

'No, Gerard left.'

'Hang on, I'm on my way. Call 999 now!'

She turned to Zac. 'It's Serena. She's overdosed. Gotta go.'

'I'll come with you.'

'No. Stay here. I'll call you.'

She started running. It was quicker to get there on foot – a taxi would have to go the long way round. Out of the park gates, past the shops, cut through the alley to the estate. She raced through the joggers and pram pushers, her long legs striding out, hair flying, heart hammering.

Chapter Seven

Gasping for breath, Maya reached the block of flats and found what she hoped was the right staircase. She sprinted up the steps onto the concrete landing. Which way to go? She hadn't been to Serena's flat for ages and wasn't sure. Which number was it – 201, 203, 205, 207? At 209 the door was slightly open, pairs of high heels lined the hall – they could be Serena's. She pushed and went in.

'Leona?'

'In here.'

Serena was lying flat on her back, one arm thrown out, her head at a slight angle, her eyes half closed.

'Get her up!' Maya ordered, stooping down. She slipped an arm underneath Serena's back and lifted her. 'Help me! She's heavy. We have to walk her, keep her awake.'

Between them, they managed to pull her upright, but as they walked into the kitchen, Serena's legs dragged behind her.

Leona's voice was shrill with panic. 'Oh, my God, she's not moving, she's dead!'

'No, she isn't. She can't be,' Maya said, desperately. Propping Serena's head back against the wall, she slapped her cheeks. 'Come on, Serena, wake up!' Briefly, Serena's eyelids flickered, showing the whites of her eyes.

'Oh, my God,' Leona sobbed. 'She's totally gone.'

Maya put her fingers on Serena's wrist. 'No, she has a pulse. When did you ring for the ambulance?'

'I don't know! Ten minutes ago, as soon as you told me.'

'Good. What did she take?'

'I don't know.'

Maya's face tightened, she glared accusingly at her friend.

'I don't know, honest,' Leona protested. 'She was with Gerard, they were out of it when I got here. '

Although Serena was slim, her lifeless body was heavy.

'I can't hold her no longer,' Leona moaned.

'OK. We'll sit her down,' Maya said.

They managed to manoeuvre Serena onto a kitchen chair and hold her steady between them. Leona, kneeling at the side of the chair, started to sob, spilling the story out in spasms.

'When I got here she was wasted. Her arm was tied and she was, like, droopy – I knew she wasn't right. Gerard just laughed at me, said she'd be OK – it was her first time mainlining so it had, like, a big effect. But then she fell sideways. He tried to get her to open her eyes. I could tell he was spooked. He pulled her up and she just went over again, then he got his stuff together and took off, cleaned up – needles, everything.'

Maya leaned forward and saw that Serena's face was covered with a sheen of sweat and her lips were white. Slapping her cheek again, she spoke loudly, urgently, 'Serena, wake up. Serena, can you hear me? Wake up!'

Leona was adding her own cries. 'Where's the ambulance? Where's the ambulance? Please, please, come quick.'

'Did you call her mum?' Maya asked.

'No, I. . .'

At that moment they heard a siren. Relief swept through them. Maya told Leona to hold Serena steady on the chair while she ran down to meet it. When she returned with the paramedics, Serena's head and arms were hanging down lifelessly and Leona was sobbing. Maya felt helpless as the medics lifted Serena and laid her down on a stretcher. They were unhurried, calm.

Leona came over to Maya, her face streaked with tears. 'It's bad, isn't it?'

Maya put her arm round Leona. 'She'll be OK. She has to be.'

'One of you will have to come with us,' the woman medic said. 'They'll want to know what she's taken.'

'I don't know,' Leona spluttered.

Maya took her by the shoulders, hugged her and then said, firmly, 'You go. Tell them what you know. I'll try and find Gerard. All right?'

Leona nodded.

'Come on, love,' one of the paramedics said. 'We have to get her to hospital fast.'

* * *

A crowd had gathered outside, emergencies being a regular source of entertainment on the estate.

'What's wrong with 'er?' a sharp voice asked, as

91

they loaded Serena into the ambulance.

'Get lost,' Maya snapped.

'She's a goner, innit?' the boy said.

'No,' Maya said. 'She'll be fine.'

As soon as the ambulance drove away, siren blaring, Maya started running, racing up the road to the boarded-up houses, running furiously, fire in her eyes and heart. If she got her hands on Gerard, she'd punch the truth out of him.

A black BMW was parked in front of the house. Gerard was in the passenger seat, slumped forward with his head in his hands.

Maya banged on the window, yelling, 'What did you give her? What did you give her?'

Gerard looked up. His eyes were bewildered, his face was tense; he actually looked scared. Then he turned to the driver, a big, thick-set man, and said something. The engine started. Maya hammered on the window but it was no use, the car accelerated and sped off down the road. 'OM 6' was all she could distinguish from the number plate.

* * *

Drained and anxious, Maya arrived home. Helen was in the kitchen cooking dinner.

'I wondered when you were going to turn up,' she said.

'Did you get my message?'

'Yes, but you missed Simon. He called round to see how we were. He had some news about Pam. She's fine, nothing to worry about, her mission's going well but she's going to be out of touch for a few days.'

'Where is she?'

Helen dished up a steaming shepherd's pie as she spoke. 'He didn't say.'

'I hate it when I don't know where she is. It never used to be like this. Mum always trusted me.'

'I know,' Helen said, putting dinner plates on the table. 'And she still does trust you, but you know what her thoughts are. She feels more protective after what happened in the summer. It all worked out fine, but it could have gone either way.'

Maya sat down at the table. She hadn't thought about eating all day. The dinner smelt delicious but she was on edge, worrying about Serena. Maya had gone back to her flat after Gerard had driven away. Serena's mother had arrived on the scene and looked to Maya for explanation. There was no way to soften the news – her daughter had overdosed.

In a state of shock, Serena's mum had reacted as if

Maya were responsible, hurling questions at her that she couldn't answer.

'So, how was your day?' Helen asked.

Maya blinked and almost choked on a piece of broccoli. Helen, sitting opposite her, was eager for news, anxious to know that her granddaughter was settling back into her old life after the trauma of the summer.

Maya's mind flashed over the day's events. A battered friend, a drugs drop, a life-threatening emergency. She looked up at Helen's expectant face, her soft grey eyes shining, silver-streaked hair framing her face. She smiled and forked up a piece of pie.

'Fun,' she said.

'And the party? Did it go OK?'

'Yes, it was great. They'd gone to so much trouble.'

Throughout the rest of the meal, Maya tried to keep her tone light while she chatted to her gran. It would have been a relief to explain what had happened to Serena and share the worry about her friends, but any mention of drugs would send Helen into a mad panic, particularly with Pam away.

All the time she ate, Maya was waiting for a call or a text from Leona. It was hard to get the picture of Serena's wasted face out of her head.

Please be all right, she said over and over again to herself. Please, Serena, you have to recover.

If only she could talk to Pam she'd feel better, but Pam was out of reach and that must mean her mission was delicate and dangerous.

'Have you got any homework to do?' Gran asked.

Jolted back to reality, Maya remembered she had a History assignment to finish.

'Bring your books into the sitting room. I've got some emails to write. We'll have a cup of tea in there and I made a chocolate cake.'

Maya cleared the table and filled the kettle before going up to her room to collect books and paper.

Before she went down to sit with Helen, she quickly called Zac. He answered right away.

'What happened? I've been waitin' for your call.'

'Sorry, I didn't mean to cut you out. I just thought if Serena was in a state it was better to go on my own. Oh, Zac, I'm so worried about her, she was totally out of it. We walked her round but she wasn't responding at all.'

'So, she went to hospital?'

'Yes, Leona went with her. She promised to call but I haven't heard a thing.'

Zac was positive and comforting, reminding her

how difficult it was to make phone calls in hospital. 'Soon she'll be callin' you and tellin' you Serena is home.'

Maya wanted to believe him and it made her feel calmer just talking to him. She gathered her books, went down to the sitting room and tried to concentrate on writing up her History project. But the picture of Serena's ravaged face, her bloodless lips and blank eyes haunted her.

Then her mind turned to Pam. Where was she? She imagined Pam in various world hot spots – somewhere out east; Afghanistan, Yemen, Somalia. It all fitted, the long cotton dresses, the shawls and sandals, the last minute trip to the hairdressers when she'd returned with her naturally blonde hair darkened. 'Just fancied a change!' It hadn't sounded very convincing at the time and now she realised it had all been preparation for a dangerous mission.

Oh, Mum, where are you when I need you?

Up in her room, Maya tried to sleep, but the night was long and full of disturbing dreams. When the alarm chimed from her mobile she wasn't in the best of moods. But she had made a decision. Before she went to school, she called Simon, her mum's deputy.

Simon listened carefully as she explained how Gerard

had moved in on her friends, selling them drugs.

'He doesn't care,' she said. 'He left Serena to die. This girl I met, Kay, she says he's part of a big gang and he's trying to take over the estate.'

'This isn't my field,' Simon warned, 'but I'll pass it on to the Drug Squad. They'll set up surveillance.'

'They'd better hurry up, before he hurts any more people,' Maya said. 'Serena's in hospital.'

Simon promised to call a friend in the Drug Squad right away, but he warned her that if Kay was involved she'd probably be arrested too.

'If she's willing to inform on the gang there should be some leniency, but a criminal record would damage any application for residency. And don't expect quick, drastic action – you know how these things are. It's the big fish they'll want.'

Maya remained silent for a moment, mulling over the information.

'Are you all right? Are you in any danger?' Simon asked.

Maya hesitated. She wasn't sure. Would Gerard come after her because she knew about Serena? She remembered his scared face at the window of the car last night.

'I'm OK,' she replied.

'All right, but if anything worries you, I want you to let me know. Thanks for the info, I'll be in touch.'

On her way to school, Maya took out her mobile and checked it for the tenth time to see if there was a message about Serena. She was disappointed – there was no news and every attempt at contacting Leona failed.

Arriving at school slightly late, she found to her horror that she'd completely forgotten about a Maths test and went into panic mode, while Evie badgered her to tell what had happened to Serena. The Maths teacher had no time for their whispering and ordered Maya to take her book and sit at the front.

In morning lessons, Maya went through the motions of listening and taking notes, but her mind was elsewhere. Behind her, she heard classmates whispering Serena's name – the gossip had spread. On the page in her Science textbook she saw Serena's face.

It was impossible to concentrate, last night's emergency played over and over in her head. Sometimes she feared the worst – Serena was dead – other times she saw her walking away from A&E with her usual cheerful, 'What's 'appenin'?' greeting.

Between lessons, Evie was begging for every gory

detail and Maya tried again and again to call Leona, but her phone was still switched off.

'It's bad, innit?' Evie said, wide-eyed.

Maya shook her head. 'I don't know, Leona's not answering.'

'Because she don't want to,' Evie said. 'She's so broke up, she can't talk, and that can only mean one thing.'

Maya gave her a warning stare. 'We don't know anything yet. If Leona's at the hospital again then she can't use her mobile – you have to switch phones off.'

Just before lunch break, Maya was called out and told to report to the head's office. She swallowed nervously as she slipped past questioning eyes and strode down the corridor. In the reception area, she sat clasping and unclasping her hands, her mind flying over the events of the past few days. She wasn't surprised, when she was finally called into the head's office, to find not only Ms Pearce, the head teacher, but also two people in casual clothes, a middle-aged man and young woman who introduced themselves as detectives from the Drug Squad.

Their opening questions were sharp and searching. Maya felt she was on trial and very firmly denied knowing anything about the drugs Serena had taken or being involved in taking any herself.

'I was at the flat because a friend called me. Please tell me – is Serena going to be all right?'

'It's too early to say yet. She hasn't regained consciousness.'

Maya sat back in the big leather chair. This was a nightmare. 'I don't know what she took, but I do know who supplied her with drugs,' she said. 'I can help you.'

Chapter Eight

At the end of lessons, Maya headed for the toilets and hung out there until she thought most students had left the premises. The news of the emergency ambulance and Maya being there had spread and people whispered behind her back and pointed at her as though she were somehow responsible.

All day she'd been bothered with questions and had to keep repeating the same useless answer, 'No, I don't know how Serena is. Yes, I have tried but I can't get in touch with Leona.'

Wandering down the school drive, she mulled over the interview with the Drug Squad detectives. They'd listened to what she told them all right, yes, they'd listened, but there was something that didn't sit right – she could tell they were more interested in the gang connected with Gerard's drug dealing than in Serena's collapse. Of course, she understood it was important to catch the big fish, the smugglers and distributors, but she wanted Gerard caught too.

At the end of the interview, the detectives had made no promise to get back to her, and when she'd offered to point Gerard out, they'd declined. Their modus operandi, Maya knew, would be slow – meticulous observation, a painstaking gathering of evidence to try and follow the chain back to the smugglers and suppliers – but she wanted action. While they waited, Gerard would be selling his wares.

And she was worried about Kay. If the cops caught Gerard, they'd catch Kay too. She had to warn her. The detectives had told her not to talk to anyone – 'Mum's the word,' the older guy had said in a patronising tone. Slightly insensitive, she thought, since her own mum was nowhere near and he possibly knew it.

Her mood darkened as she walked down the school drive. Head down, she pressed her face into the folds of a scarf – in one day the weather had turned from summer to autumn. Near the bus stop she saw a familiar figure standing leaning against the fence.

'I wait a long time,' Kay said accusingly.

'How did you know where to find me?'

'Uniform.'

'Why didn't you call me?'

'Gerard take my mobile. Anyways, I have to see you face to face – we have to talk.'

'What's happened?'

Kay's face wrinkled like screwed-up paper. Her words were disjointed and sharp. 'Last night, Gerard give my friend Leila a fix. She close her eyes, fall on the floor. Gerard is angry, he shout. He push us all away, lock the door. This morning, Leila is gone.'

Her eyes glittered with rage. 'Leila is my friend, she look after me when we come to the UK. Gerard say she is stupid, she take too much stuff, but it is not true.' She sniffed and wiped her nose on her scarf. 'Today I ask Gerard, "Where is Leila?" and he tell me she left, she is gone. But her coat is on the chair and her boots are on the floor! She would not leave without clothes and with nowhere to go.' Biting back tears, her voice shook with emotion. 'I think she die. He take her body away.'

As Kay's words slammed into her brain, Maya felt sick. Serena and Leila – it was too much of a coincidence. She put a hand on Kay's shoulder and fumbled in her blazer pocket to find a tissue to give her.

'Last night my friend Serena was taken to hospital. She had a bad reaction to some stuff Gerard gave her. Do you think it was the same drug he gave to Leila?'

Kay nodded. 'Gerard mix powder into heroin. He want to make more money. He don't care. All the time he sell bad stuff.'

Maya swallowed. 'What? You mean, even if he knows the stuff might kill someone, he'll still sell it?'

Kay closed her eyes briefly and frowned. 'He have to. He owe money to his boss. No excuses. You cannot mess with this gang or you will end up with a bullet in your brain.'

Maya stared into the distance, scanning over the purring traffic to the hockey field and far tower blocks. Her emotions were swirling – a boiling cauldron of anger, sadness and helplessness. Part of her wanted to turn away – this was too big a problem – but she knew she had to try and do something. By the time the Drug Squad had gathered their information and decided to act, more people could have died.

'Where are the bad drugs?' she asked Kay.

'In the house.'

'Can you get Gerard and his dog away?'

Biting at her lip, Kay blinked away tears. 'Will you find out what happen to Leila?'

'I'll try.'

Kay nodded. 'Gerard will go to meet his gang at six o'clock. He always take Gunner with him.'

By the time Maya had outlined her plan, Kay was calmer. It was a simple plan – quick, decisive and hopefully effective.

* * *

Back home, Maya prepared for action. She called Zac, who agreed to meet her in the little square on the estate. Her clothes had to be as functional and nondescript as possible, so, in her bedroom, she pulled out a dark blue hoodie, black T-shirt and black jeans. She dressed quickly, then screwed her hair up into a ponytail and stowed her mobile in the front pocket of the hoodie. Before she left the room, she picked up a photo of herself and Pam that was on her dresser. It had been taken at the police cadet training centre; both their faces shone out with happiness and pride. It had been a fabulous day, a treat for Maya's fifteenth birthday and Pam had been so pleased with Maya's prowess on the assault course, the driving circuit and shooting range. At the end of the day, Maya had decided that she wanted to follow in Pam's footsteps and join the security services.

'I have to do this, Mum,' she whispered, looking at Pam's image. 'You wouldn't approve, but I know you'd understand.'

There was just enough time to collect a few essentials – torch, screwdriver, pliers – which she stowed in a cloth bag. Then she dashed downstairs and into the kitchen. A note on the worktop from Gran read:

Chicken and plenty of salad in the fridge. Love you. Back at 7.

Maya opened the fridge, pulled off a piece of chicken and hoped she'd be back by seven o' clock too.

* * *

'What's it all about? It's him, isn't it? Gerard?' Zac's face was full of concern. 'He lives here, doesn't he?'

Maya nodded. 'All I want you to do is to keep watch. He shouldn't be back for an hour, but if you see him coming, call me, pronto.'

Zac put his hand on her shoulder. 'I don't like it. He's unpredictable. If he finds you in there, he'll go crazy.'

'That's why I want you to keep watch.'

'Why are you doin' this?'

Maya took his hand. 'I wouldn't do it if I didn't have to. Trust me. He's got something that it's dangerous for him to have, something very important.'

Zac sighed. 'OK. But I don't like it. Let me come in with you.'

Maya gestured with open hands. 'Then who'd keep watch?' She smiled at him. 'Look, it's all right. I know he's out – I won't be long.'

She strode forward, leaving him on guard, keeping watch from a doorway of the flats opposite. Crossing the road, she faced the sign on the gate, *Beware of the dog!* She fervently hoped Gerard had taken Gunner with him.

The gate swung back easily but the wire fence was a problem. She caught a thickly wound strand at the top and pulled but nothing happened. Next she tried the bottom, stuck her foot under it and tried to lever it up. There must be a way to pull it aside, but how? She tried again, the wire ripping at her fingernails. Then she saw a loose piece of wood at the side, pulled that and a piece of netting came away to reveal a gap just large enough to slip through. She glanced back over her shoulder, then sped down the side of the house. Pausing at the back door for a few moments, she listened – all was quiet. She bent down and peered through the keyhole. Nothing was going on in the kitchen, there was nobody about. She tried the door – it was locked.

Sliding along the back wall, she came to a low sash window, took the screwdriver out of her pocket, pushed it into a gap at the bottom of the frame and jemmied the window up. It opened enough for her to get her fingers in and push the window open. Dark material was stretched tightly across the frame. There was nothing she could do but pull it down. Wrenching the curtain made a loud tearing sound; she waited, her body half inside the room, half out, ready to dodge back if anyone came.

If there were people around, nobody had come running, so she pulled herself up, slid her legs over the sill and stepped into the room. What a tip! Cartons of takeaway food, mouldy plates, plastic bottles, screwed-up newspaper, a charred cushion and a tin tray blackened with soot. She picked her way over to the door that led into the hall and, as quietly as she could, opened the door. Putting her head out into the dim hallway she listened – nothing – then a faint scuffing sound and a creak of flooring. Kay had warned her that other people lived in the house.

Cautiously, she stepped forward and tiptoed to the bottom of the stairs.

The first few steps made no noise, then one creaked loudly. She waited, ears straining – a sharp muffled sound came from above her and she froze. What if Gerard hadn't taken Gunner with him? What if he was asleep and had just woken up? Kay had told her not to worry because Gerard took the dog everywhere, but the animal had an injured paw, so perhaps he'd left him at home. There it was again, a cry, not a dog, though – human.

Creeping up several more stairs, she peered up onto the landing. All doors were closed. Kay had instructed her – first door on the right. If she made it into the room she could pick up the bag, slip back down and climb out of the window before anybody saw her. She pulled up the hood, tucking her ponytail inside.

Her heart was hammering as she stepped onto the landing and tiptoed towards the first room. Stretching out her hand, she reached for the doorknob but was stopped in her tracks by a sudden loud cry. It went on and on, turning into a dreadful, keening sound – empty, helpless, desperate. It was a sound she couldn't ignore.

The cry was coming from the room opposite and

Maya turned and tugged open the door. A single bare light bulb illuminated the space; four mattresses were laid out and on each lay a young girl, hands tied, feet hobbled, mouth taped, eyes staring helplessly.

Maya reeled back in shock, then her eyes rested on the girl nearest to her. She was the one moaning and crying, the sound edging out from silver tape which had come loose on one side of her mouth.

Maya bent down. 'What's going on? Who are you?'

The girl rocked and swayed, her light brown hair tumbling around her face.

Maya reached out and ripped the tape from the girl's mouth. 'Sorry,' she said, as the girl winced.

The girl stopped moaning. Maya put a hand on her shoulder. 'Who are you? Who's done this to you?'

The girl looked up, her brown eyes huge and sad. 'I am Annika. They brought us here. They. . .'

The girl's next words were lost as Maya was alerted by her mobile vibrating. Zac was sounding the alarm! She had to get out, and quickly.

'I'm sorry. I'm sorry,' she said, spreading her hands wide and backing out of the room. 'I'll come back, I promise, I'll send help.'

In a mad panic, she dashed onto the landing, wrenched open the door of the next room, strode over to a built-in cupboard and opened it. Just as Kay had said, there was a dark blue holdall on the bottom shelf. She pulled the bag out and sped downstairs.

Chapter Nine

Descending the stairs, Maya heard a scuffing, scratching sound and, to her horror, Gunner appeared below her. He stood on the bottom step, panting, his tongue lolling sideways, a deep-throated growl coming from his stomach. His fiery eyes were fixed on her, his jaws bared in a vicious snarl. She stood perfectly still and swallowed hard. Then the whole picture came into focus. Around Gunner's head was a white plastic cone; he couldn't attack – if he did, he'd bite air.

Slowly, very slowly she edged down the last few steps, holding the bag in front of her. The dog snarled and snapped as she came close but he couldn't reach her. She passed him nervously, swinging the bag behind her legs to protect herself. Voices! There was somebody in the kitchen, but if she could make it to the window, there was still a chance of escape.

One, two quick noiseless strides; she was swinging the bag through the open window, a knee bent ready to climb out, when behind her, a voice shouted, 'Stop, right there!' and she heard an ominous click.

'Drop the bag. Turn round.'

She obeyed the order. A tall, stocky, ginger-haired guy wearing a denim jacket was pointing a gun at her. Behind him was Kay.

The man stuck the gun in his belt and grabbed Maya by the arms. 'Get the bag,' he told Kay. 'Who are you working for?' he snarled at Maya.

'Nobody,' Maya answered.

His fist struck the side of her face, sending her reeling; her vision blurred and she tasted blood.

'You're lying. You're working for Creek.'

'No. I've never heard of him.' Maya grabbed onto a chair and levered herself up. The room span. She steadied herself, then, cradling her bruised face in the palm of her hand, she stared down the barrel of the gun. 'I'm not working for anybody. I. . .'

A sharp voice interrupted. 'Gunner! 'Ere Gunner!' Gerard came into the room with the dog. 'I know who she is,' he said. His sharp eyes were on her, his mouth turned up in a familiar sneer. 'Shoot 'er; she needs disposin' of. 'Er mum's a cop.'

'What?' The ginger-haired guy seemed confused.

Gerard pointed at Maya. 'She don't work for Creek. 'Er mum's a cop – big 'un, top of the 'eap. She'll 'ave us all down, Ginge.'

'What? What you got us into, you bloody fool?' Ginger snarled. 'You're for it if Stefan finds out.'

Maya saw a look of panic cross Gerard's face. 'I was only doin' what I was told, movin' in, groomin' – getting the kids 'ooked. She's one of their mates.'

'She needs getting rid of,' Ginger said.

'Yeah, shoot 'er,' Gerard urged.

The gun pointing at Maya blurred, seemed to grow and expand. She braced herself, ready for the explosion, the throb of pain. She held her breath as Ginger nodded. Then he lowered the gun.

'Yeah, but not here. We'll take her with the girls,' he said.

Maya could hardly breathe, she felt like a cord was around her neck and somebody was pulling it tighter and tighter. Her eyes locked onto Kay's. Had Kay betrayed her – did she want her dead?

'Put her upstairs. Tie her up, then she can do nothing,' Kay said.

Gerard's eyes narrowed as he glared at Kay. 'You'd like that, wouldn't you?'

Kay's eyes were frightened. 'Why do you say that?'

'I've just worked out your little game. Ask yourself, 'ow did she know the bag was 'ere? 'Ow did she know where to find it unless somebody told 'er? 'Ow did she know I'd gone to the vet's with Gunner? I know about your meetin's, remember my mates is everywhere. You and 'er, you're in this together, ain't you? 'Ow much are they payin' you for the information?'

Gerard had hold of Kay's neck and was pushing her backwards as he spoke. 'You think you can make a deal with the cops. I've sussed your game, but they won't give you what you want. They'll use you.'

'No, no!' Kay shrieked. 'I did not do this.'

Suddenly Ginger stepped forward. 'We're wasting time!' he roared. 'What sort of an outfit are we running here? Makes us look like a bunch of amateurs. Stefan won't be pleased.' He gestured at Maya with the gun. 'Search her and give me the bag.'

With a leery grin, Gerard stepped forward. He picked up the blue holdall and handed it to Ginger, then he ran his hands over Maya's hoodie, taking her mobile out of her pocket. He pulled the cloth bag containing the screwdriver, torch and other implements from her shoulder.

'Give it here,' Ginger ordered. The mobile went into his pocket, he looked in the cloth bag and then threw it in a corner. 'Right,' he said, waving the gun, 'let's get the girls and get outta here before we're raided. Whoever she's working for, this place is dead.'

Maya felt something poke at the back of her knees. She flinched. Gunner had padded into the room and was sniffing round her and Kay.

'Gunner can smell a rat,' Gerard sneered. 'That's it, my old mate, you sniff 'em out, traitors, eh? What we goin' to do with 'em?'

'Bring them both. Shove them in the van,' Ginger said. 'If this girl's who you say she is, there could be some money in it.'

He turned away, strode to the door and shouted into the hallway. 'Ivan, Terry! Go and get the girls and you other two, come in here.'

Maya heard footsteps on the stairs, then she cringed as two guys in black tracksuits appeared. One was thin and wiry, the other built like a tank, his bull neck and stomach bulging.

'Make sure you wipe this place down,' Ginger ordered. 'We don't want the cops tracking us down.

But before you see to that, escort our two guests to the van.'

The men said nothing but the thin one grabbed Maya in a vice-like grip, marched her into the hall and pushed her through the kitchen. She knew it was no use resisting, so she walked calmly and quietly down the path and obediently ducked to get through the wire fence. Outside, a big white van was parked at the kerb. Her eyes raked the opposite pavement as the man's fingers dug into her arm.

Please let Zac see me, she prayed.

She was pushed forward so that her face was pressed up against the side of the van; her arm was wrenched painfully up her back while the beefy guy pulled some keys out of his jacket pocket and tried them in the lock of the van's back door. The more he fiddled with the lock, the more she hoped that any minute she'd hear a siren and police cars would appear. But the lock turned, the guy pulled open the doors and heaved Maya into the back of the van as though he was throwing in a parcel. She landed painfully on her elbow and then Kay was subjected to the same treatment, landing beside her with a soft moan.

At first neither Kay nor Maya spoke. Kay was

breathing heavily, grinding her foot into the floor and uttering curses.

'What happened?' Maya asked quietly. 'Why did you come back to the house? Did you shop me? You never told me about the girls!'

Kay spoke in low urgent tones. 'Everything go wrong. Gerard leave to deliver the stuff. But I did not know these new girls come. Some men want to look at them. I try to stop them coming to the house, but they suspect me. I did not betray you.'

'Where will they take us?' Maya asked.

'Maybe the warehouse. Tomorrow they will kill us both,' Kay whispered.

'No.' Maya reached for Kay's hand. 'Don't say that, something will happen. My friend Zac was watching the house. He'll tell somebody what happened – we'll be rescued.'

At that moment they heard voices, the doors were flung back and light briefly flooded the van. The four girls from the upstairs room stood at the doors.

'Go on, get in,' a man's voice ordered and he pushed one of them forward so that she cracked her knee on the lip of the van. Crying softly, she crawled in and Maya glimpsed her terrified eyes before the man roughly pushed the others inside and slammed the doors. Then they were in darkness again. Maya squeezed Kay's hand. She heard a girl whisper. The engine started up and they pulled away fast. Maya and Kay edged closer and clung to each other, trying to stop themselves from crashing sideways as the van swung round corners.

'Where will they take us?' one of the girls asked in English.

'We don't know,' Maya answered and another girl started to cry.

Chapter Ten

The van was driven at high speed and Maya and the other women were thrown about as it dipped and swayed. Finally, after about twenty minutes of uncomfortable bouncing, they came to a sudden stop. The engine was turned off and front doors opened and closed.

It was very dark in the back now and Maya couldn't make out Kay's features, but she felt her bony shoulders as they leaned against each other. Neither of them spoke and there was no sound from the other girls. It was as if they were all holding their breath, waiting to see where they were and what would happen. Then the doors at the back rattled and were thrown open.

'Right, get out!' a voice commanded.

Daylight had faded, a single light was glowing in the distance, but from where she was sitting, Maya couldn't make out any of her surroundings. She waited, trying to stay calm, letting the other girls scramble out.

Kay edged forward. 'We are at the warehouse,' she whispered.

After the girls had shuffled forwards, Maya stepped down, and the man Gerard had called Ginger grabbed her roughly by the arm and marched her towards the building. At the small inset door she hesitated, having to stoop to avoid the low door frame. Ginger was right behind her and gave her a strong shove so that she scraped the top of her head as she went reeling into the cavernous space of the empty warehouse. Blinking, she took a moment to recover, then saw three men staring at her.

'Which one is it?' demanded a craggy-faced man in a shiny suit.

'That one,' Gerard said, pointing to Maya.

'She workin' for Creek?' the shiny-suited man asked.

'She's a cop's daughter,' Gerard said.

The man in the suit turned his gaze on Gerard and Gerard shrivelled.

Shiny suit is the boss, Maya thought, as he advanced towards Gerard, jabbing, slapping and shouting at him.

'You brought a cop's kid here?'

A look of sheer panic flew across Gerard's face as he dodged the blows.

'Think about it, Stefan. She could be useful. 'Er mum's a top cop. We could get money for 'er.'

Stefan grabbed Gerard's throat. 'We're not in the ruddy kidnappin' trade. How's she mixed up in this?'

Gerard's eyes bulged. 'She was a mate of the kids on the estate.'

Stefan hoisted Gerard off his feet and shook him. 'So, what was she doin' in your house?'

'She was tryin' to steal my stuff,' Gerard gasped. 'She and Kay, they're in it together.' He pointed at Kay. 'She thinks she's gonna get somethin' out of it, thinks the girl's mum will help 'er, stupid cow.'

Stefan let go and Gerard staggered back.

'Is that right?' Stefan asked Kay. His voice became softer, but took on a chilling note. 'Are you doin' the dirty on us?'

'No. He is the dirty one,' Kay protested, pointing to Gerard. 'He double-cross you. He is cutting drugs to make money.'

'She's right,' Maya spoke up. 'I haven't told the cops anything. My mum didn't ask me to steal the drugs, she wouldn't let me do anything so dangerous. I was trying to get the heroin because it's poisonous. He gave my friend some and she's unconscious – in hospital.'

'And my friend Leila, she disappear after he give her bad stuff. Her clothes, her shoes. . .'

Gerard got up, grabbed Kay by the arm and shoved his hand over her mouth, stifling her words. 'Don't listen to 'er, she's talkin' bullshit.'

Stefan sprang towards him, pulled out a gun and waved it in Gerard's face. 'Shut up!' He levelled the gun at Kay's head. 'All of you, shut the hell up!'

There was immediate silence. Gerard and Kay froze like statues; the four women clung to each other and shuffled backwards to take refuge behind a brick pillar. Maya tensed, ready to act if any shooting started. None of Stefan's men spoke. The air crackled with tension, everybody wondering what Stefan's next move would be.

What nobody expected was laughter – a rolling, gritty sound like pebbles pushed by the tide.

'This is unbelievable,' Stefan said, lowering his gun. 'Unbelievable,' he repeated, still cackling. He looked over at Ginger. 'We've nearly done it – we're so close to pullin' off one of the biggest drugs consignments ever to reach these shores and this happens. What do you think, Ginge? Should we clip 'em all?'

He strode over to Maya and put the gun to her forehead. 'Are you on the level, cop's daughter? Are you tellin' me the truth? Is he double-crossin' me?'

'Check if you want to,' Maya said coolly. 'Serena's in hospital, Leila's disappeared – the drugs in the bag are contaminated. That's the only reason I was stealing them. I haven't told anybody about your operation because I didn't know anything about it. I thought Gerard was just a dealer. I had to destroy the drugs to stop other people getting hurt.'

Stefan shook his head. 'Had to? What are you, Miss Community Service?' Another short, sharp laugh turned into a sneer and his face grew angry. He threw his arms out in exasperation, waving the gun and spitting out words like fireworks. 'I don't know which one of you's lyin' and I don't care! What a ruddy cock-up! Months of plannin' and this. . .' He turned to his men. 'Get 'em out of my sight while I think what to do.'

Maya, along with Kay and the other girls, was seized and marched up some wooden steps at the back of the warehouse. They went quietly, it was no use resisting tough men with guns. Upstairs, they were pushed inside a dimly-lit room which held a rickety table and some benches near the far wall. Kay sat down, shaking. Maya put her arms round her.

'It'll be all right,' she muttered.

'No, they will kill us. Stefan does not want any problem, not now, not with the big delivery. We will die.'

Maya turned away; she didn't want Kay to see that she was terrified. Downstairs Stefan was deciding their fate and he was seething with anger. If she could convince him she hadn't informed on the gang they might have a chance, but he wasn't in the mood to listen.

Get real, Maya, she told herself, unless you escape, you're doomed.

The desperate sobbing of a girl sitting opposite reminded her she wasn't the only one in trouble. Annika, the girl who Maya had found tied up, had her arms round a girl who was crying.

Sensing that Maya was staring at her, Annika looked up and met Maya's eyes.

'Where are you from?' Maya asked.

'Macedonia. This is my sister, Tanya,' she said,

stroking her sister's hair. 'They tell us we can have good husband in the UK but when we arrive here, they tie us up and take our passports.'

Maya looked at the two girls, who were hardly any older than herself. 'You came here to get married?' she asked.

'It is the only way,' Annika explained. 'In our country, we have no work, no money, no hope.'

Maya reached out and put her hand over Annika's, and her heart filled with pity for these girls.

Annika's sister Tanya raised her head. 'We have become nothing,' she said, sniffing back her tears. 'Men tell us we have to work for them, we have no rights. We have to do what they say. They treat us like slaves.'

Annika nodded. 'See,' she said, pulling up her sleeve and showing Maya a huge bruise on her arm. 'I ask for information and they hit me.'

Another girl, who looked to be the oldest of the group, a girl of about nineteen with strong, dark, good looks, spoke up in clear English. 'It is disgusting,' she said. 'They treat us like animals.' She sniffed at her armpits. 'I am disgusting. I smell. We have had no wash, no food for three days.' She clenched her fists on the table. 'I gave all the money I have to come here.

They said I can choose a good husband.'

Maya sat in the growing darkness, feeling desperate. She wanted to help the girls, but could do nothing when she was a prisoner herself.

Kay leaned her head on Maya's shoulder. 'I am in big trouble,' she said. 'Gerard tell them I am a traitor. I know their business. They will show no mercy.'

'I don't think Stefan believed him,' Maya whispered, but they were the last words she had the chance to say – suddenly the door opened and Ginger, Gerard and the boss entered, accompanied by three heavies.

'Right, you four are goin' to your new residence,' the boss announced, looking over at the girls. He rubbed his hands together. 'You'll be given new names, identities, then a wash and brush up before we introduce you to your place of work.' He moved closer, his eyes travelling over each of the girls. 'Not a bad lot, not bad at all. You two,' he ordered, signalling to two of the heavies, 'take them to the hostel.'

He laughed as the girls were herded out. 'Like a bit of company do you?' he said, as they passed him.

The door slammed behind the girls. 'She's bad news,' the boss said, pointing at Kay. 'Get rid of her.'

The third man pushed Maya aside and seized

Kay's arms. She protested, screaming in her own language and kicking out at him. Behind her, Maya tried to grab Kay's waist and pull her back, but Ginger strode over. His elbow jabbed into Maya's neck and she fell back, choking. Her eyes were streaming, she coughed and clawed her way onto her knees. Blinking, she raised her head and was just in time to see Kay being bundled out of the door. At the last moment, Kay hung onto the door frame and managed to turn round and look at Maya.

'Please, help me,' she screamed. 'Do not forget me!'

'Take her away,' Stefan shouted. Then he turned his gaze on Maya, his eyes glowering beneath a shock of silver grey hair. 'You're trouble, too,' he said.

Ginger hauled Maya to her feet. Stefan took out his gun and levelled it at her chest. Maya's head span into space, she coughed and trembled while he made a soft explosive sound –'Ppff!'

Stefan raised his eyebrows and moved closer to her. 'Frightened, cop's daughter?'

'You have a gun,' she said.

He laughed cruelly. 'I have devised a plan,' he said, 'a little entertainment.' He put his hand out and Ginger handed him the blue bag which contained Gerard's stash of drugs. Thrusting his hand into the bag he pulled out a small foil-wrapped package and held it up to the light. Then he shoved the package at Gerard. 'You take a hit of this and we'll see who's tellin' the truth, eh?'

Gerard went pale. His eyes darted round the room, as if looking for escape. Then he took a deep breath and smiled. 'Yeah, just what the doctor ordered.' He snatched the package and held it up. 'Can't say better than that – a dose for free. This stuff is clean, man, pure.' He looked round. 'Anyone wanna join me?' He stared round the room. There were no takers, but his gaze settled on Maya. 'She should try some.'

Maya's heart fluttered. 'I don't take drugs,' she said.

All eyes were on her, sizing her up, then the boss went over to Gerard and stood in front of him. His voice had an icy, menacing authority. 'You wouldn't ruin my business, would you? You wouldn't do anythin' to get me a bad reputation, would you?'

He whipped a knife out of his pocket and thrust it near Gerard's face. Gerard flinched back against the wall, then slithered sideways. 'No, no, Stefan. I respect you, respect.' He sounded out the last word lengthening the first vowel. 'We do business. You know me. I ain't gonna cross you.'

'We'll see,' Stefan said, sliding the knife back in his pocket.

At a nod from his boss one of the heavies stepped forward and punched Gerard hard in the stomach. Gerard doubled over gasping.

'You and the girl, you both take the stuff,' Stefan ordered. 'We'll see which one of you's alive and kickin' in the mornin'. Then we'll know who's tellin' the truth.'

Chapter Eleven

A door was unlocked, a light switched on and Maya and Gerard were pushed inside a long, bare room at the top of the warehouse. Maya lost her footing and fell onto a lumpy, stained mattress. A strong smell of sweat and urine rose to meet her as she rolled over, sat up and then moved as far away from Gerard as she could.

Ginger came into the room and dumped the blue holdall and a plastic bag on the floor.

'Right,' he said. 'Let's get down to business.'

He took the foil package from Gerard, put it down on the floor and opened it.

'This one of your specials?' he asked, laughing at Gerard, who was still lying sprawled on the mattress.

Taking a burner out of the plastic bag, Ginger lit

it, placed some powder on a metal spoon and heated the contents. He watched the spoon, carefully waiting until the powder turned to liquid. 'Mm, nicely cooked,' he said. 'Right!'

Reaching into the bag, he drew out a cellophane packet, tore it open and extracted a hypodermic needle. Maya was mesmerised, her brain seemed to have turned to mush. She couldn't think. There was no hope of escape. She imagined the prick of the needle and poison being forced into her veins. In the morning, the men would return and find her body.

'Who's first?' Ginger asked, pointing the needle at the ceiling.

Maya shrank into the corner. 'Please, don't do this,' she begged. 'That stuff is bad. I swear it is. My friend's in hospital. I don't know if she's alive or dead.'

Ginger sniffed. 'Ain't nothing to do with me,' he said. 'I'm just following boss's orders.'

'Ask him, ask him,' Maya pleaded, staring at Gerard. 'Ask him what happened to Leila, she's missing. He killed her with the drugs he cut.'

'That right?' Ginger asked.

Long seconds ticked by. Maya drew up her knees and hugged them tightly, trying to stop her body from shaking.

Then Gerard took off his leather jacket, rolled up his sleeve and thrust his arm forward. 'She's a lyin' cow. Come on, give me a dose.'

Maya didn't want to watch and yet she couldn't tear her eyes away. With utter fascination, she stared as Ginger knelt down beside Gerard. From his pocket, Gerard pulled out a wide piece of elastic and Ginger wrapped tightly it round his arm.

Ginger pursed his lips and frowned as he flicked at Gerard's veins. 'They're shot,' Ginger said. 'Like shrivelled worms – can't find a spot.'

'I'll do it myself,' Gerard snapped.

He took the needle, pinched his skin and plunged the point into his arm. Within moments, his head went back, he sighed and smiled. 'Nothin' wrong with this shit, man.'

He pulled out the needle and crooked his arm. Then he glared at Maya. 'Do the princess now. Do friggin' Mulan over there.'

Maya backed away. 'No, no, please. I don't want any. I've never had any drugs – nothing, not even a smoke.'

'You were nicking our stash,' Ginger said.

'I told you. I was just trying to stop people getting hurt.' Her voice was hoarse, her tongue dry, she couldn't speak properly, the words wouldn't come out. 'I didn't want m-money . . . I . . . just . . . wanted to. . .'

Ginger got up and stood in front of her. He kicked her leg and she cried out in pain. 'Shut up. Don't try that crap with me, cos I ain't interested. You come on our patch and you take the consequences. Your hours are numbered, darling.' He looked across at Gerard who was now grinning, his head lolling forward. 'He's happy, so what's your problem? You're gonna spend your last few hours high as a kite.'

Leaning forward, he took hold of Maya's shoulders, his squashed nose and freckled cheeks almost touching her face. 'Pity I'm not spending the night in here with you,' he chuckled.

Full of revulsion, Maya twisted her head away. He laughed and grabbed her arm. 'If you never mainlined before should be no problem – nice, fresh, juicy veins.'

Maya held her arms rigid, tugging her sleeves down and squirming away from him. He made a grab for her. She ducked and struck out with a fist, catching his ear. In return she received a stinging blow on her forehead. Kicking out, she wriggled underneath Ginger's arm, made for the door and yanked at the handle. It was locked. She felt arms around her waist, was lifted off her feet and thrown back onto the hard mattress.

A shout from outside was followed by heavy banging on the door. 'What you doing in there? We have to split.'

When the door was unlocked, it swung open and Stefan stood there, looking grim. 'Kay was right,' he said. 'Nobody's seen Leila. She's disappeared.'

Holding her throbbing forehead, Maya sat up.

'So,' she said, shuffling forwards and giving Stefan a challenging glare, 'Kay didn't betray you. Gerard was cutting the drugs to make money for himself. He was ripping you off. She was telling you the truth.'

'Shut her up, will you?' Stefan said, gesturing at Ginger.

'My pleasure,' Ginger said.

He seized hold of Maya's shoulders, but Maya squirmed away from him.

'What about Kay? She didn't betray you – you can't hurt her.'

'Jesus Christ! Get her off my back!' Stefan shouted, waving his arms.

This time Ginger got a firm hold on Maya, pulling her arm up her back. Maya squealed as Ginger gave her a hard push, sending her reeling to the back of the mattress. She rolled over, breathless, while Stefan went over to Gerard and prodded him with his foot. Deep in a stupor, Gerard slid sideways and keeled over.

'Pathetic little shit,' Stefan said.

'What are we going to do about her?' Ginger asked, scowling at Maya.

Stefan snorted and swore. 'We'll see to her in the mornin'. I don't want her blood on our hands. When the cargo comes in, they can take her out with them.'

'You won't hurt Kay, will you?' Maya shouted.

Stefan turned to look at her, his face dark with anger. He took a step towards her, his fists clenched. Maya cowered, thinking he was going to hit her, but he stopped and satisfied himself with kicking the edge of the mattress.

When she dared to look up, he had a half twisted smile on his face.

'What do you care about Kay?' he asked. 'She's scum, a whore, a junkie.'

'I don't want you to hurt her.'

'Why would I hurt her? A pretty girl like her, she can be useful.'

They left, locking the door behind them. Maya

sank down on the smelly mattress. Her chest was heaving, her breath stuttering in and out in strangled gasps. She put her head in her hands and closed her eyes. She'd escaped the needle – that was a miracle and she offered up grateful thanks to whatever spirit was watching over her – but she was still a prisoner.

Footsteps rapped down the stairs, she heard muffled voices. A door banged, car engines started up outside, exploding into life then fading away. After that, there was silence. Had they all gone?

Gerard was totally still. His face was ashen. Maya leaned down to check if he was breathing. His eyelids slid open; he chuckled and, lifting his head slightly, muttered, 'All right, princess?' Then he took a few deep, rasping breaths and shivered so violently his teeth rattled.

Maya didn't know if his reaction was normal or not – she remembered reading a leaflet in PSHE at school – *Regular heroin users experience an initial feeling of euphoria followed by relaxed drowsiness.*

He'd certainly been happy and relaxed, but the shivering didn't seem right. There was nothing she could do to help him, though. She had to think about her own situation. Stefan's last words had left her full of fear. 'Cargo comin' in, they can take her out with them.' That's all she was to him, baggage to be got rid of. She had to escape.

An angry kick at the door was met with absolute resistance – it hardly vibrated. She scanned round the frame but failed to see the tiniest crack. The room offered no hope of an escape route, either. There was no furniture, nothing to use to smash the door with. The ceiling was high and angled, a single beam running across the top; the one window was heavily-boarded and there were no roof lights or any roof space to climb into. A single bare light bulb dangled from a crooked piece of flex and on the opposite wall hung a stained sink.

As she stood scanning the room, a thump on the floor made her spin round and she saw that Gerard had rolled so that he was lying on his back, one arm flung out, his mouth open. A sheen of sweat covered his face and he was taking short, shallow breaths. He was reacting just like Serena – she had to get help for him.

Crawling over to him, she pulled his leather jacket from underneath him. He didn't protest, so she delved into the pockets. Her fingers touched his flick knife, then some coins, but not the thing she was looking for. She shuffled closer and patted his jeans pockets.

Nothing. What had he done with it? Her hands groped underneath his neck, she lifted the mattress, but there was no sign of his mobile phone. Ginger must have taken it just before he left.

There was no hope of calling help for Gerard or herself, but she had to do something. Her gaze settled on the high window. Thick boards were nailed to the outside of the window so the glass would have to be smashed before she could get her hands through to try and lever off the boards.

Visualising a plan of the warehouse, she guessed that the window was at the front, facing onto the towpath. Even if she could break it open, from what she remembered it was a hell of a long drop down. And she didn't know if all the men had gone. Had anybody been left behind to act as a guard?

With regret, she looked down at her trainers – no hard heels for breaking glass. Casting her eyes round for a weapon, her eyes settled on Gerard's boots – they were heavy and studded. If she could get one of them off and stick her arm inside it, then she could hammer at the glass and be protected from cuts. If somebody heard her and came running, well, at least she'd tried.

Gerard's foot had no intention of aiding her

mission. His leg was heavy, the boots hard to unbuckle. At first she was afraid he'd fight her off, but she soon realised he was in no state for that. He was almost comatose. Growing braver, she pushed and pulled until she managed to ease one boot off.

With a quick glance towards the door, she raised her arm and smashed the first pane of glass out. The noise crashed and echoed as she started punching at the boards. Any moment somebody would come running, but she didn't care – in her desperation she banged and thumped, scattering wood and glass. The two boards across the middle splintered easily and fell away. Brushing aside pointed fragments, she hoisted her leg up and knelt on the windowsill. It was dark outside but there was just enough light to see below. It was a long drop, too high to risk jumping down.

Despair flooded through her. A piece of glass punctured her jeans and pierced her knee. She scrambled back into the room and saw blood oozing through the dark material. Behind her, Gerard gave a little moan. She was on the point of going over to check on him when a light moving on the surface of the water caught her attention and, leaning out of the window, she saw a boat sailing along the canal – a houseboat. She shoved her hand out of the window and waved frantically, but the boat didn't falter. It went downstream, her eyes followed the lights until they'd almost disappeared and then, in the periphery of her vision, she noticed something else.

Leaning forward, she peered sideways and saw a metal pole sticking out of the brickwork. It looked as if it had been used as a pulley at one time and near to its base hung a heavy chain. If it had been used to haul up sacks of cargo then hopefully it would hold her weight.

The pole jutted out over the canal, so if she could manage to shimmy along the pole, she could drop into the deep water. It was a crazy plan but it just might work.

Casting a glance back into the room, she saw that Gerard was looking very pale and a sticky mess of vomit had stained the corners of his mouth. She watched his chest pumping – he was gasping for air; it didn't look good. Striding over, she turned him onto his side but there was nothing more she could do to help him. She had to work fast – soon it would be completely dark. Her main priority was to smash the remaining boards and escape.

With all her strength, she hammered at what remained of the window frame and it gave way, falling with sheaves of glass, wood and plaster to the towpath below. Wasting no time, she knelt on the windowsill, put her head out and judged the distance to the pole. It should be possible to swing her body sideways and grab. The worse that could happen was that she could jump and fall. The best that could happen was that she could jump, catch hold of the pole or chain, climb on top of the pole and edge out over the canal. Did she fancy a swim? Not really, but it would be better than breaking her neck. Of course, she could also sit back down and wait till morning, when she was going to be transported to God knew where and disposed of. Her options were not great.

But there was one important thing she had to do before any attempt to escape. Climbing back into the room, she snatched up the blue holdall containing the drugs, leaned out of the window and threw it as far as she could. It landed with a splash and the contaminated drugs were swallowed by the canal.

With a feeling of triumph, she hoisted herself up to stand in the window. It was a narrow space but almost as tall as herself. Arms outstretched, she held onto both sides of the brickwork and felt a cool breeze on her face.

Turning her head sideways, she estimated the leap – the pole, about a metre and a half away, was angled upwards from the wall. She'd only get one chance – she'd have to use the brick wall for leverage, propel herself sideways and try to grab the pole. She took a deep breath, gave a slight shudder. The words, 'Don't look down' flashed in front of her eyes. It was like her first bungee jump, standing on the lip of a bridge over the canyon, the wind in her hair. No, wrong, it wasn't like that at all, because then she'd had a safety device. This was heart-stoppingly scary. Another breath, a deep swallow – push off and fly.

She missed the pole by centimetres; her stomach fell out of her mouth. Plummeting downwards, something rough grazed her cheek, her fingers grasped wildly, clutching at the rusty chain. Legs dangling in mid-air, she hung on. It was still too far to jump down, she'd escape with broken limbs at best. The only possible solution was to shimmy up the chain to the pole and then edge out over the water.

It took a lot of courage to take one hand off the chain, but she had to do it. Slowly, hand over hand, she started to climb. Behind her, the brick wall rumbled, the pole juddered and she was jolted downwards. The earth came up to meet her, she gasped, closed her eyes and braced herself for the fall, but a moment later, things settled and she was still hanging on. Praying the bolts would hold, she began to climb again as quickly as she could, until she was just beneath the pole. With a mighty effort, she kicked and swung her body up to hook one foot over the pole. For terrifying seconds she was immobile, suspended ten metres above the towpath, her energy almost gone. She took a deep breath, gritted her teeth and hauled herself up to sit astride the pole.

In the distance, she heard a car engine, tyres rolled along the towpath, headlamps flashed. A vehicle came to a stop directly below her. The sound of keys in a lock, the scraping of a door, footsteps tramping up the stairs, reached her.

She imagined the scenario. On Stefan's orders, one of the gang had returned. When he opened the door to the room, he'd find her gone. Any moment he'd see the smashed window, look out and spot her. She was a sitting target.

Her brain was telling her to move, but she couldn't. The thought of a bullet ripping into her back made her freeze in panic. But the explosion didn't happen. Instead she heard footsteps thumping back down the stairs. Stefan's watchman hadn't spotted her.

Move, you idiot, you have a chance! she told herself.

Gripping tightly with her hands and feet, she edged forward to the end of the pole. She was almost at the end hanging over the water when somebody shouted and a powerful torch beam flashed over the dark water and opposite bank.

'Where are ya?' a voice shouted. She was sure it was Ginger.

The beam swung wildly, lighting up patches of rough grass and slimy waterweed. It flashed along the towpath. She heard the man cursing, panting as he ran, then he came back and the beam of the torch swung to the other side. As long as he didn't look up, as long as she could keep her balance, she was safe. But then the pole creaked, the torch beam swung upwards, illuminating her legs. The man shouted. Her balance disturbed, she started to tilt sideways and then she fell.

The water hit her like a wall of ice – stinging, freezing. Gurgling, bubbling sounds filled her ears as she plummeted down; the water was thick and dark. Something grazed her leg, long strands of weed wrapped around her. She kicked hard for the surface, but her clothes were like weights dragging her down.

It took a mammoth effort to swim up and raise her head above the water level. Choking and coughing, she spat out foul-tasting water and tried frantically to gulp air. It was imperative to get to the side and climb out, but a crack of gunshot sent her ducking down again.

Underwater, she plunged down, holding her breath until she thought she'd burst. Bullets peppered the water above her. There was nothing she could do to save herself – either she'd drown or be shot in the head.

Swim, swim, a voice was telling her, swim to the side, there's a chance, a slim chance he won't find you, if you surface under the platform.

She hadn't been aware of spotting it, but an image had registered – there was a metal platform jutting out over the water.

Making small rippling movements, she propelled herself forward until she could hold her breath no longer, then she surfaced and gulped. The top of her head bumped against a flat piece of slimy metal. She'd made it, she was under the platform. If she kept absolutely still, then she might not be detected. Gently moving her arms to keep herself afloat, she managed to keep her nose and mouth above water level. But the man wasn't giving up. He'd heard the splash; he knew she couldn't swim far in her clothes.

Footsteps thumped on the hard mud.

'Where are ya? Did I hit ya? Are you down there? Come to a watery end?' He laughed – a harsh, joyless sound.

There was a clanging noise over her head and she could tell her pursuer had stepped onto the platform. He shuffled and grunted. She heard him flop down and guessed he was peering into the water. If he leaned over far enough, he'd be able to see her!

She couldn't hold out much longer. The small movements she was making weren't enough to keep her afloat. She was sinking. Icy fingers wrapped around her. Chilling spikes of water pierced her skin; her cells, blood and bone were freezing. Her brain was numb, she couldn't think. There was no escape. If the man with the gun didn't leave, she'd sink into a watery grave.

Chapter Twelve

Underwater, Maya's head sank slowly as her feet rose. She could hear singing; she could see flowers, clusters of brightly-coloured petals dancing in the soft current. Relaxed and silent, she lay, supported by the water that was slowly entering her mouth, her nose, her ears and lungs.

Ginger was above her, pointing his gun at the water. He waited for a few minutes, then shrugged his shoulders and swore. There was no sign of the girl. Either he'd shot and killed her or she'd drowned. He played the beam of his torch over the sides of the canal. They were steep and slippery. Nobody could climb out without help, particularly not if they were fully-clothed or wounded. Stefan would be happy – he wanted rid of the girl, well, that was sorted!

The beam from his torch swung over the water one more time, then, satisfied, he turned to walk back to the warehouse. There was nothing more he could do tonight and he'd made too much noise already. He stood listening for a moment, worried his gunshots might have drawn the cops. Then he started to walk away.

Further down the river, an engine started up, a houseboat began to move. Air trapped inside Maya's body gurgled, her clothes ballooned, taking her up to the surface. The chunky boat ploughed through the dark water, heading upstream. The wake rocked Maya to the side, her head banged on the platform and she opened her eyes. In front of her, a thick chain dangled into the water. She coughed, spitting out rancid bile and gulping in air. With her last bit of strength, she grabbed the chain and hauled herself up onto the platform, then crawled, gasping and choking, onto the towpath.

She couldn't breathe properly, her lungs weren't working. She was like ice. Rolling onto her stomach, she pulled up her knees and tried to hug herself, but her hands were like lumps of frozen meat flapping uselessly in the dirt. A violent spasm shook her; putrid canal water poured from her mouth and ears, her eyes watered, her throat burned, then she heaved her guts up.

'Bit cold for a swim.'

She could hardly make sense of the words, but heard the laughter and looked up to see faces peering down at her.

'She's soaked,' one of them said.

'It's a mermaid, it's a mermaid,' another voice joined in.

'I reckon she should go to 'ospital,' another voice said, as a coughing fit seized Maya.

She felt a hand on her shoulder, a face came close – a big square chin, squinty eyes. For a moment she saw him clearly before he dissolved. His features rippled as if she was back underwater; his voice was muffled, water sloshed and slopped in her ears. Coloured lights drifted and circled her head. Something soft and warm touched her neck and then she was rising and jolting and falling into oblivion.

'It's all right, lads, I know her. I'll take care of her.'

'She should get some treatment. She was, like, drowned.'

'Could have brain damage.'

Maya's eyes flicked open. Strong arms were holding her, beery breath on her face, ginger eyebrows like orange caterpillars bristling at her. A freckled fist clamped round her leg.

'Yeah. I'll call an ambulance. No need for you to worry, lads, you've done your bit. Blimey, if it hadn't been for you, she could have been out there all night – died of exposure. Heroic thing you done.'

'We heard some shootin'. Wasn't nothin' to do with her, was it?'

'Nah. Machinery over at the works. Often hear it at night.'

All Maya could do was lie and shiver, her teeth rattling, her skin prickling, her face and scalp stretched tight. Something was covering her but she couldn't feel its warmth. She closed her eyes, trying to think and sort out what had happened. The lads who'd found her had handed her over to Ginger. She was back in the warehouse. After all her effort to escape she was a prisoner, once again.

The faces melted away, the voices faded. She heard Ginger's voice.

'It's my niece, lives down on the houseboats, was just going home; must have fallen in. I'll call an ambulance. You've been fantastic, lads. No, it's all right. I'll see to her now.'

Laid out on an old sofa at the back of the warehouse,

Maya tried to lift her legs, attempted to get up, but it was no use, everything span. She was vaguely aware of being lifted up and carried, then she landed with a bang, her frozen limbs jarred, her head jolted.

'Back where you started, princess.'

Ginger was standing over her, his arm blurred as he waved a gun. There was no fight left in her to knock it away. All she could do was lie and shiver.

* * *

The next time Maya opened her eyes, she looked up at a bare light bulb dangling from a wooden beam above her head. At one side of the beam, the ceiling seemed to sag and the plaster was stained with watermarks. When she turned her head, a course blanket grazed her cheek – somebody had covered her up, but she was cold. A chill breeze blew in through the smashed window; underneath her body, the mattress was cold and damp. When she moved, her joints were stiff and painful; the jeans she was wearing were twisted tightly round her legs as if they didn't fit right. When she tried to move her hand, she found she couldn't separate her wrists – they were bound together.

Raising herself up on one arm was an effort, but she

managed it and squirmed into an upright position. Looking down, she saw thin rope wrapped around her wrists. It wasn't an expert job, so hopefully it wouldn't take too long to wriggle her hands free. Slowly, awkwardly, she turned round and saw Gerard lying on his back. One arm was thrown out, his face was almost as grey as the blanket that covered him, his mouth gaped open and his eyes were staring up at nothing.

Crawling over to him, Maya's heart fluttered as she looked down at his blank face. She swallowed hard, turned her head away, wanted to crawl back to her own mattress without touching him, but she had to make sure. Easing the blanket down, she wriggled her fingers until she could touch his wrist. There was some warmth, but she couldn't feel a pulse.

Without freeing her hands, she couldn't help Gerard or herself. It took a while, twisting and turning, her wrists rubbed raw by the rope, but eventually the binding slipped off and she was free. The next task was to get warmer. She was so cold she could hardly think and violent shivers were rattling her bones.

Deliberately focusing, she controlled her mind.

Think of one thing at a time, just one thing. Warmth, if you get warmer you'll be able to think.

On a corner of the mattress, behind Gerard's head, was his leather jacket. She leaned over and pulled it to her, sliding it over his face. He didn't move. She slipped her arms into the jacket, then slowly, clumsily, undid her jeans and wriggled out of them. She pulled the blanket from the mattress and wrapped the dry part around her legs.

Gerard needed help. He was barely alive – if he got to hospital he might have a chance. She began to feel more focused, her body was waking up – she paddled her legs, slapped her thighs. His jeans! Her eyes ran over his body – slim waist, long legs, her height. She tugged his remaining boot off and laid it aside, then squinted at his belt buckle. Her fingers gaining strength, she worked quickly, tugging, undoing, pulling. His body was pliable, he didn't protest, he was beyond that. It seemed a terrible thing she was doing and yet she knew it was right. If there was a chance to survive she had to take it.

Wriggling out of her wet underwear, she threw it aside. Gerard's jeans were a good fit when the belt was pulled tight, and she felt instantly better for having something dry around her. He was heavy to lift and made no response as she pulled his T-shirt over his head, then she laid him back as gently as she could on the mattress. His bare chest was thin and bony; he was no threat now. Quickly, she slipped off the leather jacket, put on his T-shirt and pulled the leather jacket on again. That was much better – she was warm and dry.

Scrabbling around, she searched for her trainers. They were nowhere to be found. Gerard's boots? She pulled one on and reached for the other lying under the window. She tipped it upside down to empty out any fragments of glass, then slid her bare foot inside.

Just as she was fastening the boots, she heard a heavy tread. Somebody was climbing the stairs. Throwing the blanket back over Gerard, she dived for the mattress and covered herself up. The door rattled and Ginger entered.

She pretended to be asleep, but when the side of his shoe prodded her head, her eyes opened. He loomed over her, his legs apart, his stomach bulging beneath a tight black T-shirt, the bottom of his bulbous chin covered in thick ginger stubble. He leaned down and wrenched the blanket away from her.

'So, what's been going on here? Untied yourself? Thought you'd escape again? You're a barrow-full of trouble.'

'He needs help,' Maya said, sitting up and looking over at Gerard.

'He's all right. Happy tripping, just sleeping it off.'

'He's not all right, he's unconscious.'

Ginger laughed and kicked at the mattress Gerard was lying on. Gerard didn't move. 'He dosed himself up, stupid moron,' Ginger muttered.

'Yeah, with bad drugs,' Maya snapped. 'He'll die if you don't get him to hospital.'

'Good try. What you going to do? Shout for help while I call an ambulance?'

Suddenly Ginger was on top of her, rolling her onto her back, clawing at her neck. Maya tried to knee him but he was heavy, his weight holding her down.

'Stupid bitch!' he spat at her and then started to suck at her neck, his hard body pressing down on her. She squirmed sideways as his hands groped all over her, hands on her breasts, squeezing, pinching. She tried to poke at his eyes, but his fist came up, knocking her hand away and smashing into her chin. Tears flooded her eyes.

'Get off me! Get off me!'

He levered himself up, pulling his trousers down. She clutched at his face, clawing and scratching. She screamed in fury, twisting her body trying to get out from under him, but he was too much for her – too heavy, too strong.

He started pulling at the belt she'd put on, trying to undo the buckle. She managed to get her fingers round his ear and twist hard. He yelled in pain and then they both froze as a tortured gasping sound came from beside them.

'What the. . .?' Ginger muttered and, grabbing a handful of hair, he pushed Maya's head back and peered over her.

Maya raised her head so that she could see Gerard. His face seemed to have turned blue, his head was arched back, his eyes bulging. Deep, rasping breaths raked his lungs, his mouth flapped open, the air stuttering and echoing as he choked.

Mesmerised by Gerard's fight for breath, Ginger's hold on her slackened. With a mighty effort, Maya pushed his body off her.

'He's dying,' she shrieked.

Sliding over to Gerard, she snatched up a piece of blanket, cleared his mouth and nose of vomit and, at the same time, slipped her hand into the pocket of the leather jacket she'd stolen from him.

'Call an ambulance,' she said again. 'He needs help.'

Ginger stared at her then scowled. 'I ain't calling no ambulance. Serves the little sod right.'

Shuffling across the mattress, he made a grab for Maya, but this time she was ready for him. Gerard's flick knife was in her hand and she stood over Ginger, brandishing the blade near his eyes. He reeled back, surprised, muttering curses.

'Stay there,' Maya said. 'Don't come any closer.'

Ginger wasn't used to taking orders from a girl. He thought he could take her, but when he tried to stand up, his feet became entangled in his trousers. Off balance, he fell backwards, sprawling on the floor.

Maya didn't need a second chance. She leapt over Gerard's body, wrenched open the door and clattered down the stairs. By the time Ginger had recovered she was a blur in the distance.

Chapter Thirteen

The towpath was dark. Maya had no plan – there was no time for a plan. It was sheer instinct that directed her feet. She remembered a bridge, but how far was it? There were no lights on the path and she lurched and stumbled in Gerard's ill-fitting boots. A string of twinkling fairy lights hung in the distance – a houseboat.

She heard a vehicle coming towards her. Looking for a place to hide, she veered off the path and threw herself down a sharp dip, rolling amongst the undergrowth. She pressed her body into nettles and thorns as the vehicle's headlights flared across the towpath. It was driving slowly, coming closer, tyres deep in the soft ruts of the path. She held her breath, blood pounding in her ears. It was the white van, with Ginger at the wheel. He looked sideways as he drove past. She thought he'd spotted her, but he didn't stop.

When the sound of the engine faded, she uncurled from her hiding place, rubbed at her skin where the nettles had prickled and slowly stood up. If she could make it to the bridge, she'd be safe.

* * *

'Who is it?' a voice sang out, when Maya leaned over the side of the boat and knocked on the wooden deck. 'What do you want?'

It was a woman's voice. Maya could vaguely make out a figure sitting on the prow of the boat. There was a glow from a cigarette. She seemed to be alone.

'Can you help me?' Maya asked.

'Who are you?'

'My name is Maya Brown.'

As she spoke, Maya's body slumped forward, her strength gone. She felt the cool wood of the boat's deck beneath her cheek.

'Come on up,' the woman said.

Maya's hand scrabbled for something to hold onto; she tried to pull herself up, but her legs were too heavy. She tilted sideways and fell against some steps. Her head rolled back and she saw a shining band of stars. The air was cool on her face. Strong hands grasped her under the arms, supported her weight. She floated, bumped against something hard, sank down. A soft, light cloud surrounded her. Somebody was singing softly, tunefully. Warmth spread through her bones. She rolled over and slept.

* * *

She dreamt of water, a swirling dark ocean, an underworld of drifting shapes and wafting weeds snagged at her hair, giant fish with razor teeth swam towards her, a man's bloated face rippled past – he was grinning, the thick ginger stubble on his chin like spikes from a sea urchin. The world was rocking.

Opening her eyes with a start, Maya couldn't understand what was happening. She thought somebody was shaking her, but nobody was there. Where was she? She sat bolt upright and banged her head on a shelf above, then, as she looked around, she remembered the woman, the canal boat – she was on it and it was moving.

Throwing back the quilt, she stumbled out of the

bunk. The floor was cold on her feet, a cool, sharp breeze blew in through the open door. Light flooded her eyes as she peered out. The woman was at the helm, steering the boat.

'Where are you taking me?' Maya demanded.

Wearing a long red skirt, black hair blowing in the wind, the woman looked at Maya with amusement. 'Don't worry. You're not being kidnapped. I'm not a friggin' pirate.'

Maya blinked and chewed on her lip. 'Sorry. I woke up and the boat was moving.'

'Yep, we've been to pick up supplies. You were spark out last night. By the looks of your face, you'd had a rough time.'

Gingerly, Maya touched her face, explored the swollen contours with her fingers. One of her eyes ached and her cheek was sore.

'I'm goin' to cook you breakfast,' the woman said. 'And by the way, my name is Rose.'

'Breakfast?'

'Meal at the beginnin' of the day,' the woman said, enunciating the words slowly and firmly. 'You break the fast of night – food.'

'Oh, yes.'

'How are you feelin'?'

'OK.'

'Go and freshen up. Bathroom's small but everythin' works. Use anythin' you like; clean towel in the cupboard. Some Dettol in there too, dab some on those scratches.'

The bathroom was tiny, there was hardly room to turn round, but there was a shower. And warm water – bliss! Undressing, Maya caught sight of her face and did a double take. She leaned closer to the mirror. Wow! Ginger had hit her hard – it looked like she'd been ten rounds with a boxer. One side of her face was swollen, her left eye was puffy and half closed. She touched her cheek gently and winced.

Gathering a towel, antiseptic and some soap, she undressed and slipped into the shower capsule. It was wondrous and reviving to wash the rank-smelling canal water from her body and out of her hair. When she emerged and was drying herself off, she discovered lots more scratches and bruises but there were no deep cuts – a smear of antiseptic cream should do the trick.

Dipping her head, Maya returned to the main cabin and sat on the bunk, pulling on Gerard's leather jacket and boots. The barge gave a shudder and bumped against something. When she looked out of the small window, she saw it had returned to familiar surroundings. On the opposite side of the canal were the warehouses.

Looking towards the warehouse, she spotted a white van parked outside and reacted quickly, throwing herself back down on the bunk. She knew she couldn't be seen – she'd be a shadow behind the tiny boat window, but, even so, a nervous shudder ran through her. She gulped and hugged herself, remembering Ginger's attack the previous night.

As she lay trying to calm herself, her mind was full of questions. Who was at the warehouse? What was going on inside? Were the gang still looking for her and what had happened to Kay?

Chapter Fourteen

From the main cabin, Maya watched Rose opening bins and cupboards in the galley kitchen. It was fascinating how a whole kitchen was packed into such a small space. Rose herself seemed rather aloof, though kind enough to be cooking breakfast and taking care of her, which was very hospitable considering she must be wondering what had brought Maya, bruised and battered, to her boat in the middle of the night. She must have heard the gunshots, Maya thought, but she didn't seem interested in asking any further questions. An offer to help with breakfast had been rebuffed with an abrupt comment.

'You think there's room for two people in here?'

While Rose was busy, Maya looked round for a

phone. She had to reassure Helen she was all right. If Zac had seen her shoved into the van last night, he would have raised the alarm and Helen would be frantic. Plus Simon would have a whole gang of people searching for her.

'Could I use your phone?' she asked Rose.

'Knife and forks in that basket,' Rose replied, turning round and pointing. 'Pull the table out.'

Maya did as she was told, pulling up the small tabletop and wedging a leg under it so that it was stable, then she laid out knives and forks, salt and pepper. Rose brought mugs of tea to the table and then plates of toast, scrambled eggs and tomato. She didn't speak until she'd sipped her tea and had a bite of toast.

'That's better,' she said, and then, brushing back her dark hair, she gave Maya a direct questioning look. 'So, what's this all about?'

Maya wondered what to say. The truth seemed improbable, but she felt she ought to give Rose an explanation in return for her hospitality. It was also evident that she wasn't going to get the use of a phone until she'd satisfied Rose's curiosity.

'A warehouse down there is used by criminals,' she told Rose. 'They're drug dealers. One of them gave my friend a fix of heroin that was bad. She ended up in hospital and I was trying to stop him doing it again. Then, er, well, it's complicated, they sort of captured me and I escaped.'

Rose raised her eyebrows. 'Somethin' to do with the gunshots?'

'Yes.'

'You're a bit young to be tacklin' drug crime, aren't you?'

Maya nodded. 'Yes. I was trying to help a friend and one thing led to another. '

Rose's eyes narrowed. 'Sometimes it does well to leave things alone. Let the criminals deal with each other.'

'I can't do that, they've got my friend. Have you got a phone?'

'Nah. Can't stand the things.'

'Not even a mobile?'

Rose chuckled, her brown eyes gleaming. 'Do I look like the sort of person who has a mobile?'

Maya took a gulp of tea. 'I have to be going.'

'Sit down,' Rose ordered. 'Finish your breakfast. There's a payphone at the pub at the end of the towpath. I'll take you down there when you've eaten. Have you got any money?'

Maya shook her head, but then had another thought and felt in the pockets of the clothes she was wearing. Slipping her hand into Gerard's jeans, she pulled out a tight wad of notes. Her heart turned over.

'I . . . I seem to have acquired some,' she said. Her face flushed hot with shame. It was terrible to use drug money, but she'd deal with her conscience later – it was time to get going.

* * *

At the other end of the phone, Helen's voice was tight and shaky. 'Oh, thank God!' was her first exclamation when she heard Maya's voice.

All Maya could do was apologise and squirm with guilt as she heard the pain and worry in her gran's voice.

'Where are you? What happened?' Helen demanded.

'I'm all right, I'm fine. I'll tell you everything when I get back. I'm near Camden. I'll be home soon. I'll get a taxi.'

'How on earth did you end up there? Your friend said. . .'

Maya didn't let her finish. 'Gran, I'm OK. Don't worry. I'll see you soon.'

Rose was waiting in the bar of the pub, talking to the cleaner.

'How was that?' she asked, when Maya reappeared.

'Difficult.'

'Not surprised.'

Maya grimaced. 'Thanks for helping me.'

Rose nodded. 'You'd better get home quick.'

Maya said goodbye and hurried away. Walking down towards the main road, she saw people going about their everyday business and suddenly remembered it was Tuesday and she should have been at school. How had she got mixed up in all this? Never again would she take that short cut! The last few days had been horrendous. She'd been mugged, chased by a vicious dog, almost injected with a fatal dose of heroin, battered and narrowly escaped being raped. If you added that to the drama of the summer – it was enough danger for a lifetime.

She stopped walking and closed her eyes, tried to breathe deeply and calmly, but failed. Was she crazy? Shouldn't she just walk away from all of this? Her face screwed up in horror as she remembered

Ginger's hands on her, his rancid breath hot on her face, panting, pulling at her clothes. She opened her eyes and looked down at the red circles on her wrists. She turned her palms upwards and saw her hands shaking.

Don't fall to pieces now, she told herself, you're still on the gang's patch and could be spotted at any moment. Go home!

'Turn left at the end of the towpath, plenty of taxis there; or you'll see a bus stop in front of a café.' Those had been Rose's directions.

Follow Rose's directions, don't think about anything else, just concentrate on getting home. Breathe, breathe!

There were no taxis. None. She scanned the road up and down and then started to run. She flew past the converted flats, past two walkers with dogs, past a fenced-in scrapyard, and didn't stop running when she left the towpath road, but continued as she turned into a busy street. In a blur of images, she noticed the café and bus stop but didn't slow down. People stared at the tall girl racing along, long legs striding out, blue-black hair streaming behind her, dressed not in running clothes but in big boots, leather jacket and jeans.

Then she saw a bus coming down the street. It would stop at the end of the road, the towpath was a dead end, it had to turn back, go south. Abruptly she pulled up, turned and raced towards the bus. Three people were waiting at the bus stop. Maya leapt on board just as the doors began to close.

* * *

When Helen opened the door, she looked anxious and pale. On seeing Maya, she stepped forward, threw out her arms and hugged her granddaughter. 'Thank God, you're safe!'

'I'm so sorry, Gran. I couldn't call you. I would have, if I could.'

'What happened? Where've you been. I've been worried sick,' Helen breathed, holding Maya at arm's length. 'You're hurt. Your face is all swollen and. . .' She gently cupped Maya's face in her hand. 'Oh, Maya, what on earth's happened to you? I thought you'd been kidnapped. Why the hell didn't you get in touch with me?'

Maya tried to speak normally, but her voice was shaking and she had to bite back tears. 'I'm sorry. I lost my mobile. I knew you'd be worried.'

'Worried! I was frantic.' The expression on Helen's

face was by turns furious, then desperate, then sympathetic. She clasped Maya's arm and pushed her through to the kitchen. 'You've got a lot of explaining to do.' Her eyes scanned Maya's face. 'Did somebody hit you?' She put a hand over her mouth. 'Oh, Maya!'

There were tears in Helen's eyes. Helen, who was always so calm and practical, never seeming to be put out by anything, was crying, and Maya realised just what she'd done.

'Oh Helen, I'm so sorry. Don't worry, I'm OK.'

A strong sob shook Helen as Maya kissed her cheek. 'If only you'd called and explained where you were. I thought the worst. I couldn't help it. Kidnap, murder – I was distraught.' She blew out a big puff of air. 'I phoned your friend Leona – couldn't get a reply, then I tried Evie, she didn't know where you were. I was just about to call Simon when he phoned me. Your friend Zac had got in touch with him, told him you'd been driven away in a van. He gave Simon the registration number but the plates were false, they couldn't trace it. They've been working all night to find you.'

'Did you let him know I'm safe?'

'Of course. He's coming over.'

'The press aren't on to it, are they?'

'Not yet.' Helen pulled out a chair and sat Maya down. 'And lucky for you, Simon couldn't contact Pam, although by now the news might have filtered through. You have to tell me what this is all about.'

Maya nodded. 'I know. It's complicated. I got mixed up in something that I shouldn't have got involved with. But I was safe last night – a nice woman on a houseboat let me stay with her.'

Helen looked incredulous. 'A houseboat?'

'Yes,' Maya said, brushing back the hair from her eyes. 'She was very kind.' A sudden coughing fit shook her, she gasped for breath and when she spoke her voice was hoarse. 'Can I tell you the rest when Simon gets here?'

Helen shook her head and rolled her eyes. 'All right. As long as you promise me you aren't hurt or in danger and. . .' She stopped speaking abruptly as she noticed Maya's unfamiliar leather jacket. 'Whose clothes are you wearing?'

Maya got to her feet. "I . . . er. . . I'll explain later. I'm fine, honest. Just let me go and have a shower and change and then I'll tell you everything.'

A real sense of warmth and relief flooded through Maya as she walked into her bedroom. The cool white curtains, crimson duvet and black framed photographs that she'd thought were so stylish now looked familiar and comforting. She glanced at the photos of herself and Pam and sent a mind message.

Come home soon, Mum. I need you.

Slipping into the bathroom, she closed the door. Safe, she was safe. She'd escaped, she'd survived – but only just. Standing in the shower, her thoughts darted to Kay and the other girls. She had to convince Simon to act quickly or they might be lost forever.

What would you do, Mum? What can I do? She pictured her mum's face. And the message came back loud and clear.

You have played your part, Maya. Leave it to the experts.

* * *

Helen was bathing Maya's face with antiseptic when Simon stormed in. He took one look at Maya and exploded.

'What's been going on, Maya? What the hell have you been up to?'

His blond hair was flat, his nose was pink and his eyes watery. He didn't look half so cool and attractive as he usually did. Maya could tell he hadn't slept all night.

'I'm sorry. I was trying to help my friends and then one thing just led to another. Have you spoken to Mum?'

Simon's eyes narrowed and he lowered his voice. 'No, I didn't personally have that pleasure. She can't be reached directly – somebody had to pass a message on. No doubt she was woken in the middle of the night and told her daughter was missing. Don't imagine she got much sleep after that.'

'Simon,' Helen said quietly. 'Let's listen to what Maya has to say.'

Helen dropped the cotton wool swab she was holding into the bowl, asked Simon to sit down and took the bowl over to the sink. 'I'll make us some tea and then Maya will tell us what happened.'

Maya took a sip of tea and swallowed. 'OK. I told the Drug Squad about this boy, Gerard. He was selling drugs to my mates, some Es, maybe, and other stuff, I'm not sure what – he was trying to get them hooked. But he was dealing hard drugs, too, coke and heroin. I hoped the Drug Squad would get him, but they seemed more interested in locating his contacts, the suppliers, dealers, whatever.

'Anyway,' she continued, 'after Gerard gave Serena some heroin he'd cut, she ended up in hospital. Then this girl I know, Kay, told me her friend Leila had taken the same stuff, courtesy of Gerard, and she'd reacted badly too. Kay wanted to look after her, but Gerard wouldn't let her and in the morning Leila had disappeared.'

Simon and Helen were listening closely and didn't interrupt as Maya took another sip of tea.

'All Leila's things were there, coat, shoes, but she was missing. Kay thinks she died and Gerard hid the body. So, Kay begged me to steal the bad drugs and get rid of them before more people were harmed.'

'So why didn't you call the Drug Squad?' Simon snapped. 'Or me? You know I'll always listen.'

Maya looked down, biting her lip. 'I don't know. I suppose I should have, but it was sort of an instinctive reaction. If I didn't act quickly, Gerard would sell the drugs and more people would die.' She put her cup down and turned it round. 'It seemed like a simple answer – go into the house, steal the bad stuff, flush it down the loo. After that the Drug Squad could sort it out.'

'You can't do this sort of thing,' Helen said, 'take on dangerous criminals. You could have got yourself killed.'

Maya nodded. 'I know, Gran. Maybe it was a stupid

thing to do, because they caught me and I was lucky to escape. But at least I know where they hang out, where they stash their stuff, and I found out that it's not just drugs they're dealing in. They bring in girls, too – young girls, not much older than me. They use them in clubs, make them go with men – it's horrible, Gran. They're nice girls, but they're poor, and in their own country they don't have a chance. We have to rescue them.'

Simon folded his arms and shook his head. 'I am lost for words. You thought you could tackle an international drug and sex trafficking ring by yourself?'

'No!' Maya disagreed hotly. 'Of course not! All I knew was I had to act quickly – to stop people being hurt. It was a desperate situation. It wasn't until I went into the house that I realised all the things Gerard was mixed up in.'

'It was irresponsible, Maya,' Helen said quietly, 'totally irresponsible to try and sort it out on your own.'

Maya touched her hand. 'I know and I'm sorry I worried you. But while we're sitting here, Kay and the other girls are in the gang's hands and those men are ruthless. Ginger is just a thug and Stefan is mean and cold-hearted. He won't have any worries about getting rid of the girls if they don't cooperate. We have to find them and rescue them. I can't let them down.'

At this point, the doorbell chimed. Helen went to answer it and returned with Zac. He was not looking his usual bright, confident self. In fact, he looked scared, his arms jiggling by his sides, his eyes darting around the kitchen.

Simon turned an icy gaze upon him. 'So, you're the young man I was talking to last night? Maya's spy – keeping watch.'

Zac ignored him and made a beeline for Maya. 'Oh, my God! What did they do to you?'

'It's all right. I'm fine.'

'You don't look fine. Did they hurt you?'

He knelt down and took hold of Maya's hand. She put her head on one side and smiled at him.

'It's OK. Just scratches, no real damage.'

'It was so scary, I thought I'd never see you again. I saw them takin' you and I didn't know what to do. There was too many. I couldn't do anythin' to stop them. Then afterwards, I felt like a coward cos I didn't even try.'

'Good job you didn't. They would have killed you.'

'I called the number you gave me.'

'I know. You did right.'

'I was goin' crazy. Couldn't sleep all night, thinkin', wonderin' where you were and what was happenin' to you. Are you really all right?'

Maya looked down at her hands, her voice was a whisper. 'I . . . there was . . . one of the men. . .' She raised her eyes and looked at Zac. He put his hand on hers. Helen gasped, Simon stared. Conscious of their attention, Maya put her hand over her mouth, sniffed, then sat up taller in her chair and brushed back her hair. Then, in a much stronger, firmer voice she said, 'For a few moments it was scary, but I handled it. The man was coming on to me but he tripped and I ran. There was no way that fat slug was going to catch me.'

Helen put her hand to her throat. 'Oh, Maya!'

'I'm fine, Gran. The main thing is, I dumped the drugs – they're at the bottom of the canal.'

Zac nodded. 'You done good. They was poison.'

Simon cleared his throat. 'Good?' he snapped. 'You got yourself mixed up with a notorious drug-smuggling, trafficking operation, an outfit the Drug Squad tell me they've been tracking for two years. This gang is clever, brutal, ruthless – they don't

179

forgive, they've got eyes everywhere and,' he paused dramatically, 'now they're after you.'

'Simon!' Helen warned.

Simon walked away, speaking as he paced about the kitchen. 'Well, it's true. I'll have to put a watch on the flat. You can't do this, Maya. You can't take things into your own hands.'

Maya stood up. 'So, I see my friends getting into trouble – nearly killed – and I should just turn my back?'

His face was stony. 'No. You should inform the proper authorities.'

'That's exactly what I did, you know that.'

Simon spread his hands in exasperation. 'If you want to be a special agent, Maya, one thing you're going to have to learn is patience. That counts for all of us. We rarely move as fast as we'd like, but gathering evidence gets us convictions.'

'But what Maya's done is sound,' Zac said. 'If you've been lookin' for these guys for two years, then Maya's found them.'

'If only it worked like that,' Simon replied. 'They'll be on the back foot now. They'll lie low.'

'But we can't just leave it,' Maya said. 'This is not just about drugs any more. They have Kay and Tanya

180

and Annika and the other girls, and they'll bring in more. Girls who come here with hope. Girls like me, from Kosovo and all the other places where their lives are hard and they have nothing. And they think in England they'll have a better life and then when they get here they're just exploited. The criminals don't care, they traffic in human misery. I want them caught and I want the girls released.'

Chapter Fifteen

Simon's face was grave when he came back into the room. 'You're not going to like this.'

Maya, Zac and Helen stared up at him questioningly.

'I relayed the information about the girls, gave the Drug Squad the location of the warehouse. They want to interview you again.'

'Don't tell me,' Maya said, 'they're not going to do anything yet. They're not even going to try to rescue the girls.'

Simon sat down. 'Maya this is huge, bigger than we imagined. The gang that Gerard was involved with is operating a chain of criminal activity which runs from China across Europe to the UK. The Drug Squad have been watching them for months, Interpol is involved.

The gang bring in drugs and girls via Eastern Europe. They run several clubs where they put the girls to work as hostesses – get them hooked, exploit them and use the clubs to distribute supplies of heroin and other drugs.'

'So, what you're telling me is that, in the grand scheme of things, Kay and Tanya and Annika and the others are not that important,' Maya said dully. She sighed bitterly. 'Individuals don't matter. The cops will wait until they have all the evidence they need and by that time Kay and the others will all be junkies or dying from some horrible disease they've picked up.'

She banged her cup on the table. 'What more evidence do they need? I've told you about the warehouse and they must know where the clubs are.'

Simon pursed his lips and looked into the distance, then he focused on Maya. 'Look, I shouldn't tell you this, but there are intelligence reports that there's a big shipment coming in from Europe, sometime in the next month. They want to catch the gang and their European contacts red-handed.'

Maya slumped forward, elbows on the table and sighed. 'So that's what Stefan was talking about. He said they were setting up something big.'

'Did he give any details?'

'No.' She scratched impatiently at the red marks on her wrist. 'What am I supposed to do now, forget the whole thing? Those men tried to kill me, they're selling drugs to school kids, controlling girls with drugs so that they can pimp them.'

Simon folded his arms and nodded. 'That's exactly what you do – you let specially-trained people take care of it. But first give me all the information you can, write it all down and I promise you it will be followed up. And there's one other thing.'

'What?'

'If this gang has the connections I think they have, it won't take them long to find you. We'd better put you under protection immediately. Category one.'

Maya looked horrified. 'No. I don't want to be confined to the house. I've only just gone back to school. Put me on watch, please! The gang don't know where I live and there's no way Gerard can find out now.'

Simon raised his eyebrows. In answer, Maya nodded.

'I'm pretty sure he's dead. He was in a terrible state and nobody was helping him.'

'And Kay?'

'She won't give me away.'

Simon tapped his fingers on his jeans while he was thinking. 'Maybe you're right. We don't want to do anything to alarm the gang. The best way to draw them out is for everything to appear normal. You go to school, see your friends. I'll make sure you're discreetly tailed.'

Maya pulled at a strand of hair, puckering up her face. 'I don't like it. It doesn't feel right. I just go about my normal everyday life while Kay and the other girls suffer.'

Simon stood up and held out his hands, gesturing, palms upwards. 'Let's face it, Maya. These girls are just a few out of many.'

Maya's cheeks burned. 'I know them, Simon. If I close my eyes, I can see their faces. And you know, I was once like that – a little girl without any hope. It could be me in that stinking brothel.'

For a moment there was silence. Helen looked shocked, Zac looked away.

But Simon always had an answer. His voice was smooth and practical. 'Then that's why it should be important to you to stop this horrible trade, not just for the girls you know but for all girls.' He pulled his mobile from his pocket and examined it. Then, turning back to Maya, he said in a brighter voice, 'Your mum will be home soon. You'll feel better then.'

'Yeah, course I will,' she answered. And she would, she knew she would, everything was better when Pam was around, but she couldn't fix everything and while she was completing her mission, time was running out for the girls in captivity.

'Right, let's get a few more details before I leave,' Simon said.

He asked Helen's permission to take Maya into another room so that he could question her in more detail. While she was explaining the trail of events that led from her first sighting of Kay to her plunge into the canal, she heard Helen and Zac talking and laughing in the kitchen. It made the catalogue of events she was relaying to Simon seem bizarre and almost unbelievable. She wasn't even sure she believed it herself – the past couple of days had seemed like the scenario for an action movie.

'I didn't go looking for adventure, you know,' she said to Simon. 'It just happened.'

Simon pursed his lips and regarded her with an expression of wonderment. 'Couldn't you just rent a few DVDs, watch *The X Factor*?'

For the first time that day, Maya laughed. 'Yeah, right.'

Simon put away his laptop and stood up. 'Confirm all this in your report,' he said, moving towards the door.

After saying goodbye, he stood on the doorstep, looking out for a moment, then he turned to Maya. 'Don't think I don't value what you've done, Maya. You're intelligent and brave; you'll make a great agent, if that's what you want to do.' He reached out and patted her shoulder. 'I'll send somebody to pick up your report tomorrow. You're on to something big here. Drugs – not my department, but smuggling illegals, a cross-country operation – I may get a look in. Drug Squad are wily devils, like to keep things to themselves, but if it gets passed on, I'll keep you informed.'

'Thanks,' Maya muttered.

Before he turned to go, he looked hard into her face once more. 'But leave it now, understood? And tomorrow get yourself checked over. Swallowing putrid water can do nasty things to you.'

She nodded, closed the door and returned to the kitchen where Zac was stirring something inside a big pot on the stove. He looked up when he heard her enter and smiled.

'Your gran is teachin' me how to cook.'

'Great,' Maya said, and suddenly she felt very tired.

Helen, ever watchful and astute, advised, 'You should go and rest.'

Zac was tasting his cooking and looking very pleased with himself.

'Want to go into my room and play some music?' Maya asked.

He looked questioningly at Helen. 'Go on,' she said. 'I'll finish the curry.'

The bedroom was bright with evening sunshine, the breeze gently ruffling the leaves brushing against Maya's window.

Zac's eyes lit up when he entered. 'So, who else sleeps in here?' he asked.

Maya laughed. 'Just me, I have a lot of stuff.'

'I can see that,' Zac said, wandering round the room. 'Hey, loads of books. You read?'

'I read.' Maya thumped down on the sofa. 'Zac, I have to think.'

He sat beside her and looked serious. 'You not happy 'bout Kay.'

'No, how can I be? Those men were evil. Ginger, the guy who . . . you know . . . he had a gun. He shot at me. If Kay kicks up a fuss, they won't hesitate.'

Zac came and sat beside her and put his arm around her.

Maya turned to look at him. 'Kay has to have a chance. She hasn't lived yet. She's been in one bad situation after another; her family killed, con men promising her a new life in England then betraying her, living on the streets."

'It sucks,' Zac said, softly.

She took his hand and stroked his fingers. 'I promised to help her. Fat lot of use my promise was – just like all the others, I failed her.'

Zac slipped his arm round her shoulders. 'You aren't responsible for what them men are doin'.'

Maya leaned against his shoulder. 'There has to be something I can do.'

'*We* can do,' Zac said. 'I want to help. It was horrible when I saw those heavies takin' you. I wanted to do somethin', but if I did they'd have got me too – then there'd be nobody to tell Simon.'

'You did the right thing.'

'Yeah, but it didn't make me feel good. I want to do somethin'.'

Maya held up her hand. 'Wait, I'm thinking.'

* * *

When Helen called upstairs to say dinner was ready, a fragrant aroma of spices was in the air and, sitting at the table with Helen and Zac, Maya felt some sense of normality returning.

The curry was delicious, but she found it hard to eat anything. Her mind was turning. She knew Simon was right – the only way to break the circle was to catch all the players – the dealers, the smugglers, the traffickers and drivers. And so the Drug Squad, with the aid of Interpol, would gather information, set up surveillance, wait for the right moment and then strike. But all that time, Kay and the other girls would be in danger. By the time the ring was smashed, Kay might be dead.

'This is amazin',' Zac said, waving his spoon over his almost-empty plate.

Gran smiled. 'Plenty more. You eat, I'll keep it coming.'

Zac emptied his plate and held it up. 'Most meals in our house come out of cardboard,' he said.

Gran moved from the stove and plonked the casserole dish down in the middle of the table. 'Here,' she said turning the ladle towards Zac, 'help yourself and there's more rice in the dish.'

He grinned. 'Thanks. Won't say no.'

Out in the hallway, the house phone chirped. 'I'll get it,' Maya shouted, pushing back her chair and racing into the hall.

It was a surprise to hear Pam's voice. 'Maya! Thank God you're safe. Are you all right?'

'Yes, I'm OK, Mum, really.'

Then came the serious words Maya dreaded. Pam never shouted at her and rarely told her off, which made her warnings all the more significant. There was no use protesting – Maya knew it was deserved.

'My mission is crucial,' Pam said tersely. 'I'm involved in sensitive and delicate negotiations. I can't abort this mission to come home and deal with you. I have to be able to rely on you while I'm away.'

'I'm sorry, Mum. I'm really sorry.'

Pam's tone softened slightly. 'What on earth were you up to? Where were you?'

An answer was tricky. Maya didn't want to lie, but it was no use worrying Pam with all the details while she was so far away, and it was complicated to explain. 'I was trying to help some friends and I came into contact with a nasty gang. But I've handed it on to Simon and he's dealing with it. So don't worry.'

'Well, Simon seemed pretty concerned. Are you sure you're telling me everything?'

'I'll fill you in when you come home, but honest, I'm fine – everything's OK. I just should have told Helen what I was up to.'

'Yes, you should and make sure you do that from now on.'

'Yeah, I love you, Mum, miss you.'

'Miss you too, darling.' Pam sniffed, and Maya knew that, as tough as her mum was, she was holding back the tears. 'You know you always come first,' she continued, her voice breaking slightly, 'but I need a few more days, then I'll be home. Will you be all right?'

Silence crackled over thousands of miles. It would be fantastic to have Pam home, to have her help and support, but Maya knew how important her mum's job was. It was no exaggeration to say that world peace could depend upon her.

'No, Mum. Please stay and finish what you have to do.'

'All right. Be careful, Maya, understood?'

'Understood.'

'I love you. See you soon.'

'Love you, Mum.'

It was a sober Maya that returned to the kitchen table. She gave Gran the news – Pam would be home soon.

'So, why aren't you jumping for joy?' Helen asked, eyeing Maya suspiciously.

'It's great, I'm really happy Mum's coming home, course I am.' She looked over at Zac, who was still eating, but her food sat on her plate, largely untouched, and now she couldn't face another mouthful. She was flooded with sadness. 'It just seems so unfair for me to be happy when Kay's in deep trouble.'

Helen put a hand on Maya's arm. 'You can't make the world right for everybody, Maya.'

There was a few minutes' silence, which Zac broke by offering to wash up. Maya looked at him in surprise.

'What?' he exclaimed. 'I do it all the time at home.'

'Offer appreciated,' Helen said, 'but I'm going to stick it all in the dishwasher.'

For a moment Zac was floored. 'Oh, right,' he said. 'I should get one of them.'

Upstairs, Maya closed the door to her room, went over to the window and gestured for Zac to follow. 'Can you stay for a while?'

Zac nodded.

'I want you to help me,' she said. 'It's nothing dangerous, I promise, no direct action – just research. We have to find out about Stefan's organisation.'

She put on some music while she told Zac what she wanted to do. He listened then put his arm around her and pulled her close. 'You are crazy,' he said.

Half an hour later, he went downstairs and said goodbye to Helen in the kitchen, while Maya crept through the hall and out of the front door. She checked the street, but couldn't see anybody watching the flat – friend or foe. It was only a matter of time, though, before Simon put one of his team on watch.

Chapter Sixteen

Standing behind a wall opposite the squat, Maya and Zac were relieved to see there were no cars parked outside the house – the street was empty. Peering through a hole made by crumbling bricks, they could see the house clearly; one of the upstairs windows was open, a curtain flapping in the breeze.

'Nobody home,' Zac said, staring at the open window.

'Yeah, somebody would have closed that,' Maya whispered.

'Can't be certain,' Zac said softly.

'No, they won't come back,' Maya whispered.

'So, why we whispering?' Zac replied, in a slightly louder whisper.

They smiled at each other and broke some of the tension. But watching the empty house was one thing, to enter it was another. Fresh in Maya's mind was the terror of staring down the barrel of Ginger's gun. It wasn't the first time a gun had been pointed at her, it probably wouldn't be the last, but it was something you couldn't get used to.

Crossing the road to the house, she had to control her thoughts and ignore the fear. Standing in front of the house, Maya experienced a moment of panic and clutched at Zac's arm.

'You don't have to do this,' Zac said.

'I know,' Maya said softly. 'But actually I do. If I can discover anything that may help rescue Kay, then I have to do it. She spoke up for me and that may have saved my life.' In a firmer, bolder voice she added, 'Don't worry. The gang won't dare come back to this place, now their cover's blown.'

Despite her brave words, she approached the house cautiously, creeping up to the side gate, grateful to discover it open, the wire fence broken down. Continuing down the side path and round the corner of the house, Maya reached behind her and put a steadying hand on Zac's shoulder.

'Listen!'

A faint tapping sound could be heard from the kitchen.

'Stay there,' Maya said, and she continued moving forward until she could push open the back door and peer into the kitchen.

The place had been cleaned up. A horrible smell of rotting food and grease emanated from some bags of rubbish in a corner, but the surfaces had been wiped clean. Holding her nose, Maya tiptoed into the hall and stood, listening and waiting. There was no sound to indicate that anybody was in the building, so she pushed at the door which led into the living room. The room was empty, the window still open from when she'd tried to make her escape. Behind her, a sudden loud creak spooked her.

'Only me,' Zac said softly.

'Oh my God! I thought you were Ginger,' Maya said. 'Forgot for a moment you were with me.'

Zac grabbed her hand. 'Well, I am.'

Maya gave him a faint smile.

'I'm so glad. This place gives me the creeps.'

She pulled two pairs of thin rubber gloves out of her pocket.

'Here, put these on – don't want to mess up any evidence. Let's get to work and get out of here fast.'

They wiggled their hands into the gloves, then crept upstairs, pausing and listening, until they were finally on the landing. All the doors were open and it took only moments to check that nobody was inside the rooms. The house was deserted.

'So, what we goin' to do now?' Zac asked.

'We look for clues, anything they've left which tells us about the organisation.'

'OK.'

Maya went into the room with the soggy mattresses. There wasn't much to find: a few rags, a piece of rope, some bent scissors, smoky plastic bottles. She lifted a mattress, but there was nothing underneath. She was just about to give up when Zac called.

'Come and see what I've found.'

Zac was standing at the end of the landing with a heavy padlock in his hand; he gestured to a door which had heavy bolts on it. 'Mostly locked, I guess, but the padlock was undone. Perhaps someone left in a hurry. Come and see – it goes through to next door.'

They went through the door which led onto the adjoining landing. Zac dipped into a room and Maya followed. To her surprise, she found herself in a pleasant bedroom. It was a world away from the scabby rooms with the stained mattresses next door. A king size bed with black leather headboard dominated the centre of the room and the sheets on the bed looked freshly laundered. Two big red velvet cushions lay in the centre of the duvet, lined up on a white unit were bottles of aftershave and other toiletries, an iPod and a stack of magazines.

'Gerard's hideout?'

'Yeah, I reckon,' Zac said. 'Good cover, eh? A palace in a squat.'

Maya was busy looking round. She went over to a side table and lifted up a cigarette lighter. 'This has got his name engraved on it – Gerard Lesanne. I doubt if he'll be back here to claim it.'

'Easy come, easy go, I guess,' Zac said.

'Zac! Gerard's probably dead.'

'Oh, yeah, well, I didn't. . .'

His voice tailed off and Maya wasn't listening, anyway. She was checking out a newspaper she'd picked up from a pile.

Zac came over to her. 'That's Russian or Polish,' he said looking at the newspaper. 'Somethin' like that, anyway.'

'Russian,' Maya said. She set it aside and picked up a leaflet. Opening it up, she saw, spread across the centrefold, photos of women, most of them young girls. At the top of the page was a heading – 'Omega Brides'.

'Look!' Maya pointed. 'I'm sure that's Annika . . . and her sister.' Her gaze swept over the rest of the photos. 'I get it. Omega finds husbands for some girls, but that's just a front, to make them seem legit. The most attractive girls they keep and get them hooked on drugs so they can control them.' She rolled up a couple of leaflets and a newspaper and stuffed them inside her jacket. 'I'll send these to Simon tomorrow with my report.'

Zac picked up a leaflet and looked at the girls. 'It's horrible. Some of them don't look any older than us.'

Maya nodded. 'I know. Let's get out of here. This place gives me the creeps – Gerard sleeping in here like a king and next door girls tied up, lying on filthy mattresses and crying their eyes out. How could he do that?'

Zac put his arm round Maya's shoulders. 'Come on. Let's split.'

* * *

On the doorstep to Maya's flat, Zac whispered goodbye and gave her a quick hug.

Sliding her key into the lock, Maya turned it and edged the door open. Thank goodness the alarm system didn't go on until later. She could hear the TV in the sitting room – Helen, slightly deaf, had it booming. She was watching a rerun of *Inspector Morse*.

If she could just get through the hall to the bottom of the stairs, Maya thought, then she was home and dry. Three quick strides and she was on the bottom step. Swiftly she mounted the stairs and dived into her room. Hopefully Gran hadn't noticed her absence.

She was just removing the leaflets and newspaper from inside her jacket when there was a knock on her door.

'Maya?'

'Just a minute!' Stuffing the papers under a school file, she slung her jacket on a chair and went to the door.

'Oh, you're still dressed!' Gran exclaimed.

'Yeah, I know. Don't worry, I'm going to get ready for bed in a minute – switch my brain off and fall into a deep, dreamless sleep.'

'I shouldn't think so, after all the adventures you've had,' Helen said.

'Err. . . I'm going to try, anyway.'

'Well, before you go to sleep, I want to look at those cuts and scratches and put some more ointment on them. You never know what germs could have got into them in that water. You need to be on antibiotics.'

'How did you know about the canal?'

'Simon. He phoned about ten minutes ago. I was going to come up but I thought you were asleep – then I heard you. Did you come down for something?'

'Oh, just a glass of water.'

'Right. Well, Simon said he'll send a car round tomorrow evening to pick up your report. We're possibly not going to tell Pam how you escaped. A half-drowned daughter is something she doesn't need to think about.'

'Thanks, Gran,' Maya said.

'Yes, well, you were very naughty. First thing tomorrow I'm taking you to the doctors.'

'Gran, I'm all right.'

'You were coughing earlier.'

'I know, but I'm fine now. I'll go and see the school nurse tomorrow. She can check me over.'

'We'll see. But you have to promise you're going to keep out of trouble from now on.'

Maya rested her chin on her gran's head. 'I promise I'll try not to get into more trouble.'

Once Gran had kissed her goodnight and had been reassured for the tenth time that Maya really wasn't hurt any more than the obvious cuts and bruises, she left her to sleep. As soon as her footsteps faded, Maya spread the stolen papers out on her bedroom carpet.

A hundred young women's faces looked up at her. Some were fresh and innocent, some were heavily made-up, several wore skimpy clothes, adopting fake sexy poses, and a few had serious faces, but one thing they all had in common was their eyes – they were full of hope. How many of these girls had Omega brought to England and exploited? On the top of the paper was a website address. Booting up her laptop, Maya accessed the site. Men could peruse the site and choose a prospective bride. Only brief details about the girls were given: their names, height, weight, hair colour, body measurements and what country they came from – Albania, Romania, Kosovo, China, Thailand, Philippines. At the top of the page was a phone number.

Chapter Seventeen

The next morning, it took a big effort for Maya to get out of bed. Dazzling dreams held onto her; the night had been full of sleeplessness and turmoil. She staggered into the bathroom and stood for a long time under the shower, letting the stream of hot water ease the ache of her muscles. She examined her body. Glistening under a sheen of water, the cuts and bruises took on a life of their own, marking her skin with livid scars.

Wrestling with Ginger and her fight for survival underwater had taken their toll. The bathroom mirror was too steamed up for her to see her face properly, so, putting on a dressing gown, she went back into her room. The swelling on one side of her face had subsided, but her cheek had a bluish tinge and above it, her eye was ringed by a dark circle. There was a cut on her chin and scratches on her neck. Make-up should conceal some of the damage, though not all.

Trousers were a good option. Actually, she hated the shapeless, navy blue trousers that were the school alternative to skirts, but today they'd act as a useful cover-up and, together with a long-sleeved shirt, would conceal most of her injuries. After quickly pulling on her clothes, she applied some make-up. Leaning close to the mirror, she tried to decide whether the effect was better or worse.

By the time she'd finished treating and drying her hair, she was hot and sweaty. This was not a good way to start the day.

To think deeply requires a calm mind.

Pam's voice! When she heard it, she realised with surprise that it had been absent. She used to hear it all the time when Pam was away. If she was scared or worried, she'd think of something Pam had said, but recently, Pam's voice had been missing without her realising it.

She walked over to the window, opened it and took a deep breath. She felt strange, unnerved. She'd lost the connection with Pam without even noticing. Had she outgrown it? Was she becoming more independent, or was it because she knew Pam wouldn't approve of what she was doing?

From the window, she looked down on the scene she knew so well; the old square dappled in early morning sunshine, the beech trees forming a border round the little park. What scene had greeted Pam upon waking – stark mountains, dusty plains? Like her mission, it was a mystery. Maya tried to picture her mum, but all she saw were Pam's grey eyes looking at her with serious questions.

'I know, I know,' Maya whispered. 'But you didn't see how desperate those girls were – they were crying, feeling ashamed, as if they'd done something wrong. It's not their fault, it's foul, inhuman. They're prisoners, probably somewhere nearby. I can't just ignore them, Mum, I can't.'

A woman in bright summer clothes hurried along the pavement, tripping in high red shoes. Two mothers supervising a line of children in neat uniforms – the walking bus – rounded the corner and crossed the road. One of the children broke away from the line and was ushered back into his place.

'If you'd met Kay, you'd want to help her, just like you helped me. You remember how I was found in a ditch, filthy and starving? I had this dream that a girl with gold eyes pushed me in there to save me. It could have been Kay.

'I have to try and find out about Omega, Mum. You do understand, don't you? I have to help Kay.'

She touched the ruby ring which had been a birthday present from Pam.

Be careful my darling, I'll be home in three days.

Maya smiled.

Got you, Mum, I promise I won't take any unnecessary risks. See you soon.

While closing the window, a heavy, bald-headed man sauntering along with a newspaper under his arm caught her attention. He was wearing jeans and a combat jacket. He stopped, leaned back against the railings, opened his newspaper and began to read. Maya didn't miss his direct glance up to her window, and then he spoke into a wired headset. She dodged back, a burning question in her brain – was he Simon's man or one of the Omega heavies? Just as she'd decided to take another peek, the house phone next to her bed rang.

Quickly she crossed the floor and picked it up.

'Don't worry,' a male voice said. 'He's my man.' With a flood of relief, she recognised Simon's voice. 'He saw you looking. He'll tail you. There'll be somebody on watch till Pam's back.'

'Can I catch the bus?'

'Yes. Carry on as normal. If the gang are watching we don't want to alarm them.'

Down in the kitchen, Helen was listening to the radio and making toast.

'I thought I heard you,' she said. 'You're not going to school, surely?'

'Yep,' Maya replied, taking a piece of buttered toast.

'I was just making you breakfast, I was going to bring it up on a tray.' She gestured to a tray neatly-laid with a cloth and crockery. 'How're you feeling?'

'I'm all right. Honest,' Maya said. 'I haven't coughed once and I don't want to miss athletics practice.'

'You sure you're up to it?' Helen asked. She pulled down her glasses and inspected Maya over the top of them. 'Your face is rather a mess, darling. Have a day off.'

'I am a bit tired, but I can't let the team down.' She took a bite of toast and chewed slowly. 'Don't worry, Simon's men are out there, watching me. Bye, gotta go.'

'What about that report Simon wanted?'

'I'll do it when I get home.'

When the door closed behind her, Maya surveyed the street. Her bodyguard was still pretending to read his newspaper. Her eyes swept over the pavements and square; thankfully there was no sign of Ginger or any gang members. Even so, as she hurried towards the bus stop, she was glad Simon's man was following.

Leona and Evie were sitting together on a tabletop when Maya entered the tutor room.

'Where've you been?' Leona shouted. And then she looked horrified. 'What the hell happened to you?' She grabbed Maya's arm and pulled her close. 'Who hit you?'

Maya turned away. 'I was sick, I fainted, fell down.'

'Yeah? Looks like you been street fighting.'

Maya turned away and dropped her bag on a table. 'How's Serena?' she asked, hoping to ward off more questions.

Leona's face puckered. 'She's improving but they don't know what damage is done yet. They're runnin' tests. Could be her liver is damaged.'

'Oh, no! Poor Serena.'

'You never called,' Leona said accusingly.

'I tried loads of times but your mobile was off.'

'Yeah, when I was in the hospital. What about yesterday?'

'My mobile . . . er . . . got stolen.'

'Somebody took it while you were sick?' Evie asked.

Leona frowned, her eyes narrowed and she leaned closer to Maya. 'What are you up to? Nobody gets their mobile stolen twice in one week – not even you.'

Maya stepped back and held up her hands. 'Thanks for your sympathy, guys.'

Leona gave her an examining stare. 'You seen Gerard?'

Maya shrugged and adopted a baffled look.

'Don't go getting any ideas like you're gonna get him back for what he done to Serena.' She put her arm round Maya's shoulders. 'I know you done all that training with your mum and you can do karate and stuff but we heard he's part of a big gang. Anyways, the cops is after him.'

'I hate him,' Evie said, with real venom. 'I hope they get him.'

The image of Gerard lying on the filthy mattress bloomed vividly in Maya's head and a sudden stab of sadness for him surprised her.

'I'm pretty sure he's dead,' she whispered.

Leona's eyes shot open. 'Dead? Gerard?'

Maya pulled her friends close. 'Don't tell anybody. I'm not supposed to even know. I shouldn't have said that.'

'You didn't have anythin' to do with it, did you?' Evie asked, her eyes goggling.

'No,' Maya said. 'I heard it from somebody my mum knows. They reckon the gang wasted him for cutting drugs. Their reputation was on the line, see?' She held up her hands in warning. 'You can't talk about this to anyone. I don't even know if his family knows yet.'

'Well, I for one don't care,' Evie said. 'He deserved it.'

'Nobody deserves to die so young,' Maya said quietly.

Leona sniffed in a dismissive manner. 'I feel stupid to be taken in by him.'

'Yeah, I thought he was well nice,' Evie agreed. 'How wrong can you be?'

Maya stepped back and undid her bag, fiddling with the catch, then she squinted up at her friends.

'You see what can happen. Please don't mess with drugs any more.'

'Don't worry. I'm never touching dope again, no Es, no tabs, no fags, no alcohol – it's all crap,' Leona said fervently.

Evie nodded seriously. 'Me too. I been to see Serena in hospital; she's done in. That face was not Serena's face – her skin was all dull and dusty, her lips broke out in sores. She is one mess.'

Leona's face puckered into disapproval. 'She's gonna get better, I know it. You'll see, Serena will come back stronger and better. She'll be wiser, for starters.' She patted Maya's shoulder. 'Let's go and see her tonight. Cheer her up. OK?'

* * *

It wasn't until lunchtime that Maya had a chance to borrow Leona's mobile, then she rushed off to the quiet space at the back of the gym. Luckily most students were getting lunch and there was nobody about. Pulling a sheet of pictures out of her pocket, she called Omega.

A woman with a sweet, syrupy voice answered. Maya thought of Kay and did an impersonation of an Eastern European accent, saying she was living in London as a student.

'I love England. I study to be an engineer but now my studies are finished, I must return to my country. Can you find an English man for me to marry?'

'We do this for girls we bring into the country,' the woman said. 'We don't deal with girls who're already here. My best advice is to return to your own country and apply there.'

'How do I apply?'

'Well, you fill in the forms online or you contact our nearest agent and arrange an interview.'

'Why must I return? I can fill in forms in this country.'

The woman hesitated. 'How old are you?'

'Nineteen.'

'What is your name?

Maya thought fast, putting together the names of two different girls she'd seen on the sheet. 'Dania, Dania Ballack,' she said.

'Describe yourself to me.'

'Tall and er . . . I have blonde hair, brown eyes.'

'Are you beautiful?'

'Men say this.'

'Fat or thin?'

'Slim.'

'So why can't you find someone to marry you?' the woman asked, suspiciously.

'All the men I know are students. No money,' Maya said firmly.

The woman on the other end of the phone was silent for a moment, then she gave in. 'All right. Come

here at eleven o' clock tomorrow morning and we'll
see what we can do.'

'How do I visit you?'

Maya wrote down the address and when she
put the phone down she felt triumphant. She was
a jump ahead of Simon and the Drug Squad. If she
acted quickly, she just might be able to get information
that would save Kay and the girls and smash
the gang.

Back in the classroom, Maya joined her friends
and listened to them making plans for the weekend.
She felt a million miles away – in her head she was
plotting her next move. Tomorrow she'd skip school
and go for the interview with Omega.

'Cinema, then pizza,' Evie said, jolting Maya's
elbow.

'Oh, OK, count me in,' Maya agreed distractedly,
still making plans. And suddenly she had a good idea.
'Hey, my mum should be back on Saturday. She said I
could have a party.'

'Oh great! When?' Evie asked.

'Well, not this Saturday, cos she'll only just have
got back, but the weekend after. I want to do a fifties
party. You know, all glam, like old Hollywood film
stars. I'm going to be Marilyn Monroe.'

The girls stared at her. 'You're joking?'

'No.'

Leona grinned. 'Hello! Blonde hair, white skin?'

Maya shrugged. 'You racist or something?' She laughed. 'I just fancy the dress, you know, that white one with little pleats, where it's blowing up all round her. And I'll get a blonde wig.'

Evie rolled her eyes. 'Oh, yeah, you could easily pass as Marilyn.'

'Well, it's just for fun. How about we go up to Covent Garden before we go to the hospital? We could go straight after school and look for a wig and clothes?'

'Yeah, that'll be a laugh,' Leona agreed.

* * *

The girls were familiar with Covent Garden, they knew most of the buskers and circus acts that inhabited the square; they liked the young American guy who played the guitar outside the East shop and the small woman whose brave operatic voice swelled through the indoor market. Maya didn't get the guys covered in paint who stood like statues.

'Can never see the point in that,' she said, as they passed Abraham Lincoln.

'What do they do when they want to pee?' Evie asked.

'Must ruin their paint job,' Maya laughed.

They made their way to the indoor market, past the racks of richly-coloured Turkish bathrobes, the tourist trophy caps and trinkets.

'Who's that guy followin' us?' Evie said, turning round suddenly.

Looking over her shoulder Maya shrugged. 'You seeing things?'

'No,' Evie replied.

Leona gave Maya a serious look. 'You've got somebody watching you, haven't you? Like you did before?'

Maya nodded. 'Yeah. But don't look round, he'll get embarrassed.'

'What's up, then?' Leona asked.

'Just a precaution till my mum gets back,' Maya said.

'Thought they was supposed to be invisible,' Evie whispered.

When they reached the wig stall they forgot all about their guardian angel.

'We haven't just come to try on,' Maya said to the stallholder, who was eyeing them suspiciously. 'I want a blonde wig, Marilyn Monroe style – a good one.'

The woman looked at her with amusement. 'How much do you want to pay?'

'I'll decide when I see what it looks like,' Maya replied.

She sat down in the chair and the woman presented a selection of blonde wigs. The first ones she tried on looked hideous.

'I look like sunburnt Barbie!' Maya protested.

'Why don't you go as Cleopatra?' Evie suggested.

'It's 50s Hollywood. I want to be Marilyn!' Maya said, suddenly turning her head to look at Evie, so the wig fell half across her face. That had them in fits of laughter. 'Can you find something better?' she asked the woman.

'I can but it'll cost you.'

'I don't care,' Maya said. 'My mum's paying.'

The woman pursed her lips then seemed to relax and enter into the fun. 'You're in luck. I had to hang on tonight for a supplier. I've got something I think you'll like.' She turned and went to the back of the stall pulling out a silver box. When she placed it in front of Maya and opened the lid, Maya knew it was going to be right.

'Real hair,' the woman said.

'Ugh!' Evie exclaimed in disgust, but when the woman had pulled Maya's own hair tight and scooped it under the wig they were all surprised. The wig looked as if it belonged to her; the silvery-blonde tresses framed her face and her skin shone lighter.

'Just your eyebrows,' the woman said. 'Let's lighten them a little.' She reached for a small bottle of gold.

'That looks like nail varnish to me,' Maya said anxiously.

'No. It's a fine powder, you'll see, it works like magic.'

When she stroked some of the powder onto Maya's eyebrows they harmonised with the wig and Maya was a perfect sun-kissed blonde.

'Fabulous,' she said, thrilled at the sight of herself. 'Might go blonde for real.' She turned to look at her friends. 'How do I look?' she demanded.

Leona had put on a pink wig and Evie's head was covered in chestnut curls. They were joking around, but when Maya asked her question they knew she was serious.

Leona stared her up and down. 'You look great,' she said.

'Yeah,' Evie agreed. 'You'd pass for a blonde.'

Satisfied with her purchase, Maya paid and strode out. 'Now for the clothes,' she said.

Behind her, Leona whispered to Evie, 'What's she up to?'

Afternoon was turning into evening and most of the stalls were closing, but they caught one stallholder packing dresses away. When Maya told him what she wanted, he produced a slinky white number that wasn't exactly Marilyn Monroe, but Maya said it would pass. All she secretly wanted was something short and tight that she could easily slip into her schoolbag.

'I want some boots now,' Maya announced, linking arms with her friends.

'Marilyn Monroe did not wear boots,' Evie stated firmly.

'Yeah, I know," Maya agreed. 'But I want to get some boots in case I change my mind about the costume.'

Evie made a face. 'Nobody except peasants wore boots in the 1950s,' she declared with authority – she was doing Textiles at school. 'Fashion boots are sixties.'

'All right, I own up,' Maya smiled. 'I have a fetish for boots – knee-high, shiny leather is what I want.'

Leona and Evie exchanged glances. They were convinced their friend was plotting something.

'OK. Let's go to Shoos. Hope your guardian angel likes shoppin',' Evie said, with a mischievous glance over her shoulder.

* * *

The boot-buying trip had her friends tottering about in ridiculously high heels, while Maya tried on all sort of boots she'd never normally wear. She settled on some knee-high black patent leather with high heels, and then the three girls caught the bus to the hospital.

Serena had been moved from Intensive Care to a High Dependency ward. After they'd rung the bell, waited and washed their hands, a nurse sitting at the central station gestured to a side room.

'Serena's in there. She'll be glad to see you. Her mum was here this afternoon, but left about an hour ago.'

Maya followed Leona and Evie into the room where Serena was hooked up to a machine and she saw that what Evie had told them earlier was true. Serena looked dreadful, hardly recognisable, all sparkle and life had evaporated. She lay smudged against white pillows, a plastic tag round her thin wrist, her skin dry and powdery, hair dull and dark circles under her eyes.

'Hi,' she said, trying to raise a smile when she saw them. 'Good to see you.' Her voice was thin and raspy; her fingers fluttered weakly. She tried to lift her head and sit up, but lay back with a sigh. 'I don't seem to. . .' she started to say then lost the words. Before she turned her head away, Maya saw a trickle of a tear.

'Hey,' Leona said, moving round the bed, and reaching down to give her cousin a hug. 'Look, we brought you some mags, chocolate bars, cos we thought the food in here might be crap, and a surprise.' She lifted out the bag of Soap and Glory toiletries they'd clubbed together to buy. 'For when you get up. Pamper yourself.'

'Thanks,' Serena whispered.

An awkward silence fell, none of them knowing quite what to say. Then Serena turned her head towards Maya, and between long breaths she managed to tell her, 'The cops were here; wanted to know about Gerard. He's dead, fell in a canal.'

'Stoned out of his head, probably,' Evie said.

'Evie, that's not very kind,' Leona said, glancing at Serena.

Serena closed her eyes. 'Dead,' she muttered. 'Gone. I can't . . . I keep seein' his face.' She coughed, her mouth contorting as she tried to breathe.

'Shall I call a nurse?' Leona asked, anxiously, bending over her.

Serena waved her away and motioned for some water. After she'd sipped from a straw, her breathing calmed. 'I know he was bad news, but he deserved a chance, you know? Everybody deserves a chance.'

'He nearly killed you!' Evie exclaimed.

Tears welled in Serena's eyes. 'It wasn't just him. I shouldn't have taken the stuff. I was stupid.'

'Yeah, you were stupid,' Evie said.

'Evie!' Maya and Leona said together.

Evie held up her hands. 'All I'm sayin' is, I guess we've all learnt a lesson.'

Tears trickled down Serena's cheeks. Maya passed her some tissues and Leona held her hand.

With blurry eyes, Serena tried to speak again, her voice breaking at intervals. 'I thought he was cool. I thought he was different, he always had money and he bought me things.' She heaved another big sob and sniffed. 'Evie's right, I was stupid. He was just usin' me.'

'Oh, darling. Wait till you get outta here,' Leona said. 'You will get the best boyfriend ever. We'll have a party for you. Strictly no drugs.'

Evie's mobile buzzed. 'Oh no, forgot to switch it

off!' She answered it and held it out to Maya. 'For you. Be quick or the machines might stop workin'.'

It was Zac calling and Maya arranged to meet him at Victor's café. She wasn't sorry to leave the hospital room, because seeing Serena looking so ill made her furious. Escaping into the balmy autumn evening was blessed relief.

* * *

Zac was waiting for her when she arrived. The café was busy and he was sitting at a small table by the window. She borrowed his mobile to check in with Helen and then they ordered some drinks.

'So, what's happenin'?' Zac wanted to know.

Maya leaned forward. 'Well, for a start, somebody's following me.'

'No!' Zac said, his eyebrows drawing together in a big frown.

'Look, see over there.' Maya pointed to a man in dark jeans and a hoodie. He was standing in the rain opposite the café. 'Hm, a different one. The other must have gone off duty.'

'What?'

She smiled. 'I'm under guard. Simon was worried

Omega would track me down so he's put a tag on me.' She smiled. 'I've led him over half of London today.'

Zac took another glance. 'I'm glad he's watchin' you,' he said. 'Omega's dangerous and you know too much about them.'

Maya told him of her plan to find out even more by going to the interview the next day.

'You're the only person that understands,' she said. 'I'm trusting you totally. Nobody else must know what I'm doing. Simon would tell me "no way", but I have to try and find out where they took those girls and . . . Kay.'

Zac nodded. 'I'm listenin'. You can count on me, but. . .' He frowned. 'You're just goin' to the office, just for information, yeah? But how you goin' to get away from your shadow?'

'I have a plan,' Maya said.

'Wait,' Zac said holding up a warning finger.

'What?'

'Did you buy a new mobile?'

Maya's face fell. 'I was too busy thinking about my disguise.'

Zac exploded. 'You got to have a phone – you cannot go into this situation without a mobile. I need to know you're safe. Everyone needs to know you're safe.'

Maya looked into his dark brown eyes and smiled. 'OK. You're right. I should have thought. Let's go and buy one.'

* * *

After buying a new phone, they were on their way back to the flat, Zac trailing slightly behind Maya, their hands loosely linked, when turning the corner into the square, Maya stopped dead and pulled back. The street was busy, but she was developing some kind of homing instinct when it came to danger.

'It's them!'

'Who?'

'Two of them – waiting for me.'

She leaned back against a wall, her eyes glazed over, and she was breathing fast. Zac stood in front of her like a shield, she put an arm on his shoulder to steady herself.

'You sure?'

'One of them's Ginger.'

'OK. So what we have to do is stop here and tell the cop guy.'

Maya turned and looked back. 'Can't see him. I think we lost him on the high street.'

'Call Simon.' Zac held out his mobile.

'I can't.'

'Why not?'

'If Simon's men come running, the gang will know I'm being watched.'

Zac stared into her eyes. 'You are one tough lady.'

Maya kissed his forehead. 'It's all right,' she said, shaking a carrier bag. 'I have plan B.'

* * *

A dark-haired school girl wandered into an office block, telling the guard she was meeting her mum. In the bathroom, Maya set to work, while Zac stood outside, waiting. He watched a few office workers leave, listened to a couple of tunes on his iPod, then a tall, blonde-haired woman, in a short, white dress and high-heeled boots came strolling out of the offices. She was very attractive, but not his type – a bit too obvious. He looked away, wondering how much longer Maya was going to be. The blonde woman came closer and grabbed his arm. His eyes goggled.

The woman laughed. 'It's me.' Maya was triumphant. 'You didn't recognise me!'

'Wasn't lookin' for no hooker.'

'Thanks,' Maya replied, pretending to be offended. She was as tall as Zac in her high-heeled boots and had to lean down to put her head on his shoulder.

'Walk me to the flat,' she said. 'Put your arm round me, like I'm your girlfriend.'

'Pleasure's all mine.'

It was a long walk up the street, Maya tottering in her boots, hiding her face on Zac's shoulder. 'Are they still there?' she whispered.

'Yeah, keep your head down.'

She couldn't see Ginger as they walked past, but she sensed him and trembled. At the door to the flat, she handed Zac her key. They were inside by the time the two gang members thought to check them out. All Maya had to do then was face Helen.

'What on earth have you got on?' Helen asked.

'Forgot to tell you,' Maya mumbled, before she darted upstairs. 'Own clothes day at school.'

'Own clothes!' Helen exclaimed.

Chapter Eighteen

Later that night, when Zac had left, Maya called Simon.

'You said you'd tell me if there were any developments,' she said. 'Has anything turned up?'

'No, no news,' Simon replied. 'But I have got something to say to you. Where the hell is the report I asked for? I could have saved my assistant a journey.'

Maya gulped. The events of the day had taken over and she'd completely forgotten about writing the report. 'I'm . . . I'm so sorry,' she stammered. 'I didn't have time, you know with school and everything.'

'Well, let me have it tomorrow without fail – all the details in hard copy. I'll send somebody over about eight o' clock tomorrow night to pick it up. By the way, Gerard's family have been informed. They were told he'd fallen in the canal.'

'I know,' Maya said.

There was a short silence until Simon spoke. 'All right. Don't forget, eight o' clock tomorrow evening.'

When Simon clicked the phone off, Maya wondered if she'd deliberately forgotten to write the report. Tomorrow, after her visit to Omega, she might be able to write something really useful.

Her dreams that night were dark and disturbing. She was running and running, trying to catch someone, then she fell into deep water and at the bottom, amongst dense weeds, was Kay. However much she pulled, Maya couldn't free her, she was trapped.

In the morning when she woke, her duvet was rumpled and damp with sweat, her head full of scary images. Looking out of the bedroom window, she checked the square and saw a new minder leaning against the park railings. His street gear gave him away – regulation hooded top, lumberjack shirt and jeans. It was slightly worrying that she could spot him so easily.

Later when she was walking to catch the school bus, she was aware of him trailing behind. She knew the drill from the previous term when a kidnap threat had restricted her movements. He'd follow her to school until he was certain she was safely inside the building and couldn't leave the school grounds until he met her at the end of the day.

To avoid alarming the man, she'd have to be clever – make him think everything was normal by catching the usual bus and walking into school. Then, after registration, she'd split.

A whispered conversation with Leona and Evie during registration ensured their support. Maya didn't tell them where she was going, but asked them to cover for her – if any teacher asked about her, she'd gone to the sick room.

When the bell for first lesson sounded, Maya headed towards doors that led out into a tarmac area, skirted the Science block and made her way round to the front exit. There was no other way in or out since the school had been newly-surrounded by railings and fences. Striding purposefully down the front drive, she hoped nobody would challenge her – and luckily they didn't. True to form, her minder had returned to base while she was safely inside school premises. At the bottom of the drive, she headed towards the nearest Tube station.

Sun was dappling the streets as she walked from Leicester Square up to Soho. It was an exceptionally warm day for September; a street sweeper was belting out a Green Day song and tables on the pavement were occupied by early coffee drinkers. The dusty doorways shadowed by bouncers and hostesses at night were empty now and the streets looked bright and colourful.

It took three trips up and down the street before she spotted the Omega offices. Crammed between a restaurant and shop selling flamboyant party wear was an entrance bearing a laminated sign – Omega Introductions.

It was an hour before her interview, adequate time to transform herself. The plan was risky. Hopefully her fake Eastern European accent would pass, but if somebody asked her to speak her native language, she'd be sunk. The few words she remembered would hardly convince.

Walking past the Omega sign, she continued up the street and went round the corner, looking for a coffee shop that she thought might have a decent lavatory. She chose a stylish, modern place and, once inside, ordered a cappuccino and croissant then sat watching customers come and go. She checked her watch every few minutes, willing the time to pass swiftly, thinking about the questions she might be asked and what answers she would provide. Over and over she told herself that what she was doing was simple. All that was required was to go up some stairs, into an office and answer some questions. She could pull out at any time – but for some reason she began to feel more and more nervous.

Her gaze settled on the empty coffee cup in front of her; it was ringed with dried foam. Her eyes glazed over, her heart raced. She was mesmerised, frozen into silent panic.

I can't do this.

Thoughts and images bombarded her mind, she saw the glinting metal of a gun, remembered the icy cold water of the canal. And she asked herself, why was she doing this, who exactly was her mission for? Was it for Kay, who might already be dead, for the trafficked girls, to impress Simon or Pam, or for her own satisfaction?

She asked all these questions of herself, but didn't come up with answers. It was as if an unknown force were driving her, something deeply-hidden in her soul had to fight for justice – action made her feel better. One day she'd face her demons and think things through, but not yet. Standing up, she gathered her bags and walked towards the toilet – time to transform.

Taking off her school uniform, she stuffed it into

her schoolbag, then slipped on fishnet tights, her new boots, the white dress, and added a bit of bling in the form of a gold pendant and hooped earrings. She screwed her hair up into a ponytail and carefully pulled the blonde wig over it, tucking in any stray strands of black hair. The magic marker for her eyebrows came next and she painted them a light golden brown. Concealer hid the bruises, pale foundation lightened her skin, glossy pink lipstick brightened her lips. The only sign of her skirmish with Ginger was the cut on her chin – painting over it with the magic marker made it almost disappear.

When she looked at herself in the mirror, the transformation was total – a different girl looked back at her, the only distinguishing features she couldn't change were her large almond-shaped eyes.

Turning her head sideways, she made sure none of her own hair was showing under the wig, smoothed the fringe and pouted. Yes, she could easily pass for somebody older than her fifteen years.

Red nail varnish was the finishing touch. She painted carefully, then waved her fingers under the hand dryer. Transferring her purse and new mobile to a small silver handbag, she suddenly realised that she hadn't considered what to do with her schoolbag.

It was scruffy and not the sort of thing you'd take along to an interview, plus if anybody looked inside it, they'd find evidence of a different identity.

Loud knocks pounded the door. Maya opened it.

'Sorry, I get ready for an interview,' she told the girl, who was waiting to clean the toilet.

The girl ran her eyes over Maya's high-heeled boots and short, tight skirt.

'Hm! Hope you get the job.'

Maya started to walk away and then turned back. 'Can you look after my bag for me while I go for the interview? It is not nice – it spoil the look.'

The girl looked amused. 'Yeah, all right,' she said. 'How long will you be?'

'Maybe one hour. Can you put it somewhere safe?'

'I'll stick it in the back with my things,' the girl offered.

'Thank you,' Maya said, handing over her schoolbag. 'I will see you later.'

As she walked along the street, the white dress clung like a second skin, the hooped earrings jangled and the outsize gold locket bounced over her low neckline. When a man in a sharp business suit whistled at her she winced, but at least she knew she'd achieved the desired effect.

Taking a deep breath, Maya pressed the buzzer marked with the Omega logo. A voice answered and she announced her name. 'Dania Ballack.'

When the door release was pressed, she climbed a flight of dingy stairs and opened the door into a small office. Behind a desk with a sweep of empty worktop sat a tiny woman with a pale face and shiny dark hair. She rose to meet Maya, stretching out a bony hand.

'Hello, I am Sonja Selkoff,' she said.

A clutch of gold bangles jangled, her smile was bright, her eyes searching. From the carefully-applied red lipstick to the crisp pinstriped suit and white blouse, she was immaculate.

Maya met her eyes and gave her false name without a flicker. 'I am Dania,' she said. 'Dania Ballak.'

'Can I get you anything – tea, coffee?'

'No thank you,' Maya replied in perfect English and then, swiftly correcting herself, she added with a strong accent, 'It is all right. I just drink coffee at a snack bar.'

'Right, let's get down to business, then,' Sonja said. Sitting down, she motioned Maya to do the same, then she leant forward and smiled, showing a row of pearly white teeth. 'You are beautiful, that's in your favour. Is that hair colour real?'

'No, not real,' Maya answered. 'My hair is light brown, so I use bottle.'

Sonja gave her another quick smile, but there was no warmth behind it. 'That's fine,' she said. Opening a drawer, she pulled out a sheet of forms. 'First I want some details, then we'll talk about finding you a nice English man to marry.'

Maya spelt out her new name, gave the false address she had prepared, the phone number, the age and birthday she'd memorised.

'Can I see your passport?'

Why hadn't she anticipated this question? Of course she'd be asked for identification, what could she say? Quick thinking saved her. 'The college have it.'

The woman put down her pen. 'And what course were you studying?'

'Engineering,' Maya answered.

'Where?'

'UCL.'

The woman leaned forward. 'It takes a lot of money to study there. Engineering! A long course.'

She eyed Maya with suspicion, while Maya squirmed. This woman was sharp. She'd seen through her story, which should have been better-prepared. She looked down at her hands, twisted them together and made a quick decision. Pretending to break into tears, she sniffed and said in a broken voice, 'I apologise. I do not tell the truth. I have no papers – I am illegal.'

Sonja affected great surprise, then reached for a tissue and handed it to Maya. 'It's all right. This happens. Do you have any family here?'

Maya shook her head as she sniffed. 'No, I pay much money to come to the UK but the man betray me. He have no job for me and now I have no money to stay in my accommodation. No money to go back home.'

Sonja smiled. 'Don't worry, I can find you a job where you'll earn good money. And I'll arrange papers. Are you interested?'

'Of course,' Maya replied.

'Wait there a moment.'

When Sonja left the room, Maya jumped up and searched the drawers of the desk. There was nothing in them except blank forms. A filing cabinet revealed nothing either – it was empty. A coffee machine and a few mugs stood on a side table, but that was all.

The noise of clicking heels sent Maya hurrying back to her seat and when Sonja opened the door, Maya was sitting with her legs crossed, looking composed. That was until she saw the man who'd entered the room behind Sonja. He was a tall man with a shock of silver grey hair. It was Stefan, the boss from the warehouse.

Maya gulped, then concentrated on trying not to let her panic show.

He won't recognise me, he won't recognise me, she repeated to herself. Last time he saw me I was Maya, dressed in jeans, a hoodie and my hair was dark. Even Zac didn't know me when I was dressed like this. As long as I keep cool, I'll be all right.

But her heart beat faster as silence filled the room.

Stefan leant on the filing cabinet, facing away from her, Sonja hovered in front of him. He coughed, cleared his throat and then swore. He raised his head and spoke sharply.

'Coffee, thick and black,' he ordered.

While Sonja fussed around, producing a bottle of water and packet of coffee from her bag, Stefan muttered a string of curses and complaints. He seemed totally oblivious to Maya as he moaned to Sonja that the men he employed were incompetent and the girls were always complaining.

Lost in his bad mood, he slumped further over the filing cabinet, his elbows crooked, his head resting in the palms of his hands. Maya saw that his suit was crumpled, his face unshaven. He looked like he hadn't slept. Suddenly he reared up, patted his pockets and pulled out a pack of cigarettes.

'Not in here,' Sonja warned.

'It's my office,' he snapped and lit a cigarette. Taking a long drag to breathe in the smoke, he seemed calmer.

'Stand up!' he said with a quiet authority.

It took Maya a moment to understand he was talking to her. Startled, she got up.

'Step back from the desk."

Eyes cast down, looking at the floor, she trembled as he walked around her. He paused at her side, blew out a circle of smoke. She tried not to cough as his gaze travelled over her body.

'Look at me,' he said.

She lifted her head, quivering under the glare of his gaze. Her fists clenched, she tried to control her ragged breathing. Long moments ticked past. He stepped closer, reached out and took a strand of the blonde wig in his fingers. She flinched, thanking her lucky stars she'd splashed out on real hair.

Smiling softly, Stefan muttered, 'Yes, yes, very nice. We can certainly use you.' Turning to Sonja, he said, 'Take her over to the club.'

Sonja nodded. She handed him a cup of coffee,

patted her hair and then reached for her handbag. 'Come,' she said, beckoning to Maya.

Maya gulped down a cry of panic – everything was happening too quickly. She tried stalling for time.

'We have not finish filling out the form,' she said.

'It's all right. That won't be necessary,' Sonja replied, in clipped tones. 'Get your bag.'

Obediently, Maya picked up her handbag and followed Sonja out of the office. A sleek black car with tinted windows waited at the kerb. As they approached, a man who was leaning on the bonnet stood to attention and went round to open the doors. There was a moment, a split second when Maya could have made a run for it, but Sonja held her tightly, pushed her onto the back seat and slammed the door shut.

When the car engine started and moved forward, making its way through Soho, it was too late to escape – and Maya was panicking.

* * *

A smell of stale smoke rose up the staircase to meet them. Flanked by Sonja and the car driver, Maya had to dip her head as she entered a dimly-lit room that smelt of disinfectant and beer.

'This is the main floor of the club,' Sonja informed her. 'Over there is the bar. It's a nice easy job. We give you a pretty dress, you sit at the bar and look available. You are pleasant to customers and so they buy you drinks. The more business you get, the more money you earn. Wait here and I'll get one of the girls.'

She walked away, leaving Maya alone with the car driver. He leaned close to her, touched her wig and stroked her neck.

'You'll have no trouble,' he said. 'You're gorgeous.'

Maya reeled away from him, her skin burnt where his fingers touched. He laughed, took out some cigarettes and offered her the packet.

'I don't smoke,' Maya said.

He laughed again. 'No vices, eh?'

Maya moved to stand well away from him and looked around. Perhaps at night, when it was lit, the club might look exotic, but in daylight it was shabby and not very clean. There was a strange mix of furniture – some smart glass and chrome tables and some battered old wooden ones, and the chairs were the same, a selection of old and new. At one end of the room was a small stage, two big speakers and a mixing desk. Above them, two iron cages were suspended from the ceiling.

Her eyes were travelling over the bar with its variously-shaped bottles and optics when a door near the stage creaked and swung open. A girl wearing a tight red dress, her shoulders bare, came tottering towards her. The girl's face, caked with make-up, looked familiar, but it was only when she came really close that Maya recognised her – the eyes were unmistakable. It was Kay.

Maya was thrilled to see her and wanted to reach out and hug her, but she managed to control herself. It was obvious Kay hadn't recognised her. She watched as Kay sat down, took a cigarette from a packet and lit it. She crossed her legs and stared at Maya for a moment, then sat back and blew out a long stream of smoke. Maya saw that one of her front teeth was chipped and her neck was marked with bruises.

Glancing around to make sure nobody was within earshot, Maya leaned forward.

'Kay, it's me, Maya. Don't say anything.' Her eyes flicked round the room. 'They think I want to work here. I've called myself Dania.'

For a moment there was a gleam of hope in Kay's eyes, but then her lips pouted and she scowled. 'Why have you come? I do not need you. I am OK here.'

'You asked me for help.'

Kay gave her a withering look. 'That was a mistake. I was frightened. But now I see this is a good place. I am happy. I make customers happy – everybody is happy.'

'But you're covered in bruises.'

'It was an accident.'

Maya looked down and noticed puncture marks and more bruises on Kay's bare arms.

Kay looked away, avoiding Maya's eyes. 'It was nothing. I am OK now.'

'So, this is what you want?' Maya asked.

'Yes, this is good. I want this,' Kay said. 'You must not interfere.'

Chapter Nineteen

Kay leaned back in her chair – bitter and defiant. Maya seized hold of her arm.

'How can you be happy? They've bought you – body and soul,' she hissed.

'You speak like a crazy person,' Kay snapped back. 'Get lost. We don't want you here.'

'What's going on?'

They both jumped at Sonja's interruption and cowered when she stood in front of them. Neither had seen her enter the room. She stared accusingly at Maya.

'Do you know her? Who are you?'

Kay glared at Maya. 'I never see her before but she is a stupid girl. She say she want a husband – good English man. I tell her that is a dream. The club is better, we can get food, money, a place to live.'

Sonja smiled, her red lipsticked mouth a wide gash

in her face. 'Very wise,' she said. 'Good advice. Take her upstairs. She can have Leila's room. Show her what to do.'

* * *

Maya was fuming as she followed Kay up a staircase that led onto a narrow landing. She'd risked her life to get to Kay, only to have her concern thrown back in her face. Neither of them spoke as they passed several doors, then Kay opened the last one on the corridor. She switched on a light, stepped aside and pulled Maya into the room.

'This is your room – where you do business.'

The room was small, only big enough to hold a double bed and chest of drawers.

'Business? What, you mean . . .' a look of absolute horror came over Maya's face, ' . . . with men?'

Kay snorted. 'What do you think? We work in a bank or something? You meet men downstairs, you flirt, then you ask them to come upstairs. They pay – you get a percent.'

Kay closed the door. Maya stared at her.

'Kay, you can't want this life? It's horrible!'

Kay shrugged. 'Gerard, he beat me. I live on the street, I am hungry, then other men beat me. Here, the men are only sometimes rough. Any big trouble, I send for the bouncers.' She sank onto the satin duvet. 'Also, I can get a fix, then I care for nothing.'

'There's something better than this, there must be,' Maya said urgently. She leant forward. 'Think about what happened to Leila. Please, let me help you.'

Kay sat on the edge of the bed. 'You think you can make everything OK, Miss Rich Girl. You think everybody can live like you? It is not possible. You think I can just walk out of here? They will kill me.'

'What about Tanya and Annika and the other girls? What's happened to them?'

'They are in the hostel. It is like a prison, they cannot escape. Soon they will work here. When they get the habit, they won't care.'

Maya leaned against the wall. 'Where's the hostel?' she asked.

Kay stood up. She stared at Maya, her gold eyes hard and unforgiving. 'Do not cause trouble. They will kill you.' She seized Maya's arm. 'Go,' she said. 'We are OK. We do not want you here. Leave now, before Sonja come back.'

Maya stood uncertainly, her mind racing, then she picked up her handbag, turned and strode to the door. Yanking it open, she took one step into the corridor and found herself staring into Sonja's face.

'Ah,' Sonja said. 'You like your room?'

Choked with sudden fear, Maya was unable to speak and just nodded. As Sonja moved forward, she was forced to retreat back into the room.

Sonja stood watching Maya's face closely. 'Did Kay explain the business?'

Maya glanced at Kay, who avoided her eyes. 'Yes,' she whispered.

'And it's all right?'

'Yes.'

'Good. So that's settled,' Sonja said. 'Now come with me and see the hostel where you'll live.'

As they walked back down into the club, Sonja told Maya how lucky she was to be coming to work for them.

'We look after our girls. You have regular checks and if you work hard you can earn good money. Naturally, we charge for your accommodation and food. Do you have to send money home?'

'Yes, to my mother.'

'We will arrange that,' Sonja said. 'We will arrange everything now you work for us.'

The broad-shouldered, leering bouncer placed a hand on Maya's arm as he accompanied them to the car, then he pushed her onto the back seat and slammed the door. When she heard the doors lock, Maya felt desperate.

The driver accelerated round corners, veering and roaring along back streets as though he were in a police chase and Maya felt queasy by the time they stopped at a pair of wide iron gates. Reaching out of the window, the driver punched at an intercom on the gatepost, somebody answered and the gates opened automatically as they drove through.

'Here we are,' Sonja said, opening the car door. Maya slid across the seat and got out. They were in front of an old brick mansion, which was surrounded by high walls topped with razor wire. The gardens were neglected, weeds sprouting from every bit of soil and crevice. Climbing plants twisted around drainpipes and shadowed grimy windows.

Sonja held Maya's arm as they walked to the front door. When Sonja tapped in a code, the heavy door swung open. Propelled forward, Maya found herself in a wide entrance hall. Remnants of elegance could be seen in fancy plasterwork and a huge crystal chandelier, but paint was peeling from the walls and there was a smell of damp.

'I'll get Zena to show you to your room,' Sonja said.

'Zena will look after you.' She went over to a panel on the wall, pressed a button and spoke on an intercom. Almost immediately, a door opened at one side of the staircase and a woman came hurrying in. She was dressed in jeans and a red T-shirt. Her hair was long and dark, she was strikingly beautiful, but had an angry red scar running down one side of her face. Maya couldn't help gulping when she saw it. What kind of injury had ripped her face apart?

Zena led Maya up the stairs onto a wide landing and opened the door to a large room. At first glance it appeared stylish, with cream walls, a large double bed and mirrored wardrobes, but when Maya stepped inside, she quickly saw damp patches on the walls, the carpet was worn and stained and one particularly unwelcome feature was that the windows were covered by steel bars.

'This will be your room. It's the best room. Sonja must have high hopes for you,' Zena said. 'You'll be treated well if you behave yourself. But don't do anything to upset Sonja.' She gave Maya a warning look. 'Give me your handbag.'

'No!' Maya protested and just in time managed to put on a fake smile. 'There are some precious things inside.'

'I'll take care of it,' Zena said. 'Don't worry, I'll put it in a safe place.'

She held out her hand. Maya knew that Zena would take the bag no matter what; she stalled for time.

'Could I have a glass of water?' She sat on the bed and hung her head. 'I feel sick, the driver drove fast and I have not eaten today.'

'Of course. I'll be back in a moment.'

As soon as she'd gone, Maya looked around for a hiding place. Slipping the bank card out of her purse, she stuck it under a bedside lamp, then stuffed her mobile under the pillow and lay back on the bed.

Zena returned with a glass of water and some biscuits.

'Dinner will be at five o' clock – we eat early to give the girls plenty of time to get ready. This should help till then.' She looked down at Maya. 'I have to take your mobile. We don't allow personal phones.' She carried on staring at Maya as if she could see through the pillow she was lying on. 'All rooms are thoroughly searched on a regular basis.'

Reluctantly, Maya thrust her hand under the pillow, pulled out her mobile and handed it over.

Zena nodded. 'I'll leave you until dinner. Have a bath, if you like, in fact, I recommend it. Stefan will be over later. He likes to instruct all our new girls.'

She must have seen the look of panic on Maya's face, because her voice softened. 'You can do very well here,' she said. 'You are safe. You are cared for. Be nice to Stefan and he'll be nice to you.'

When Zena left, Maya heard a key turn, she waited a moment then went over and tried the door – of course, it was securely locked.

She wandered into the en suite bathroom, which was high-ceilinged and splendidly tiled, although some tiles were missing and there was a green stain on the bath. Behind some white gauzy drapes, the high sash window was covered by a blind. When she lifted the blind she saw more bars – there was no way out.

Feeling thoroughly miserable, she sat on the bed. Once again she was a prisoner and all she could do was sit and wait – wait for Stefan, who Zena had said ominously 'liked to instruct the new girls'. The thought of that filled her with dread.

Chapter Twenty

Time went slowly. There was an hour to go before dinner time. Maya was on the move, pacing from bed to bathroom to wardrobe. She opened the wardrobe door and found sparkly tops and dresses – clubbing outfits – and a couple of elegant long dresses. She looked through barred windows onto the back garden and saw flower beds overgrown with grass and weeds. Tall trees and bushes enclosed the boundaries, so that it was impossible to see what lay behind the house.

Several times she tiptoed over to the door and heard distant voices. One time she heard somebody crying. She wondered if it was Annika or Tanya. It was horrible that they were imprisoned, even if Kay didn't seem to want her help, she had to try and set the other girls free. But there was nothing she could do until she managed to escape or found a way of getting in touch with Simon.

And she was aware that she had caused another major incident. The minder would be expecting to follow her home from school and she wouldn't be there. Registers would be checked and questions asked. She hoped Leona and Evie wouldn't be in trouble, and then she felt a big stab of guilt about Helen.

She'd promised Gran not to get into any more trouble and she'd meant it. She'd only gone to the Omega office to gather information; she hadn't imagined ending up a prisoner.

Have I been stupid, Mum? Should I have given up? How do I get out of this one?

Although she concentrated hard at conjuring up her mum's face, the look in her eyes, the words she might say, the mind message didn't work. No answer came back – no communication.

And that's because I'm out of order, Maya thought. The thread has been broken because I've broken promises to Mum and Gran.

Then her thoughts turned to Simon. She couldn't imagine how furious he'd be. She had really messed up.

When she heard a knock on the door, her mood was grim and she just wanted to be left alone. At the sound of a key in the lock she frowned, drew up her knees and wedged herself back against the pillows on the bed.

'It's me, Zena. You have to get ready. Stefan is arriving soon.'

Maya didn't move.

The door opened and Zena entered the room. 'You have to make yourself beautiful. This is good for you. Stefan has only the best women. If you are his woman, you are favoured. No other man will touch you.'

Big deal, Maya fumed. I don't want anybody to touch me, certainly not Stefan.

Going over to the wardrobe, Zena opened the door and pulled out a dress of shimmering gold.

'This one I think is beautiful.'

Reluctantly, Maya eased herself off the bed and stood up. She had to play the game until somehow she managed to get away.

'Did you have a bath?'

'No.'

Zena looked angry. 'I told you to have bath, you are a stupid girl.'

She pushed Maya towards the bathroom, but at that moment there was an ear-splitting scream that froze their movements.

Zena recovered quickly. 'It is nothing,' she said, putting a firm hand on Maya's arm.

But another scream followed and, all senses alert, Maya elbowed Zena aside and ran to the door. The screams grew louder. A door at the other end of the landing was half open and Maya shot towards it. Behind her, Zena shouted for her to come back, a hand wrenched at her arm, but she pulled away. Pushing back the door, she stepped into a bedroom.

Annika was standing by the window. She was holding onto her sister's legs and screaming. Above her, Tanya was hanging from a curtain pole, her neck at a preposterous angle.

Maya dashed forward and righted the chair Tanya had kicked away.

'Get me a knife!' she shouted, then, climbing up, she took the weight of Tanya's body in her arms.

It took Zena only a few moments to come running back into the room with scissors and Maya cut the scarf tied to the pole. Together, they supported Tanya's body and laid her on the floor. Maya knelt down, tilted Tanya's head back, opened her mouth and breathed into her. She tried and tried, but knew it was hopeless; Tanya's spinal cord had snapped and she wouldn't respond, she couldn't breathe. In vain,

Maya felt for a pulse, watched for the slightest rise or fall of her chest. With tears in her eyes, Maya kept on trying until she was exhausted and Zena gently moved her away.

Immediately, Annika threw herself on Tanya's body, shaking and hugging her sister, shouting and crooning in her own language, then she stood up.

'You know why she did this?' she shouted at Zena. 'She was ashamed.'

Zena held up her hands. 'Be quiet!' she ordered. 'We have to think what to do.'

'Who cares?' Annika screamed.

Zena slapped her face. 'Shut up – he will kill you if you make trouble.'

Annika's arms dropped helplessly to her sides. 'I do not care. I have nothing to live for. My sister is dead.' And she started to wail.

'We should get an ambulance,' Maya said.

Zena gave her a hard stare. 'Sonja will take care of things. Take Annika to your room. Keep her quiet.'

'I will not leave my sister,' Annika protested, pulling back towards Tanya's body.

Maya understood the dangerous position they were in. Any suggestion of trauma had to disappear before Stefan arrived or he'd act swiftly to quash any trouble.

A death was not an event to mourn, but a body to be disposed of, and if Annika was a nuisance she'd be got rid of too.

'Come, you come with me, Annika,' Maya said, putting her arms round Annika's shoulders. 'You must be safe.' She hugged Annika, holding her tightly. 'Only you know the truth. You must go back to your family, tell what happened to Tanya or they will never know.'

Zena pushed Maya in the back. 'Take her!' she ordered. 'Go to your room and keep your mouth shut.'

All the fight seemed to go out of Annika and she allowed herself to be led across the landing into Maya's room. Once inside, she collapsed on the bed and sobbed her heart out. Maya sat and stroked her hair, wondering what she could do to get her away from Omega's clutches before Annika, too, wanted to die.

When Annika had cried herself out and fallen asleep, Maya got up from the bed. She was hot and uncomfortable, her head itched under the wig and the silk dress was creased and tear-stained. She went over to the window and looked out, wondering what would happen next, wondering what to do. She had no answers. The house was like a prison.

Below the window, amongst the long grass, a

few late roses were still in bloom, birds darted in the bushes. Her thoughts went back to the summer and one early morning when she'd stood in Gran's garden, dew glittering like diamonds on the lawn, the distant hills hazy in early morning sunshine, Pam stretching before they went for a run together, her blonde hair shining in the sunlight. Maya remembered how she'd grown so much taller than Pam and on their run she'd outpaced her. The next scene she banished. No way would she ever allow herself to think about the kidnap, the moment when the terrorists struck, the terror of the gunshots, the horrible sight of poor Danny, the agent who was shot dead. They were memories she wanted to blot out forever.

But then a clear image of Pam formed – it was during the rescue attempt, the moment after the blast when the world had stood still, Pam's soft grey eyes reassuring, her mouth saying words Maya couldn't hear. The message was coming through, Pam was telling her to have courage, to stay calm, to think carefully and logically.

There's always hope, never give up.

She heard Pam's words clearly and when she raised her eyes, she noticed a pale silver moon hanging over the tall trees – a summer moon. The sun had not yet gone down but the moon had risen and her mind became calm.

Right, I have to change this dress for a similar one. I have to wake Annika, comfort her and get her to give me as much information as she can – where she came from, how she got here. I have to pretend to like Stefan, I have to find out about Omega's operations and I have to find a way of relaying this to Simon. I have to escape and I have to take the girls with me.

Putting her fingers to her lips, she blew a kiss to the moon.

'I know you're with me, Mum,' she whispered. 'Come home soon and help me, please.'

Going over to the wardrobe, she thumbed through the racks of dresses and found an almost identical gold one. The straps were a bit thinner and it was shorter than the other dress, but when she slipped it on it fitted well and looked good. In the distance she heard voices, a woman shouting. She opened the door a crack and peeped out onto the landing just as Sonja came out of Tanya's room. Seeing Maya, Sonja came over to her.

'Ah, Dania,' she said. 'There's been an unfortunate accident, but I have dealt with it. We won't mention it again.'

Maya edged round the door and stood on the landing. Sonja smiled.

'Well, thank goodness somebody is looking like a dream. Stefan will be here soon and we don't want to upset him, do we?'

Her face set into hard lines as she stared at Maya.

'No,' Maya replied quietly. 'We do not want to upset him.'

Sonja nodded. 'Good. So you will finish your make-up and you will see to it that you look perfect. And then you will make sure that Annika looks perfect.' Her eyes narrowed. 'Do you understand?'

'Yes, I understand.'

Going back into the room, Maya took a deep breath and walked quickly to the bedside, then she leaned over and gently smoothed back Annika's hair.

'Annika, stay quiet. Don't shout or scream. You have to be brave. You have to save yourself.'

For a split second, Annika opened her eyes, dazed and untroubled, then pain and grief shadowed her face. 'Tanya,' she whispered.

'I know, I know it's horrible,' Maya said, putting her hand on Annika's cheek. 'But you have to get up. You have to get dressed and come to the club. It's your only chance. Do you understand?'

Annika closed her eyes. 'Yes,' she said.

Maya leaned closer, whispering, 'Listen. I want to help you. My real name is Maya Brown. My mother is with the police. I came to get information so the police can find you. I'm sorry I couldn't save Tanya. I'm so sorry.'

Annika's eyes opened wide. 'You are police?'

'Not me, but my mother. Well, she isn't exactly. . . It's complicated, but please believe me, I'm trying to help. Don't say anything to the others. For tonight we have to act as if nothing has changed, we have to pretend everything is OK. Can you do that?'

Annika's eyes were full of tears. Maya pulled a tissue from the box and handed it to her.

'You have to be brave. Please, do it for Tanya.'

Annika wiped her eyes and shook her head. 'I cannot, I cannot,' she said. 'What have they done with her?'

'I don't know. Tomorrow they will say she had an accident, but I hope that, by then, you and all the other girls will be safe.'

Chapter Twenty-one

Zena led Annika back to her room. Alone again, Maya finished making up her face and tidying her wig, as if she were preparing to go on stage. She hardly recognised the glamorous young woman who stared back at her. Smoothing the dress down over her hips, she wondered how she was going to avoid Stefan's advances.

There was a tap on the door and Sonja came in, dressed in black, her mouth carefully re-done with bright red lipstick, her bobbed hair looking darker than ever, its edges swinging in a curtain of shimmering jet.

'Ready?' she asked.

'Yes.'

'Come with me.'

Maya swallowed hard and took a nervous step forward. The mirrors on all sides of the room reflected her image – tall, elegant in gold high heels and shimmering silk, blonde hair immaculately shaped, make-up carefully smoothed and burnished – she was the front cover of a magazine.

Stefan was waiting. His eyes devoured his new protégé as she floated down the stairs. 'Hm, good, very good,' he said. 'You look beautiful, Dania.' He directed a questioning glance at Sonja. 'She is young, yes?'

Maya's heart raced. She held her breath while he eyed her closely.

'She's nineteen,' Sonja said.

A smile spread over Stefan's face. 'Then that is perfect,' he said. 'You did well.' He took Maya's hand. 'You come with me. Sonja can travel with the other girls.'

He led Maya outside to a silver Mercedes and opened the door for her. 'There you are, princess,' he said.

Driving along unfamiliar streets, Maya looked for landmarks. She saw the Elephant and Castle, then they passed over Westminster Bridge. From there she knew the route into Soho. It was a tense ride. When they stopped at traffic lights she imagined opening the door and escaping. Then it would all be over and she'd be safely at home in the flat with Gran. Her hand twitched. She glanced along the busy streets. She could soon get lost in the crowd if she ran away, but she couldn't do it. She had to see this thing through, rescue the girls and help to break Omega.

Her mind snapped to attention as Stefan began to ask her questions. How had she arrived in England? Where had she been living? She remembered to speak in broken English and invented details which she hoped sounded convincing – a desperate, cramped journey in a petrol tanker, an address for a refuge which couldn't be found, the promise of an English husband which never materialised.

Stefan laughed. 'So, you thought you'd get yourself an English husband. English men are lazy slobs. You have to cook and clean for them. You are better off workin' for me, eh?'

He put his hand on her thigh. She felt its warmth through the silk of her dress and tried not to shudder or shift away. A loud burst of music signalled a call on his mobile.

'Excuse me,' he said, politely, clipping a listening device into his ear. His tone became sharper and more businesslike as he spoke. 'Yeah, yeah. No. Don't you speak to him. Tell him I'll be there in ten.'

He switched off. 'Business,' he said to Maya. 'All the time, business. It's a very important time for me. Soon I will be the top dog.'

He caressed her thigh again. This time Maya couldn't help pulling away. He laughed.

'I get the message – plenty of time for that later. You gotta get to know me first, eh? I can tell you're a classy lady. But I tell you this – if you are mine then nobody else will touch you. That's worth somethin', isn't it?'

She reached out and touched his hand, giving him what she hoped looked like a genuinely warm smile. 'That is worth everything,' she said.

When Stefan drew up in front of the club, the bouncer she'd seen before dashed out to open the door for her, then Stefan came round and gave her his hand. Walking into the club on Stefan's arm, Maya could see she had instant status; workers shouted respectful greetings and Stefan was all smiles. He obviously enjoyed being the big boss and having a glamorous girl on his arm.

'This is Dania,' he said, introducing her to the barman. 'Stunner, isn't she?'

The barman, of course, agreed.

Stefan led her up the same stairs she'd climbed before, when Kay had taken her up to the client rooms, but this time, instead of turning into the long corridor, Stefan unlocked a door on the first landing and Maya found herself in a big room, which seemed to be sitting room and office combined. It was lit by glittering chandeliers and a thick-pile, zebra-print rug stretched between a drinks cabinet and a long, white, leather sofa. White blinds covered the windows and on a large shiny desk stood a monitor, showing views of the club's interior, the entrance and pavement outside.

Stefan gestured to the sofa. 'Make yourself comfortable. I've got a few calls to make. Can I get you a drink?'

'Er . . . just some juice,' Maya said.

'Nonsense, have a gin and tonic. How do you like it?'

'Ice and a slice,' Maya said, remembering a woman at the bar when she was on holiday, and hoping she sounded convincingly adult. She also hoped she wouldn't have to drink it all – it was important to stay alert.

'All right?' Stefan asked, standing over her as she took a sip. She nodded. He caressed her fake hair.

'Be with you in a minute, princess.'

He wandered to the other side of the room, accessed some messages on his mobile and then called someone. 'What's up?' he asked. The answer wasn't to his liking. Maya saw him tense, then he bellowed, 'I don't believe it! Too many incidents, too many friggin' problems.'

He paced the room. 'I know, I know. That little shit Gerard pulled a trick, and the girl, what's the news on her?' Pause. 'No, the one you found tryin' to nick the bag at Gerard's place, the one you let get away. She knows too much.'

Maya's heart was pounding, sweat broke out on her forehead and trickled down her face. She sat rigidly as Stefan became more and more irritable.

'She needs takin' out.' He waited a moment, listening, and then he roared, 'Well, find her!'

Going over to the desk, he banged on the polished top. 'We take delivery tomorrow. A change in venue would spook them. There's too much to lose. I haven't spent months buildin' up their trust to throw it out the window. We can do it. As long as everythin' goes to plan we can turn it around in thirty minutes tops.'

A remark from the speaker at the end of the phone elicited another angry response. 'Bring him up here. I want to see him. Bring him up now.'

Giving an impatient sniff, he went over to sit at the desk, banging the flat of his hands down and breathing heavily. Maya was motionless, hoping to be invisible, too scared to think what would happen if Stefan found out her true identity.

A few moments later, there was a knock at the door. At Stefan's bidding, in came two people she instantly recognised – one was Ginger, her tormenter at the warehouse, and the other was Zac.

She almost gasped out loud.

Don't give me away, Zac. Don't say anything.

Her mind was breaking into pieces, her body was shaking. With a massive effort, she managed to fake indifference, to avert her eyes, lean back nonchalantly on the sofa, pick at some pistachio nuts and sip her drink. From the corner of her eye, she saw Ginger had Zac in a firm grasp, leading him over to the desk.

'Sit down,' Stefan ordered and then, leaning forward so that his eyes were fixed on Zac's frightened face, he rapped, 'So, what's the story here, Ginge?'

Ginger puffed out his chest. 'Sonja saw this kid outside the office early this evening, peering in through the window. He reckoned he was looking for his sister. Then he turns up at the club, trying to get in.

in. Lucky Sonja saw him. "Something's going on with that kid," she says.'

Stefan got up, went round the desk and stood in front of Zac. 'You lookin' for Gerard?' he asked.

Zac looked down, saying nothing.

'Not talkin', boy?'

Zac still said nothing. Maya flinched as Stefan grasped a handful of his hair and pulled his head back. 'You lookin' for trouble?'

Zac's eyes were wide, his mouth tightened into a frightened grimace, but he made no sound.

'Speak, boy, or I'll cut your tongue out,' Ginger said, stepping close and flashing a flick knife in front of Zac's face.

'Like I said,' Zac managed to say in between gasps and croaks, 'I was lookin' for my sister.'

'So why did you come to my office?' Stefan asked. He let go of Zac's hair and Zac flopped forward.

'I didn't know it was your office,' Zac answered, looking sideways. 'I was lookin' everywhere. My sister left home, got this idea about being a lap dancer, makin' a load of money. My mum was frantic so I started lookin' in Soho, scoutin' the clubs.'

'How old are you?'

'Fifteen.'

'You workin' with Gerard?'

'I don't know any Gerard.'

'You one of his gang?'

'No.'

'You know Creek?' Stefan grasped Zac's throat and Zac made a horrible choking sound. Maya put her drink on the table and eased off the couch, ready to fly to his aid, but suddenly Stefan let go.

'See to him, Ginge. Can't afford no cock-ups before tomorrow.'

Ginger grabbed Zac and pulled him from the chair. Zac half turned, his eyes darting round the room, as if looking for an escape route. Maya leaned forward, met his glance and in that split second she knew he'd recognised her.

But he said nothing. She gave grateful thanks.

Well done, Zac. You're a loyal friend, and brave. It must have been so tempting to shout out to me, but you didn't. And you found me. You're incredible. I hope they don't hurt you. Please believe me, I'm so sorry I got you into this.

While Maya was worrying about Zac, Stefan poured a drink for himself and came to sit beside her. He seemed restless, tapping his feet, scratching at his neck and sighing.

'Sometimes my life is tough, you know. People just want to make trouble for me.' He took her hand and squeezed it. 'You not goin' to let me down, are you, Dania? You're my princess.'

Maya tried to look relaxed and smile reassuringly. 'I will not make trouble. I am a lucky girl with you,' she said.

Stefan slipped his arm around her shoulders and moved in for a long, lingering kiss. When he paused to breathe, Maya broke away from him, quickly picking up her drink and rinsing the fizzy tonic round her mouth.

When she put the glass down, she tried to make her voice sound casual as she asked Stefan a question. 'That boy, what will you do with him?'

'Who?' Stefan gave her a bewildered look.

'The kid who was in here just now. Will you make him talk?'

'Nah. He's no threat,' Stefan laughed. 'Just a young punk. We'll let him go after tomorrow.'

'Why after tomorrow?'

He stroked her shoulder. 'You ask a lot of questions.'

'Sorry. This is a new world for me.'

'Yeah, I understand. I like it. You're intelligent. Play

your cards right and you could be very useful to me – beauty and brains, good thing. Tomorrow's a big day. Been a long time in the plannin'. Big operation that will put me on top. Nobody can touch Omega then. Creek can go drown himself. Omega will control everythin'.'

Chapter Twenty-two

When Stefan told Maya he had to go and see to business, she heaved a sigh of relief. He took her hand, led her out of his office and down into the club.

'Be nice to the customers, but save yourself for me,' he instructed, giving her a kiss.

She had an overwhelming desire to wipe her hand across her mouth, but she resisted, and even managed to look at him sweetly. 'Of course,' she said.

Immediately he walked away, Sonja appeared at her side.

'Go upstairs to Kay,' she said. 'Annika is making trouble. If Stefan hears her, he'll go crazy. Tell Kay to keep her quiet.' She reached out and straightened the strap on Maya's dress. 'Then you keep Stefan happy.'

Maya gave her a brief nod and Sonja took hold of her hand. 'Don't get any strange ideas,' she said, giving Maya's fingers a hard, painful squeeze. 'You may be Stefan's favourite, but the front door is always watched.'

'I do not want to run away,' Maya said haughtily. 'I am happy here.' And she turned and strode towards the back stairs.

When the door to the club closed behind her, Maya stood alone at the bottom of the staircase. In front of her were steps that led up to Stefan's office suite and the girls' rooms. To the side of the staircase was a dark corridor. She walked down the corridor and found two closed doors. Reaching out, she turned the handle of one of the doors. It led to a storeroom stacked with boxes of drinks. The second door she opened carefully, pushing it back gently to reveal a stone staircase leading down to a basement. It was the most likely place to find Zac. Slowly she descended, pausing and listening. A voice rose to meet her.

'Tulips from Amsterdam,' Stefan was saying. He laughed. 'Simple, eh? Two hundred kilos of top grade heroin packed under plant pots. Street value – eighteen million.'

Maya thought she heard a sharp intake of breath. She was reeling herself. No wonder Stefan had said this was big.

'Two hundred kilos,' a voice echoed.

'And six beautiful young women. Chinese girls this time, less trouble,' Ginger added.

'What time is it on for?' a man asked.

'Early – six o' clock,' Stefan replied, 'at the canal and you'd better be sharp.'

Maya tensed, wondering if that was the end of the meeting, her legs were braced, ready to dart back up the stairs. There was a cough, a scraping of chairs and some muttered conversation. She wondered if Zac was down there listening to their plans.

'Where do we take the haul?' somebody asked.

'When do we get our cut?' another questioned.

'Listen,' Stefan said. 'The tulip van arrives six a.m. Van drives into warehouse, we unload boxes – fifty-two boxes of tulip bulbs. Terry's group starts the extraction, take out the bulbs, lift the false bottom and, magic . . . there's your stash. Meanwhile, Sonja drives up with that kid we got tied up there, the blubberin' sister of the dead girl and the body. We transfer Sonja's cargo to the Dutch van. They'll get rid of them if we bung them an extra K – no need to get our hands dirty.'

'What about the new arrivals, the Chinese girls?' a man asked.

'I'm explainin'!' Stefan shot back. 'We transfer the new girls from the Dutch van into ours, pile in the stash and we're away. Whole operation'll take thirty minutes, no longer.'

'That girl Kay needs getting rid of too,' Ginger said. 'She's a liability, always stoned, customers don't like it.'

'All right,' Stefan agreed.

'And when do we get our pay?' a gruff voice asked.

'You always get your cut, don't you?' Stefan snapped.

Maya had learnt enough. She tiptoed up the steps and moved swiftly back along the corridor.

Kay was sitting on the bed, leaning over a side-table, her fingers splayed out as she painted them with purple nail varnish.

'Where's Annika?' Maya asked.

'She is next door. I give her something – help her sleep,' Kay said.

She didn't look at Maya. Her gaze was focused on her nails, her tongue protruding slightly from her teeth as she concentrated on the task.

'Did you tell Ginger that Tanya killed herself?'

Kay's lips pouted. 'Maybe.'

'You've put Annika in danger. Stefan wants rid of

her and he wants you gone too.'

'Me. Why me?' Kay looked up, her eyes staring and frightened. 'How do you know?'

'Because they're having a meeting down in the basement. I listened and overheard him saying you're stoned most of the time and that's bad for business.'

'But Stefan likes me. Ginger want to get rid of me but I persuade Stefan to keep me. I tell him I will be a good worker.'

'Well, he's changed his mind,' Maya said, flatly.

Kay put the brush back into the bottle and blew on her fingers. 'I can change, give up the fix. I don't need it.'

Maya looked down at Kay's white face and stick-thin body. 'He means it, Kay. They're taking you out tomorrow morning. You have to try and escape before tomorrow and take Annika with you.'

Kay shook her head. 'Not possible.'

Maya sighed and tried again. 'Stefan wants rid of you. He's got new girls coming.'

Kay blinked. 'Stefan save my life, he is not a killer.'

'He wants you as long as you are useful to him. Don't you see what you're involved with?'

Kay screwed the top securely onto the nail polish and smiled. 'I am a happy girl,' she said. 'I am safe.

I have everything I need.'

Maya grabbed her arm and put her face close to Kay's. 'You have to help me. They've got my friend. They're keeping him a prisoner down there. You. . .' The rattle of the door opening made her stop abruptly.

'Customer, Kay,' Sonja said, poking her head round the door. 'He's asking for you.'

Obediently, Kay got up and straightened her skirt. 'I have business. You have to go,' she told Maya.

Outside on the landing, Sonja told Maya to go to Stefan's office. 'He's going out for an hour. When he comes back, he'll want you.'

Looking at the monitor on Stefan's desk, Maya saw him leaving with two of his heavies. She sat on the couch and wondered what to do. She could search the building and try to find Zac – devise a way for him to escape, and Annika too, but then all hell would break loose. She'd probably been wrong to encourage Kay to run away; she'd acted instinctively without thinking things through. It would be better if Stefan thought everything was going to plan, then he'd go ahead with tomorrow's transaction and the whole gang could be caught, along with their contacts. With the gang's operation smashed, Annika and the other women would be rescued. None of this would happen, though, unless she got a message to Simon. And time was ticking away.

What she needed was a telephone, but there wasn't one in the room, and she remembered that Stefan always used his mobile. Going over to the door, she glanced nervously along the corridor to check that Sonja wasn't hovering, then she started downstairs. Halfway down, she had to stand aside to let Kay and a middle-aged man pass. Kay was holding his hand and giggling.

The club was busier now; a whole row of customers were sitting at the bar. A few girls were circulating and in one of the cages a girl with no top on was dancing in a bored fashion, her body out of time with the pulsating music. A man in a business suit tried to grab Maya's hand and a young guy with a group of men whistled at her. She averted her eyes, looking instead towards the emergency exit.

'Hey darlin', you new?' The young guy who'd whistled at her jumped up from his seat and slipped an arm round her waist. 'Would you like a drink?'

Although he wasn't bad-looking, Maya's first reaction was to pull away from his eager stare, but a plan formed in her head. 'Yes, that would be nice,' she said, smiling at him and leading him to the bar.

After they settled on stools and ordered drinks, Maya focused all her attention on Mr Young Executive. She sympathised with complaints about his job and the trouble he'd had with his wife, then slipped her request casually into their conversation.

'Could I borrow your mobile for a minute? Mine has no battery.'

'Yeah, as long as you're not callin' Moscow,' the guy joked.

'No, just a quick local call,' Maya said. 'I want to book a taxi home.'

She covered the mobile with the flat of her hand and pressed it against her dress. 'Be back soon,' she said.

It was no good dialling 999, she wouldn't get the right person or have time to explain. Simon was her best bet. Standing in the shadow of the stairs, she punched in what she hoped was his number and waited. There was no reply – not even an invitation to record a message. She bit her lip, silently cursing him. Irritably, she disconnected and called home. After two rings, a male voice answered. It was Simon – he was at the flat. A splutter of words came from him but she cut him short.

'Listen!' she directed. 'Omega has a massive delivery of drugs coming in tomorrow morning, at the canal warehouse. A van is coming in from Holland bringing the drugs and some girls. It's scheduled for—'

She jumped and stopped speaking, looking round in a panic at the sound of Sonja's voice. She couldn't see her, but footsteps were coming down the stairs. There was just enough time to disconnect and slip the mobile into her knickers before Sonja appeared.

'What are you doing down here?' Sonja demanded.

'I go to lavatory.'

Sonja gave her a lingering stare. 'You can use the one in the office.'

'Oh, thank you,' Maya said. 'I was not sure if that would be OK.'

'I thought I heard you talking.'

Maya smiled. 'I rehearse what I say to customers. My English is not so good.'

'I would say you were fluent,' Sonja said, her face full of questions and suspicion.

'That is a big compliment. Thank you,' Maya replied sweetly. 'If you will excuse me, I have to get back to customers. Stefan told me – keep them happy.'

The eagle eyes of Sonja were on her back as Maya returned to the main floor of the club and Maya knew she'd have to be very careful.

'I'll give you your phone back in a minute,' she whispered to its owner. 'We are not supposed to use them on duty.'

'Yeah, that woman is watchin' you.'

It wasn't until Maya moved closer to the guy, flirting and whispering into his ear, that Sonja seemed satisfied and moved away. When she'd gone, Maya reached to retrieve the mobile.

'Been keepin' it warm for me, have you?' the guy smirked.

It wasn't easy to get rid of the guy, but when she mentioned Stefan's name he backed off. In the corridor behind the club, she checked nobody was watching and went to the door that led to the basement. It clicked open and she felt her way down the stairs in the dark. At the bottom, there was a dim light coming from the room and the sound of snoring. Edging forward, she saw a big, beefy-looking man, his thick legs spilling over the edges of a wooden chair, his head lolling forward. Behind him, sitting on the floor, his legs and hands tied, was Zac.

Maya put her finger to her lips, circled round the

guard and knelt down beside Zac.

'Untie me,' he whispered.

She shook her head. 'I can't. Stefan will suspect something's up. Nothing can spook him or he'll change his plans. He's already worried about using the warehouse.'

'I think they're goin' to kill me,' Zac said, holding up his tied wrists.

'No, don't worry. All they're interested in is getting their shipment of drugs.' Maya bent close and whispered. 'I'm sorry. Just hang on and everything will be all right.' She turned round to check the beefy man was still asleep. 'The cops will be at the warehouse. I've tipped Simon off. If the shooting starts, keep your head down.'

The guard let out a big snore, his breath shuddered as he twitched.

Zac gave Maya a pleading look. 'I want to get out of here.'

All her being was telling her to untie him, but she couldn't risk it. Instead she took his bound hands in hers and held them.

'Be strong. Everything will be all right.' Then she stood up and slipped silently past the sleeping guard.

Opening the door to Stefan's office, she was pleased

to see it was still unoccupied. She crossed over to the white couch, where she sank down. She felt tired, anxious and irritable. Her head itched like mad under the wig, but she didn't dare remove it, and she was cold in the thin silk dress. A white throw provided some warmth and she settled back, with her head on the arm of the couch. It had been horrible having to leave Zac in the basement. Would he ever forgive her? She'd surely never forgive herself if anything bad happened to him.

Pulling up her legs, she closed her eyes and her mind began to drift. She hoped Simon was at work, getting together a team of crack marksmen, hoped that Stefan's plans wouldn't change and hoped that in the morning when they arrived at the warehouse there'd be a nasty surprise waiting for the gang. Just as she was falling into a deep sleep, she remembered she hadn't managed to give Simon the exact time of the drop.

* * *

Light was burning holes in her eyes when she awoke – overhead, spotlights were blazing down. Her neck was stiff and something was wedging her body so tightly that she could hardly move. Turning her head, she saw Stefan squashed next to her, his mouth open – he was snoring. She checked her clothing – thank goodness everything seemed to be intact and he was fully-clothed too. She pulled out her arm from underneath him, rolled off the sofa onto the rug and looked at her watch. It was nearly five a.m.

Almost immediately, there was a tap on the door. It opened and Ginger came in.

'Sorry, boss, you asked me to wake you.' Noticing Maya on the rug, he said, 'Give him a kick, darling.'

Maya stood up and leaned over Stefan to shake him awake.

Ginger came over. 'Better get going, boss.'

Stefan reached out and touched Maya's cheek. 'Hey, princess. You were spark out last night.'

'Sorry.'

'Yeah, well plenty of time,' he said, sitting up and reaching for his shoes. 'Today I got business to attend to.' He tied his shoelaces, stood up and straightened his clothing. Going over to a small side table, he picked up a handgun, clicked it open and loaded it. Then he went over to a painting on the wall and moved it aside. Maya watched as he took out several more guns.

'Here,' he said to Ginger. 'Make sure everybody's tooled up.'

Ginger nodded, taking the guns from Stefan and laying them on the table.

'Give me ten minutes and I'll be with you,' Stefan said and went through to the bathroom.

Maya watched as Ginger picked up the guns, checking and loading them. She sincerely hoped that in little more than an hour he would be safely in police custody.

Scum off the streets, she thought.

But then she panicked. What if Zac or any of the girls got caught in the crossfire? What if Zac, who'd done his best to help her and had come looking for her, should get hurt? No, she wouldn't let herself even think about that – she had to believe everything would turn out well.

Getting up, she straightened her dress; the fact that it was completely creased and offered no warmth was not important when measured against the morning's plan, but even so, she shivered. It was cold and she had nothing else to wear.

The bathroom door clicked open and Stefan entered, looking fresher and newly-energised.

'Right, are we ready?' he asked Ginger.

'Yeah,' Ginger said, handing Stefan a gun.

Stefan put the gun in his waistband. 'You stay here,

princess. I'll be back.'

Reaching for her shoes, Maya made a quick decision. 'I wish to come with you,' she said.

'What you want to come for?'

'I make sure nobody cheat you. Everybody in my country cheat. I know these people.'

Stefan laughed, then went towards her, pulled her to him and kissed her. 'You're a find, baby, you're a real find.'

Chapter Twenty-three

Just as they were ready to leave, the bouncer came stamping up the stairs towards them.

'The kid's gone!'

Stefan's face darkened. 'You idiot! I told you to keep him tied up.'

While Stefan fumed, Maya was ecstatic. Zac was free!

'Find him or you're dead,' Stefan boomed.

The bouncer backed away, looking frightened. 'He was trussed up tight, honest,' he stammered. 'I reckon that girl, Kay, sprung him. Saw her slippin' the keys back – wondered what she was up to.'

Ginger spat out a string of curses. 'I knew she was up to something, her and Gerard. They were in it together . . . and the kid.'

A quiet fury took hold of Stefan. His body stiffened as he stepped up to the bouncer. Maya thought Stefan would lash out, but instead he gave an order, his voice sharp and edgy.

'Find the kid! Go after him! Now! Bring him to the warehouse.'

The bouncer looked flustered, his mouth opened to say something, then he thought better of it and hurried off.

Stefan turned to Maya. 'You, go and fetch Kay,' he ordered. 'And be quick. Five minutes, no more.'

Maya knew it was essential to do as she was told. She rushed up towards Kay's room and went in without knocking. 'Come on, you've got to get up.'

Kay's eyes were dazed, her movements slow. Maya dragged her out of the bed in her underwear and propped her up while she picked up a red dress lying on the floor and slipped it over her head. Instead of helping her, Kay flopped back against the headboard and started humming. Maya had to lift her up and support her as they walked to the office. It was hard to imagine it was Kay who'd aided Zac's escape – she seemed totally out of it. But however Zac had escaped, she hoped with all her heart the gang didn't recapture him.

As soon as the two men saw Maya entering the office with Kay, they hustled her out again. Ginger walked Kay through the club to the car and Stefan followed behind with Maya. His manner towards her had changed; the charm was gone and he was brusque and businesslike. Ginger opened the door of the black estate car and pushed Kay inside. Stefan placed Maya beside her with hardly more care and took no notice of her shivering in her thin silk dress.

Even before they spoke, the tension between Ginger and Stefan was obvious.

'I don't like it. It's too risky,' Ginger said, as he drove along narrow streets. 'That boy heard all our plans.'

'What's he gonna do? Go tell the cops? I don't think so.'

'But what if he's working for Creek?' Ginger asked.

Stefan's reply was sharp and confident. 'He's just a kid! I know what they were up to – him and Gerard thought they could get a piece of the action. Stupid little runts!' He turned round to look at Kay. 'Thought you could double-cross me, did you?'

Kay, her head resting against the window, gave no response.

Stefan reached across and patted Ginger's hand as it held the steering wheel. 'Relax. Everythin' is set up.'

'I don't like it. Too many things are shifting,' Ginger moaned.

Stefan growled impatiently. 'Quit whinin'! We can't change our plans now. It'll go like clockwork. Thirty minutes, tops, that's all we need.' He shifted back in his seat. 'Keep your mouth shut and step on it.'

Lurching around in the back seat, Maya wondered what was in store for them at the warehouse. Would Zac have managed to get a message to Simon and told him the time of the drop? Would the police be in position, hiding, waiting?

Her mind went back to the terrifying shoot-out at the mill in Leeds, earlier in the summer, when she'd helped rescue Pam. She remembered the deafening noise of the sub-machine guns, the ripping fear and . . . something else . . . the adrenalin – that thrill of terror. Then she felt ashamed. People had died, she reminded herself. It wasn't an action movie.

Focusing on the back of Stefan's head, she wondered how he'd respond to the police. Would he give himself up or try to shoot his way out?

At the pub where Rose had taken Maya to use the telephone, the car turned onto the towpath, swaying and dipping as it drove over the rutted ground. The clock on the dashboard showed 5.45 a.m.

Parking close to the wall of the warehouse, Ginger rolled down the windows and offered Stefan a cigarette. They lit up, but neither of them spoke. The air was heavy with smoke and unvoiced thoughts.

Taking a big drag on his cigarette, Stefan looked at his watch. 'Sonja should be here by now with the van. What's keepin' her?'

'I smell a rat,' Ginger said. 'It's too quiet.'

'It's six o' clock in the ruddy mornin',' Stefan snapped. 'What do you expect? Barbeques, parties? People are in bed.'

Ginger turned and scanned back along the towpath. 'No runners, no joggers, no blokes fishing. I don't like it.'

Stefan took a last drag on his cigarette then threw it out of the window. 'Shut up! Everythin' is fine. We unload the stash, deliver the money and we're outta here before anybody wakes up.'

'That girl knew about this place,' Ginger said, throwing his cigarette out and giving Stefan a sharp look. 'Gerard says she was a cop's daughter. She could have snitched.'

'She wouldn't dare say anythin'. I put some men on her tail. She won't be talkin'.'

Ginger wasn't to be silenced. 'I know what you did.

I was there watching her flat, if you remember, but she disappeared. I didn't like that and I'm not happy now. Listen how quiet it is. I got a funny feeling.'

'Shut it!' Stefan exploded. 'This is the big one. We sort this and we're kings – kings, you understand? Nobody can touch us. We'll have control. All you got to do is keep your nerve.' He looked in the rear-view mirror. 'See, here's Terry and the rest of them.' He opened the door as another car drove up. 'All goin' to plan,' he said as he got out.

After closing the door, he bent down to speak through the open window to Maya. 'You stay in the car, princess. Make sure she don't run,' he said, nodding at Kay.

No possibility of that, Maya thought, looking at Kay, who was slumped against the side window with her eyes closed.

In contrast, Maya was super-alert. She leaned forward and watched through the front window as Stefan and Ginger walked over to the other car – Terry's car. It was parked parallel to her, with the towpath in between. Four men in dark tracksuits got out and stood talking with Stefan and Ginger.

Maya scanned the banks of the canal for any sign of police presence, but could see nothing. Her heart was racing. Thirty minutes, Stefan had said. That was all the time the gang needed, and if the police weren't already in position, or if they didn't arrive soon, the gang would conduct their business and be away.

Suddenly, the circle of men spread out, moving with Stefan and Ginger into the warehouse. Then, in the rear-view mirror, Maya saw a white van approaching. As it squeezed past between the two parked cars, Maya saw that it was Sonja who was driving. She parked to the left of the wide warehouse doors and after a few moments, Maya saw her jump down from the van, walk towards the warehouse and disappear inside.

Maya squeezed between the two front seats to sit behind the steering wheel. She peered at the white van, wondering who was locked inside. Poor Annika, with her sister Tanya's body? Zac – had they caught him?

Then a silver van appeared in the rear-view mirror. It was heading along the towpath at speed. When it came closer, Maya saw the driver was sitting on the left hand side. The van came to an abrupt halt beside her, so that the towpath was completely blocked. She turned her head and read the lettering on the side – **AMSTERDAM TULIPS**. Three men got out and went towards the warehouse.

Again, she scanned the banks of the canal and the adjacent warehouses. There was no movement, no evidence of any police. Her stomach churned, she tapped the steering wheel nervously and sent a silent plea to Simon.

A loud scraping noise signalled Ginger opening the wide front doors of the warehouse. The men from the tulip van came out, climbed into their van and reversed it into the building. Then Ginger closed the doors, trapping the van inside.

There was nothing more to see, nothing more to do except wait. In front of her, the car keys dangled temptingly in the ignition. Did Stefan trust her not to drive away; were they there for a quick getaway or had he simply forgotten them?

Two of the Omega gang came out of the warehouse and took up positions on either side of the building – one leaning nonchalantly against his car, the other wandering to the canal bank. To an outsider they might look innocent, but Maya knew they were on guard.

Another rumbling noise and Maya turned her head to see a door slide back and Sonja leave the warehouse, accompanied by three of the Omega gang. They walked towards the back of the white van, unlocked the doors and opened them wide.

First to appear was Annika. Because her hands were tied behind her back, Sonja had to help her jump down. Immediately, she was seized by one of the heavies who escorted her to the warehouse and pushed her inside. The other two gang members were busy sliding a long parcel out of the white van. It was wrapped in curtaining, which Maya recognised from the hostel. She had no doubt it was Tanya's body and they were carrying her with the intention of putting her in the tulip van beside her sister.

Desperately, her eyes darted back and forth, watching for any movement, any sign that the police were closing in, but there was nothing. The only person moving was Sonja, who returned to the white van, closed the back doors, climbed into the driver's seat and reversed it, so that it came to rest between the two Omega cars, completely blocking the towpath again.

Panic bit into Maya. If police cars wanted to get close to the warehouse they wouldn't be able to get through.

As she scanned the path behind her once again, Sonja came over. Leaning down to speak through the open car window she said, 'Dania, we have to take Kay in. Help me.'

Maya's legs at first refused to move. It was as if they were stuck in deep mud and when she tried to get up, an invisible force was sucking them down. How could she hand Kay over to the Omega gang, knowing that the police might not arrive?

Sonja's eyes were hard as stones, glaring at Maya. 'Come on! We haven't got all day,' she said, pulling open the car door.

Playing for time, Maya yawned, leaned back and then slowly levered herself out of the car seat.

'What's the matter? Wake up!' Sonja barked. She grabbed Maya's arm and shook her.

'Sorry,' Maya said, sleepily.

Moving to the back door, Sonja prised Kay out and flung her towards Maya. 'Here, take her into the warehouse. I have to get something from the van.'

Maya folded her arms around Kay and Kay leaned heavily against her. She seemed hardly awake, but then suddenly she looked up, her gold eyes wide and anxious.

'Maya?'

Maya checked to see if Sonja was within hearing. 'Yes.'

'I am sorry,' Kay whispered. She pulled away,

grasping at Maya's hands. 'You are a kind friend. I do not repay you well.'

'Don't worry. It's OK,' Maya said.

'No, it is not OK. You come to the club, you want to help me, try and get me safe.' Her voice broke. 'I was stupid.' She swallowed and spoke more loudly as she struggled to get her words out. 'But I tell Zac, run, go! That was good, yes?'

'Very good,' Maya said. 'But shush. Sonja's coming.'

And, with a heavy heart, Maya put her arm around Kay's shoulder and started to walk her towards the warehouse.

Just before Sonja caught up with them, Kay stopped. 'If they kill me,' she whispered. 'Take me home, take me back to Kosovo.'

A deep shiver ran through Maya. 'Nobody is going to kill you,' she said. 'I won't let them.'

Then she saw that Sonja had a gun.

* * *

The wide warehouse doors were closed and bolted. Sonja knocked on the inset door and, when it opened, she pushed Kay and Maya inside. Most of the floor space was taken up by the tulip van, so they had to skirt round it. Sonja ushered them to the left hand side, where Stefan and Ginger stood talking to one of the men from Amsterdam.

'Sit her down there and wait,' Sonja told Maya, gesturing with the gun to an old sofa pushed up against the wall. 'Just keep her quiet till they've finished their business.'

Obediently, Maya guided Kay down onto the sofa and sat beside her. She watched as Stefan placed a bag on a work bench and inched closer to the edge of the sofa so she could hear what he was saying.

'Two thousand to get rid of the two of them.'

'And one for the body,' the Dutch man said. 'Three thousand euro and it's a deal.'

'Done,' Stefan agreed, shaking the man's hand.

'What about the new girls?' Ginger asked.

'They're in the van. We leave them where they are until we've sorted the money,' the Dutch man said. 'Come on, let's move it.'

Stefan nodded and pushed the bag towards the Dutch guy, who unzipped the top and lifted out a wad of notes. When he set about counting the money, Maya put her arms round Kay and held her tightly.

With growing fear, she watched the men; if Simon

hadn't understood her message, if the police weren't in place, could she just watch as Kay was driven away?

As far as the gang were concerned, everything was going to plan. At the back of the tulip van, boxes were being ripped apart. Terry and his men were extracting the drugs from the false bottoms and placing them in new containers. Stefan walked over to them and began checking the drugs, cutting open a few random packets and tasting the powder on his tongue.

'Good stuff?' one of the Dutch men shouted.

'So far,' Stefan replied.

Maya heard the men talking in Dutch. One of them picked up the bag containing the money and went over to Stefan and his gang.

'We have to go,' the Dutch boss said. 'We'll unload the girls and get out of here.'

Every muscle in Maya's body tensed. She couldn't let this happen. She put her arms in front of Kay and leaned her body protectively in front of her.

'Don't,' Kay whispered, putting a hand on Maya's arm. 'Do not upset them.'

Maya turned and looked into Kay's golden eyes. 'I can't let you. . .' Maya started to say, but a voice from the back of the warehouse cut across her.

'Police! Drop your weapons.'

For a split second everybody froze, then Stefan and Ginger dodged behind a pile of boxes and started firing towards the dark shadows on the top of the stairs. One of the Omega gang crawled forward, using a piece of metal as a shield, but he was picked off, rolling over and clutching at his shoulder. A bullet ricocheted off a brick pillar near the sofa and Maya slid to the ground, pulling Kay down with her.

'Drop your weapons!' the police order came again.

'Under there,' Maya whispered to Kay, pointing to the tulip van. 'Now!'

She tugged at Kay's dress and squirmed forwards. A bullet cracked the air. Instinctively, Maya dived under the van, wriggling sideways to make room for Kay. But Kay didn't join her. When Maya turned to look, she saw her lying on the floor a few metres away, holding a bloody shoulder.

Desperate to get to her and haul her to safety, Maya started to crawl out from under the van, but a sudden flash of movement stopped her. A barrage of shots rent the air. Ginger was running towards the van, shooting at the police and they were replying. Chips of concrete and brick flew, a bullet smashed the exhaust pipe near Maya's head. Gasping and choking, she rolled back, taking cover again underneath the chassis.

As she lay shaking with fear, she glimpsed Ginger's feet running along the side of the van. Above her, the chassis shook, the engine started. More shots came from the police, one of the back tyres burst. The engine throbbed louder.

He can't go anywhere, Maya thought, the warehouse doors are shut.

But, above her, the engine revved.

A terrified Maya sucked in her breath as the undercarriage scraped her head. Her nose was filled with fumes, her mouth full of dirt and her wig torn off. The van crashed forwards, splintering the doors, and Maya was left exposed in the middle of the floor, her dark hair tumbling around her shoulders.

Bullets zinged over her head towards the fleeing van. In a desperate act, Maya raised her arm.

'Don't shoot,' she shouted. 'I'm Maya Brown.'

The police stopped shooting. In the brief pause, Stefan stared out over the workbench. His eyes widened when he saw Maya, then he raised his gun.

Her reactions were like lighting – in one fluid movement she sprang up and ran for cover, dodging behind a brick pillar. A couple of shots from Stefan hit the brickwork, throwing up a cloud of dust. As she crouched, coughing and trembling, she heard a loud bang outside and, peering through the splintered doors, she saw the tulip van had crashed into iron bollards on the side of the canal. Ginger lay slumped over the steering wheel, the windscreen had been smashed by bullets and was spattered with blood.

Maya's heart lurched with pity as she thought of Annika and the girls trapped in the back of the van. They'd be terrified. But the person who needed her help most was Kay. She was still lying on the floor, blood soaking the ground underneath her. It would only take a few seconds to reach her, but she knew Stefan, behind the workbench, would be ready to shoot as soon as she moved.

I have to risk it, Maya thought. Kay needs help urgently.

She was contemplating shouting and asking the police for cover, when somebody else had exactly the same idea.

'Cover me,' Stefan yelled to his men.

Then, rattling off a couple of shots towards the back of the warehouse, he dodged out from behind the workbench, stooped down and hauled Kay to her feet.

'I've got the girl!' he shouted. 'Don't shoot!'

Maya could only watch helplessly while Stefan backed out of the warehouse, using Kay's body as a shield. Kay was like a rag doll in his arms, her chest and shoulders covered with blood. Slowly and cautiously, Stefan started to move towards his car, but the police were ready for any getaway attempt. Armed officers began to crawl into position, training their guns on him.

Sensing the danger, Stefan changed direction. One of his gang dodged out of the open door, rattled off some shots towards the police guns, then fell back. It was enough distraction for Stefan to reach the tulip van. Walking backwards, he dragged Kay to the van and wedged her behind the van door, while he pushed Ginger to one side. Then he hoisted Kay up and held her in front of him while he started the engine.

More shots blasted towards the police from his gang. Maya saw Kay pressed up against the window screen like a crazy mascot. In a raging fury, she shot forward as Stefan drove off. He was heading away from the police down the opposite end of the towpath.

'I'm Maya Brown, Maya Brown,' she screamed as she rocketed forwards. 'Don't shoot!'

Keeping her head low, she ran to Stefan's car, opened the door, started the engine, accelerated hard and set off after the tulip van.

Stepping on the gas, she pushed the car to its limit.

This end of the towpath was stony, and the car bounced and bumped over rough ground. She desperately tried to keep it on track and then ahead of her she saw the tulip van veering wildly. It was tilting to one side; the punctured tyres were deflating rapidly. As she got closer, she heard a horrible grinding noise and the van slowed, slewing towards the canal.

It hit a pile of gravel, skidded sideways and came to a halt with one back wheel over the canal side. The doors opened and Stefan jumped out, pulling Kay with him.

Maya screeched to a halt, opened the car door and started to run after them, but a crack of gunshot had her running for cover. She zig-zagged towards a half-demolished building. At the same time, a police car came racing down the towpath behind her.

Stefan fired two more warning shots, then took cover behind some trees at the water's edge.

'Stay back,' he shouted. 'Or the girl goes in the water.'

Maya heard a rustling noise behind her and turned to see two police marksmen climbing over a low fence. They were moving towards her to take shelter in the old building. From behind the pile of wood and rusty iron girders, the cops shouted to Stefan, asking him to throw down his weapon.

'You're surrounded. You cannot escape!'

Then there was silence. The air shimmered with tension. Glancing behind her, Maya saw another police marksman sliding towards her hiding place, his rifle at the ready. At the other side of the canal, she spotted two officers inching closer. Stefan saw the danger and pulled Kay flat to his body.

A click came from a gun close to Maya.

'Don't,' she whispered. 'Please don't. You might hit Kay.'

Stefan moved to the water's edge, dangling Kay over the canal. 'Come any closer and I'll shove her in.'

It was a desperate attempt and Stefan knew it. There was no way out for him. He sent two shots towards Maya's hiding place. Wood and plaster exploded. Maya dodged down, her heart hammering. When she dared to raise her head again Stefan yelled something she couldn't catch and then he stepped forward and heaved Kay into the water.

Desperate now, he ran straight for the building, firing shots in all directions. Maya crawled round a pile of shattered wood, heard the police shooting back, then stood up and raced to the canal side. With one swift movement, she leapt and dived in.

The water was icy and thick with weeds. She took a deep breath and swam down. It was difficult to see through the murky water, but she spread her arms, feeling through clinging fronds. Her fingers grasped a waving arm. Kay was rising to the surface. Maya pulled her upwards and then caught her gently round the neck, raising her head above the water. Kay coughed feebly while Maya pulled her to the side. Kay's mouth flapped open and she gasped and choked.

At this point on the canal there was no bank; the sides dropped down sheer and there was nothing to grab hold of. Maya gulped in a big mouthful of air and shouted. Her eyes scanned upwards, hoping for some help, but all she saw was sky. Holding Kay's limp body, it was hard to keep afloat and it was deathly cold – her hands and legs were going numb. She tried to wedge herself against the side, but it was too slippery and she went under. Fighting to surface again, there was a splash beside her and suddenly an extra pair of hands supported Kay's body.

'It's all right. I've got her,' a man's voice said.

Maya felt the weight of Kay float away from her. She was vaguely aware of other help arriving and she clung onto a rope that hauled her up onto the canal side.

She staggered to her knees, shivering and shaking, and saw Kay laid out on the towpath, her face deathly white. One of the uniformed men started CPR and Kay coughed and choked, spewing up canal water. Then she went rigid.

'She's in shock. Where's the ruddy ambulance?' one of the uniformed men shouted.

Maya threw her body over Kay's, rubbing her hands over her skin, trying to get some warmth into her. With a flood of relief, she heard, then saw, an ambulance coming towards them and in moments paramedics were by their sides, wrapping them in foil blankets. Practised hands tended to Kay, while Maya sat on the path, the warmth beginning to seep back into her limbs.

'Stefan, did he get away?' she asked one of the cops.

'Not likely,' he replied, pointing.

She stood up and saw Stefan, sitting holding a bloody leg. His shiny suit trousers were torn and bloodstained and he was rocking backwards and forwards, groaning in pain and cursing everybody around him.

When Kay was being loaded into the ambulance, one of the paramedics asked Maya to ride with them.

'You should come with her,' the woman said. 'You need to be checked over.'

Maya shook her head and went to Kay's side.

'I can't come with you, not now,' she said. 'But I'll come as soon as I can. Promise.' She looked back up the canal side to the tulip van. 'The girls are in there. They'll be so frightened. I have to see if they're all right.'

Chapter Twenty-four

When the ambulance drove away, Maya pulled the foil blanket tightly round her and, with as much dignity as she could muster, walked up to the officer who seemed to be in charge.

'I'm Maya Brown,' she said.

He looked slightly amused. 'I know who you are. You did a very brave thing there, diving in and rescuing that girl.'

'She's Kay. She's my friend.'

'Yes, well. There are a lot of things to be explained, but I think you need to get some dry clothes on first.'

'There are some young women trapped in that van,' Maya said, pointing to the tulip van. 'They don't know what's happening. They'll be so scared.'

She walked towards the van, with the police

officer and others following. The van was a wreck, its windscreen shattered, two bullet holes in its side and one back wheel over the water.

Maya put her ear to the side of the van and listened but could hear nothing.

'Oh no, I hope they're not hurt,' she said. Then she gently tapped on the back door. 'Annika, Annika. It's Maya. Are you OK? Can you hear me? It's all right. You're safe.' She pulled at the door handle but the doors wouldn't open. The van shuddered.

'Are you sure there's somebody in there?' the police officer asked.

'Yes,' Maya said. 'We have to get them out.'

'We'll have to wait. The van's not stable,' the officer said.

He spoke into his radio, while Maya pressed her face against the back doors.

'Annika, don't move. The van is near the water. Just wait a few minutes and we'll get you out.' There was silence. 'Annika, can you hear me?'

An answering shout came from the other side of the door.

'Hang on,' Maya yelled. 'Help is coming.'

Waiting was horrible. Maya imagined the girls inside, traumatised by gunshots and shaken by the van careering out of control. When another police officer arrived with a set of skeleton keys, she clenched her fists impatiently while he tried several, before at last he managed to unlock the doors and pull them back.

'Easy does it, easy does it,' the officer in charge said, holding Maya back.

'I'm lighter than you,' she said firmly, squeezing round him. 'Let me get in.'

Carefully keeping her weight to one side, Maya crawled to the back of the van, where Annika sat huddled up into a ball.

'Annika, it's all right, it's me, Maya. You're safe.'

Annika looked up, her face white and tear-streaked. She was shaking uncontrollably.

'Come on,' Maya said, touching her shoulder gently. 'We have to get out, the van isn't safe.'

Annika looked bewildered, but when Maya pulled at her arm she moved forward. Maya backed out of the van, then reached in and lifted a now sobbing Annika onto safe ground.

'It is over?' Annika whispered.

'Yes, it's over,' Maya said.

Just at that moment, the van creaked and lurched closer to the water.

'I have to get the others out,' Maya shouted to the police. 'Can you get somebody to stay with Annika?'

The senior police officer, standing by the van, peered into the interior. 'Nobody else in there,' he said.

'Yes, there is,' Maya said.

Before the officer could stop her, Maya slipped behind his back, carefully climbed onto the lip of the van and slid on her stomach to the front. A tapping sound was coming from the floor. The noise grew louder and there were muffled cries.

A carpet was tacked to the van's floor. The van groaned as Maya pulled at it, then there was a loud ripping sound as the carpet came up to reveal a trapdoor. There was no handle or groove to lift it. The girls had been sealed in.

'Get me something to lever this door up,' Maya shouted back to the waiting police officers. 'But be careful. Keep the weight on this side of the van.'

One of the police officers leaned his head in. 'Let us deal with this,' he said. 'It's our responsibility.'

'Just give me some kind of lever and stand back,' Maya warned.

Her cheeks were flushed, her eyes bright, and there was no room for argument in the precarious van. When somebody handed her a metal bar, she set to work. Once she'd inserted the end of the bar, the trapdoor came up easily.

Leaning over the hole, Maya swallowed when she saw a tangle of limbs and several pairs of eyes shining up at her.

'It's all right, everything is OK,' she said.

A bevy of arms and legs all began to squirm at once. The van creaked. Maya threw out an arm.

'Stop. Be careful!'

But the girls, who'd been cooped up for days on end, were desperate to escape. Maya moved aside while the young women scrabbled past her. When the last woman was out, Maya dived for the doors, jumping clear as the van lurched towards the water.

Not a moment to spare! With relief, Maya surveyed the van, with its back end now only centimetres from the surface of the canal. She certainly didn't fancy another swim. She was cold enough already, shivering in the gold dress that was plastered tightly to her body. She'd left the foil blanket inside the van.

A friendly officer saw her plight and handed her a coat. Maya gratefully slipped her arms into it and tried to do up the buttons, but her fingers were clumsy with cold. The Chinese girls were in a worse state. Huddled by the side of the van, they were hanging on to each other, shivering and sobbing. They'd been in the tiny space under the floorboards of the van – buffeted about, suffocated by fumes and unable to stretch their limbs for three days. Their clothing was crumpled and stained; all of them were hunched over, and one girl was rubbing at her legs and arms and grimacing in pain.

When a police officer approached the group, one of the girls started to shriek loudly and they clung even more desperately to each other. Maya saw that their eyes were full of fear. With her head down, she moved towards the girls and stood silently by them. Slowly and gently, she put out a hand and touched one of the girl's arms.

The girl shrank back, her eyes narrowed, and she tensed and frowned. Maya regretted her gesture but then the girl smiled shyly, clasped Maya's hand, squeezed it and wouldn't let go.

'Maya,' Maya said, pointing to herself.

The girl looked at her. Tears had formed rivulets down her grimy face.

'Lily,' the girl said.

An ambulance, followed by an unmarked police car, made its way carefully along the towpath. Both vehicles stopped and when the doors of the car opened, a tall young man with spiky hair got out. From the passenger door, a small woman in a long cotton dress emerged, stood looking around, then strode forwards. Instinctively, Maya turned. There was a split second when she didn't recognise the woman with dark, bobbed hair, but then she ran, yelling, 'Mum!'

Throwing herself forward, she dived into Pam's arms. 'I forgot you'd dyed your hair,' she said.

Pam kissed Maya's wet face. 'You're frozen,' she said. 'Oh, Maya, what am I going to do with you?'

They watched as the smuggled women were comforted and put into the ambulance to be taken to hospital and checked over. With a massive feeling of relief, Maya leaned on Pam's shoulder.

'What will happen to them?' she asked.

Pam shook her head. 'I'm not sure – they'll probably be sent back home. We'll see.'

'The gang were going to kill Kay and Annika,' Maya said. 'I had to do something.'

Pam hugged her daughter tight. 'Oh, my love,' she said. 'You can't go on pulling stunts like this.' She kissed Maya's head. 'I should be angry with you but – two hundred kilos of heroin, one of the biggest drugs hauls ever – I don't know what to say.'

'Oh, Mum, I'm so sorry,' Maya cut in. 'I won't ever do this again. I didn't mean to get in so deep.' She looked at Pam's anxious face. 'I didn't mess up your mission, did I?'

'No, it's all finished. I was staying on to tidy things up, but somebody else can do that. The main work's been done.'

'I was afraid the police wouldn't get here in time,' Maya said.

'Your friend Zac did well. He gave Simon the right information.'

'Sure did.'

Maya looked up and saw Zac in front of her. He grinned.

'Your mum told me to stay in the car, but I guess it's OK to come out now.'

Maya went to him and gave him a hug. 'Thanks, Zac. Thanks for helping me.'

'Yeah, well, you know, if your friend Kay hadn't let me out, I could be a goner. Bein' your friend is a dangerous occupation.'

Maya bit her lip. 'I'm so sorry. I didn't mean any of this to happen, honest. All I wanted to do was to stop Leona and Evie taking drugs. Then everything just escalated.'

Pam pursed her lips and shook her head. 'Things have a habit of escalating around you. From now on, you are under close surveillance.'

'What do you think's happened back there?' Maya asked, looking towards the warehouse.

'I don't know. Simon's gone to find out,' Pam said.

'I hope they've got all the gang,' Maya said. 'I hope nobody escaped.'

Pam looked at her daughter, closed her eyes briefly and sighed. 'I can tell you this,' she said. 'Despite your bravery and heroic deeds you are not going to escape a good talking-to.'

Chapter Twenty-five

At the warehouse, Maya saw three of Stefan's heavies bent over the bonnet of their cars, hands cuffed behind their backs. Stefan and Ginger, both badly injured, had been taken to hospital. The rest of the gang and the men from Amsterdam were imprisoned in an armoured van and more police vehicles were moving in to transport the drugs and other evidence away. Sonja was sitting under guard in the back of a police car.

Pam spoke to the detective in charge, then motioned for Maya and Zac to join them.

'I want a full statement from both of you,' the detective said. 'I'll see you at the station tomorrow morning.'

'Don't you think the interview could take place at

home?' Pam asked. 'We've got some hospital visiting to do and I want to check on what's happening to those poor Chinese girls. Shall we say eleven o' clock?'

The detective agreed and shook Pam's hand. As Maya and Zac turned away, he asked Pam, 'How did your daughter get involved in this?'

Pam shook her head. 'I don't know the full story yet but I am certainly going to find out.'

'Fancy yourself as a bit of an action hero, do you?' the officer joked, calling over to Maya.

Maya turned to face him, pushed back her hair and gave him a death stare. 'No,' she said bitingly. 'I just wanted to help my friends.'

The detective moved closer and nodded. Then he said, much more respectfully, 'You risked your life – not to be recommended, but you saved that girl and intercepted a major delivery of class A drugs. Well done!'

Maya grinned. 'Do I get a reward?'

Her moment of triumph was short-lived. Grasping her daughter firmly by the arm, Pam said, 'Come on. You have a lot of explaining to do.'

Maya made a face at Zac, asking for sympathy as they walked to the car. In response, Zac blew out his cheeks and rolled his eyes, indicating there was nothing he could do to help.

Maya stuck her tongue out at him, then asked forlornly, 'Can we please get home so I can get some dry clothes on before you start questioning me?'

'Yes,' Pam conceded. 'Then we're off to the hospital, where you're going to get a thorough check-up.'

Once home, there was also the matter of a big apology to Gran. Maya found it difficult to face Helen, knowing what she'd put her through.

'I promise you faithfully,' Helen said, looking at her dishevelled granddaughter, 'I will never, ever agree to look after you again. You're more trouble than when you first came to us at the age of four.'

'Oh, Gran,' Maya said, throwing her arms round her. 'You don't mean that! I am so sorry, so sorry.'

Tears welled in Helen's eyes. 'I thought I'd lost you,' she said. 'Never, ever do that to me again.'

'I promise, I won't,' Maya said. 'No more adventures. I've had enough excitement and danger for one year. Now I have to concentrate on my exams.'

'And your running,' Helen said. 'Put your energy into those races.'

'Good idea,' Maya agreed.

When Maya and her mum had showered and changed, they set off to the hospital. First stop was to check on Kay. They found her lying on a trolley bed in a curtained cubicle.

Her eyes were wild when she sat up. 'The police come,' she said. 'I think they arrest me.' She pulled back her gown revealing thick bandages swathing the top of her arm and shoulder. 'But the police cannot take me because I have a bullet.' She settled back down and closed her eyes. 'The nurse give me a drug for the pain, so now I am happy. Soon I will have an operation.'

Maya took her hand and gave it a gentle squeeze. 'Kay, this is my mum, Pam.'

Pam moved closer to the trolley and Kay squinted up at her. 'Your daughter . . . she save my life.'

Pam smiled. 'I know. You were both very brave.'

A rustling of the curtain signalled the arrival of the nurse and porter who'd arrived to take Kay to the operating theatre.

'I'll see you up on the ward,' Maya promised, 'when you're all fixed.'

Kay's eyes were closing as they wheeled her away and she started to sing softly, a song in her own language. Maya watched her go and felt suddenly nervous – how near to Kay's heart was that bullet?

'She will be all right, won't she?' she asked her mum.

'Of course, darling. They didn't seem to be unduly worried.'

'I want to be there when she wakes up.'

'You have to think about yourself, my love,' Pam replied. 'Don't you need some rest?'

'Yep, I'm tired but I'll have a long sleep tonight.'

'Come on,' Pam said. 'We need to get you checked over.'

Maya was following Pam out of the cubicle when she caught sight of a form lying on a chair. Curious as ever, she bent down to read it.

Katrina Janovich
Date of birth: 15.5.1993
Place of birth: Cuska, Kosovo

Maya's heart thumped. Cuska, that was her village – the village where she'd lived as a child, the place where her family had been murdered, locked inside a burning building. Could the girl who'd pulled her from the fire be Kay – Katrina Janovich, the little girl with the golden eyes?

'Oh, excuse me, I forgot that,' the nurse said, rushing in to pick up the form.

Maya stood aside, her head in a whirl, then she ran

after the trolley which was heading for the lift.

'Wait! Just a minute, please I have to ask Kay something.'

The porter turned. 'They're expecting her.'

'Just one second.'

He stopped and Maya went to Kay's side and bent her head close.

'Was it you? Were you the little girl who pushed me into the ditch in Cuska?'

Sleepy from the pre-operation anaesthetic, Kay's eyes were half closed and she mumbled words Maya couldn't understand.

'You must remember!' Maya begged. 'People were locked in the church – it was on fire – they couldn't escape but you pulled me away, hid me in the ditch.'

Kay smiled. 'I will have an operation.'

'We have to go,' the porter said. 'You can see her later. Anderson ward.'

And Kay was wheeled away.

'What was all that about?' Pam asked, as she joined Maya.

Staring down the corridor, Maya saw the lift arrive and Kay being pushed inside.

'I know this sounds crazy. But I think Kay is the girl who saved my life.'

* * *

All the way through the hospital check-up, Maya's thoughts were with Kay, hoping the operation was going smoothly. She patiently submitted to tests and examinations while her mind played over her meetings with Kay and the dream about the little girl with golden eyes. The information she'd seen on the form made her heart race. Kay was Katrina Janovich – a Serbian name – a girl from Cuska.

While they waited for the results of the tests, Maya filled Pam in on all the events of the past week.

Pam listened patiently, then looked off into the distance. When she turned back to Maya, her face was serious.

'I'm staying home for a while,' she said, 'where I can keep an eye on you.' She cupped Maya's face in her hand. 'Oh, Maya, you are wonderful and amazing and . . . and . . . but you can't change the world. You can't take on gangs of criminals and drug dealers and whoever else crosses your path and seems to be immoral in some way.' She let go of Maya's face and sighed. 'Part of me wants to shake you and part of me wants to give you a medal.' She stood up. 'Come on, let's see what's happening. If we can't get results of

325

the tests, we'll go home. What we both need is sleep.'

'No. I have to wait to see Kay,' Maya protested. 'There are so many things I want to ask her. And the other girls, I want to find out what's happened to them.'

'All right,' Pam said. 'I can see I'm not going to get any sleep just yet.'

A hospital volunteer took them down to a room near A&E where the Chinese girls had been placed. Sitting silently, huddled beneath white blankets, the girls were like little ghosts, but when they saw Maya and Pam, they stood up and started talking excitedly.

Amidst the cacophony of foreign words, Maya heard one girl speaking some English. It was the girl who'd given her name – Lily. The English she spoke was heavily-accented, but Maya understood from her that she had no idea why she was at the hospital or what was going to happen to her and the other girls.

'You are safe,' Maya told her. 'Nobody will hurt you. You are safe.' Maya tried to convey the message by adding some gestures, but Lily just looked more confused. She shook her head, tears in her eyes.

'I don't think she understands,' Maya said to the nurse. 'What's going to happen to them? Are they sick?'

'Malnourished and dehydrated,' the nurse said. 'They've taken some fluids but we really need the translator to show up before we give them more treatment. We'll keep them in overnight, give them a thorough check-up before we discharge them.'

'What will happen to them after that?'

The nurse's face wrinkled. 'I don't know. Poor things, they're frightened.'

Maya turned to her mum. 'Can you do anything for them?'

'Not in my remit,' Pam said. 'I would guess they'll be repatriated. I'll do my best to see they're treated kindly, though.'

Maya took Lily's hand and tried again to communicate. 'The nurse will help you,' she said. 'You are safe here, safe.' She squeezed Lily's hand gently as she spoke and felt an answering pressure.

'Thank you,' Lily said, nodding her head. Then she frowned and she looked as if she was concentrating hard trying to find words. Finally she managed, 'I go China. See family?'

Maya smiled with relief. 'I hope so.'

A ghost of a smile lit Lily's face and she stepped forward, reached up and gave Maya a hug.

* * *

Pam agreed to let Maya stay at the hospital until Kay's operation was over and she was taken up to a ward.

'Call me and I'll come and collect you,' Pam told her. 'Give Kay my love. And don't go anywhere else.'

'Mum, I'm fifteen.'

'I know. And you're more than capable of taking care of yourself. It's your propensity to take care of everybody else that worries me.'

Maya smiled as her mum left. It was great to have her home. Sitting alone in the waiting room, her mind ran over the events of the past week and she felt suddenly very, very tired. Pulling her feet up onto a chair, she rested her head against the wall and dropped off to sleep.

The next thing she knew was that she was being gently shaken awake by a young nurse.

'Your friend is fine. The operation's over and she's comfortable. Would you like to see her? Just for a few minutes.'

It took Maya a moment to understand where she was. She sat up. Her neck was stiff and one arm was numb. 'Thank you,' she said, rubbing her arm and fingers. 'That would be great.'

Kay was alone in a side room, lying on her back, her white face shadowed by dark hollows under her eyes. A drip was feeding into the back of her hand and a drain ran from her chest into a thick plastic bag that hung below the sheets. Maya sat down in a chair at the bedside.

Kay's eyes flickered and opened. 'Is it over?' she asked.

'Yes, the nurse said you'll be fine. How do you feel?'

Kay's face scrunched up. 'Like I have dope. I am floating.'

'Does it hurt?'

'I cannot feel pain,' Kay said. 'But I need a drink.'

'Here, have some water.'

Maya poured water from the jug into a beaker and put it to Kay's lips. 'Only a bit or you might feel sick.' She let Kay take a couple of sips, then put the beaker back on the bedside table. 'I won't stay long – you need to sleep. I just wanted to see you before I went home, make sure you were OK. Next time I come I'll bring you some pyjamas and things.'

'Thank you.'

Kay's eyes closed again and Maya stood up to go. She had lots of questions she wanted to ask, but they would have to wait.

* * *

The next evening, Maya returned to the hospital carrying a bag full of goodies donated by Pam and Helen. Kay was sitting up, looking much better, her eyes were bright and her hair had been combed.

'I get out of bed,' she said. 'The nurse say I am a warrior.'

Maya laughed. 'You've been very brave. Does it hurt?'

'Only if I lift my arm.'

'Good. Mum called the doctor and she said you should recover quickly. We didn't know, but the bullet went straight through – missed the muscle and just grazed the bone. You were lucky.'

Kay looked puzzled. 'I did not have a bullet?'

'No. It went in the front and out the back.'

Kay looked thoughtful, then she smiled. 'I understand. I have a hole here and a hole here.'

'Yes. It was good the bullet didn't stay inside you.'

'I am lucky.' Kay said, settling back on the pillows. 'The hospital is a very nice place. The bed is clean and the nurse is kind. Tomorrow she will wash my hair.'

'Good. That's great. I'm glad you're OK.'

Maya put the heavy carrier bag on the bed. 'Helen – my gran – went shopping. She got you lots of things. Look – cool pyjamas. What do you think?' She opened the bag and lifted out a pair of white pyjamas covered with pink lips and then a pair of blue ones dotted with cupcakes.

'Beautiful,' Kay said.

'There's a cake in there, too,' Maya said. 'Helen baked it. You can give some to the nurses if you want – it's chocolate.'

'Mm,' Kay said, sniffing and taking out a foil-wrapped parcel. 'This is a good package.' She smiled at Maya and then lay back.

Maya pulled a chair out and sat down at the side of the bed.

'Did you see Annika?' Kay asked.

'No, she's going home with Tanya's body. A sad time for her.'

'Poor Annika,' Kay said. She sighed and closed her eyes.

There were many questions Maya wanted to ask and she was trying to work out the best way to ask them when Kay spoke.

'You ask me, before the operation,' Kay said. 'You ask me if I remember a fire?'

Maya leaned forward. 'Yes. I didn't think you'd heard me.'

'I hear you.'

Kay closed her eyes again and Maya waited. She was full of impatience but she guessed if she pushed it, her important questions might never be answered. She studied the weave of the bedspread and a picture of a giant flower on the wall.

After what seemed long minutes, Kay spoke. 'I remember,' she said. 'I was there with my family. I see your people walking, pushed by men with guns. I was six years old, I do not understand what was happening. When the flames start my mother take me home.'

'Do you remember a little Muslim girl crying because she'd lost her mother?' Maya asked. 'Did you push her into the ditch to save her?'

'I do not know about a ditch,' Kay said.

Maya was swamped with disappointment. 'But I saw you. In my dream I saw a girl with gold eyes, just like yours. She pushed me into the ditch so that I was hidden; she saved my life.'

'A dream is just a dream,' Kay answered. She breathed heavily and licked her lips. 'I am Serb. My people were your enemies.' She closed her eyes and turned her head away. 'Now you will hate me,' she muttered.

She spoke so quietly that Maya only just caught

what she said. She stared at Kay's wounded shoulder, the bandages bulging under her hospital gown. Sounds and images stormed through her head. Fragments of dreams fluttered like circling bats; her mother's eyes, bright almonds like her own, a long black robe flapping as her mother let go of her hand, her hands like claws as she pushed her away.

She grasped the bar at the side of the bed. A dizzy, nauseous feeling took hold of her. She put a hand to her throat and swallowed. Then she took in a deep breath and leaning down, she took Kay's hand.

'I don't hate you. The war is over – gone – it's in the past. Whatever happened in Cuska, it's finished. We must be friends.'

'How, if there is bad blood?' Kay asked, turning to gaze up at Maya.

'Your family died, too.'

'Yes,' Kay whispered. 'All dead.'

'We are the same then,' Maya said, softly. 'Nobody wins in war.'

* * *

Three weeks later, Maya stood in her bedroom, looking in the mirror. Kay, who had been given

333

permission to stay with them while she was recuperating, was sitting behind her on the bed.

'You look beautiful,' Kay said, as she watched Maya spinning round, the tiny white pleats of her silk dress flying out.

'Am I Marilyn?'

Kay looked down at the postcard picture and did a quick comparison. 'I think you are taller.'

'Not so much in the boobs department, either. Think I could do with some gels,' Maya said, ruefully eyeing her chest.

'You are OK. Some men like small.'

'Not Marilyn's admirers,' Maya laughed. She picked up a comb and tidied the wig. 'Not as good as the original, but it'll do for tonight. Let's go down, people will be arriving soon.'

Kay stood up. She was wearing a white blouse and a flared pink skirt, clinched in by a wide patent leather belt. Maya had attached a false ponytail to the back of her blonde hair and, despite the fact that her arm was still in a sling, she looked very like Sandy in *Grease*.

A big part of Kay's recovery had been watching films and musicals. She liked *High School Musical* and *Fame* but the one she adored was *Grease*. She'd learnt many of the songs and was in love with Danny Zuko.

It had been a difficult time for Kay as she'd withdrawn from drugs. The doctor had offered her substitutes, but she'd bravely refused and consequently suffered agonies of stomach pains and aching joints. Maya had been at school most of the time and Pam back at work, so it was Helen who'd held Kay's hand and had seen her through her nightmares. And it wasn't completely over – she still had flashbacks and panic attacks, but as she twirled around so that her skirt flew out she sang, 'You're the one that I want,' and she looked completely happy.

Downstairs, Helen and Pam were in the kitchen, finishing making food. Pam was dressed as Audrey Hepburn in *Breakfast at Tiffany's* and Helen looked elegant in a long green silk dress.

The first of the guests to arrive was Zac, who was dressed as an American gangster in pinstriped suit and trilby hat.

'You look brilliant,' Maya said.

'Went down the Oxfam, didn't I?" he said. Then he raised his gun. 'Didn't know if this would be all right? I'll ditch it if you like.'

'No worries,' Maya laughed. 'Can't be a gangster without a gun, can you?'

Zac put his arm around her and looked suddenly

serious. 'You know, I still have flashbacks. I was so scared when those men were takin' you away. They could have killed you.'

'I was scared. They wanted to kill me.'

'You was unreal leavin' me with them thugs, though,' Zac said. 'If it hadn't have been for Kay...'

'What, you still haven't forgiven me?' Maya cut in.

He kissed her hair. 'You owe me, girl,' he said, with a twinkle in his eye.

Maya had him in an armlock when Leona and Evie bounded in. They were dazzling in shocking pink satin jackets, bobby socks and pumps. 'The Pink Ladies,' Leona announced, turning to show the words on the back of her jacket spelt out in sequins.

'What you doin' to Zac?' Evie asked.

'Just teaching him who's boss,' Maya laughed. 'Hey Kay,' she shouted. 'The Pink Ladies are here. You'll have to sing some songs for us later.'

Kay came over, her eyes sparkling with fun. 'I love this party,' she said.

Maya caught her by her good arm and swung her round. 'You're easy to please. It hasn't even begun yet.'

'I know. But my friends are here. I have a place to live and I am happy.'

'What's gonna happen to her?' Leona asked, as Kay walked off to help Helen hand out drinks.

'I don't know. We're applying for her to stay. We might be able to get her a student permit. But she could have to go back to Kosovo.'

'That'd be a shame.' Leona said, 'She seems so happy.'

'Yeah, she's really settled in and she loves Helen. It was tough for her coming off the drugs – she was brave.'

'Yeah, Serena too,' Leona said. 'She's a fighter. When she's better, she wants to go back to school – do her A levels, go to uni.'

Later in the evening, Maya sat watching her friends mingling with Pam's friends and colleagues – everybody dancing and laughing and enjoying themselves. Simon, dancing with Leona, looked pretty cool in dinner jacket and bow tie and Pam was staying close to a guy who was dressed in a pirate costume. He'd arrived early in the evening, bearing Maya's schoolbag and bank card, so Maya assumed he was a police officer.

While Maya watched, she thought about the girls from China, and Annika, who was already on her way home, and the other girls, rescued from the hostel, who'd been taken to a detention centre. The centre wasn't a great place, but at least they were safe and were going to be returned to their families. One trafficking link had been broken and information gathered by the police would be useful in breaking down other smuggling operations.

'Not dancing?' Pam, ever alert to Maya's moods, came to sit beside her.

Maya shook her head. 'I will in a minute. I was just thinking about the girls we rescued. I wish I could have saved Tanya too – it was horrible that she died.'

Pam sat down and put her arm around her daughter. 'You did great. You can't fix everything, darling.'

'I know. But it doesn't mean I have to stop trying.'

Pam rolled her eyes. 'Right now I want you to try and pass your exams. I think that's a big enough task.'

'OK. I'm going to work hard, get good grades and then next summer. . .'

'What?'

'I have a plan which might involve a bit of travel.'

'Any plans you run by me from now on,' Pam said, pointing a finger. 'Understood?'

Maya smiled. 'Yes, but I think you might like this one,' she said. 'I want to go back to Kosovo, to Cuska.

I think I'm ready to face my demons. I want to find out who I really am.'

Pam leaned forward and enfolded Maya in a big hug. 'For that plan you have my blessing.'

Agent profile
Name: S.M. HALL

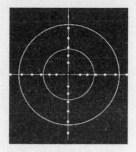

Stated occupation: Teacher of English and Drama. (Has been spotted in classrooms in Qatar, Singapore, Malaysia and Bakewell.) Sometimes poses as a writer of fiction – *Circle of Fire* is the fifth novel.

Subversive activities: recently took part in a Bed-In for Peace in Liverpool; eats pistachios while typing.

Location: between Matlock Bath, Derbyshire and John Lennon's and Paul McCartney's childhood homes in Liverpool – properties owned by the National Trust. Is this a front for digging into matters of national security, such as John Lennon's alleged scrumping of apples from Strawberry Fields? Meets high-profile individuals who visit the house, but does not betray confidences.

Distinctive features: mole on right cheek, whorls on 8 fingertips, scalp double crowned. Eye colour changeable – grey, green or blue depending on mood. Small enough not to be noticed when following a suspect.

Known weapons: rolled-up newspaper, umbrella.

Potential liabilities: putting a foot in it; worrying; speaking French badly; shouting loudly at the TV when the England squad are playing football, "Pass, pass!"

Ambitions: to win the local pub quiz, to tell one funny joke, to grow six inches, hug a mountain gorilla, plant a tree in Nepal.

CIRCLE OF FIRE
S. M. HALL

Fifteen-year-old Maya Brown's idea of fun
is time on an assault course or a shooting range.
She can't wait to follow in her mum's footsteps
as an intelligence agent.

But when her mother is kidnapped by a group
of terrorists, Maya is suddenly on her own
and determined to foil their plot.

Can she infiltrate their cell without risking
her mum's life? And is the mysterious Khaled
luring her into a trap, or is he a secret ally?

A fast-paced thriller filled with action and suspense.

If you enjoyed

Breaking the Circle

you can visit www.mayabrownmissions.co.uk
for more news and information.

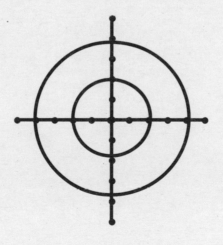